PRAISE

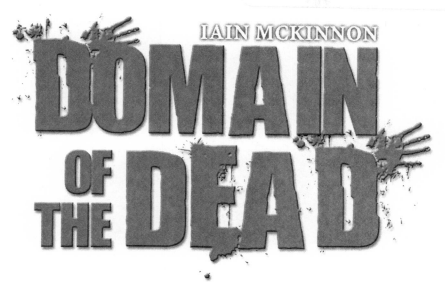

IAIN MCKINNON

DOMAIN OF THE DEAD

"Surprised me ... a quick, violent and exciting adventure."
—David Moody, author of *Hater* and *Autumn*

"Fast-Paced with great visuals."
—Z.A. Recht, author of *Plague of the Dead*

"McKinnon's grim domain is one of encroaching, inevitable horror. You will believe the end has come."
—David Dunwoody, author of *Empire*

"Deeply engaging and disturbing in all the right places."
—Travis Adkins, author of *Twilight of the Dead*

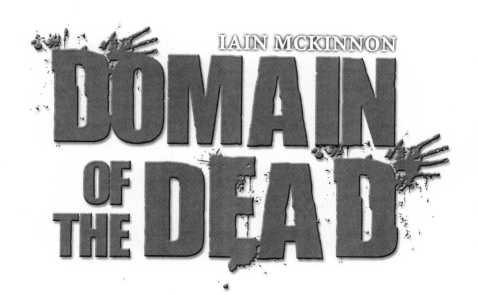

IAIN McKINNON

DOMAIN OF THE DEAD

Introduction by
David Moody

edited and designed by
Travis Adkins

cover art by
Craig Paton

Permuted Press
The formula has been changed...
Shifted... Altered... Twisted.™
www.permutedpress.com

A Permuted Press book
published by arrangement with the author

Domain of the Dead

ISBN-10: 1-934861-27-8
ISBN-13: 978-1-934861-27-1

Introduction

Got your survival plan ready for the impending zombie apocalypse? I have. I know where I'm going, who I'm taking with me and how we're going to get there. I know where I'm heading to pick up supplies along the way and how I'm going to lock my safe-house down and camouflage it and keep it isolated from the rest of the world as everything else falls apart.

But what happens if things don't go to plan?

Let's face it, how often do things in your life run smoothly? Even at the very best of times we all hit the occasional problem which knocks us off the route we were planning to take. If you think about it, it's hardly likely to get any easier as we race headlong towards Armageddon! As doomsday approaches, what if the people I find myself standing alongside as we face the hordes of the undead aren't the people I want to be with? What if they're not strong enough? What if *I'm* not strong enough? What if I find myself stuck in a rapidly-emptying warehouse, surrounded by thousands of reanimated corpses, with a mixture of pensioners, young kids and other misfits and unknowns for company? What if the days of fear and isolation turn to weeks, then months, then years...?

That's the situation Iain McKinnon presents us with at the beginning of *Domain of the Dead*—a small group of individuals who, somehow, have managed to survive against all the odds when just about everyone else has fallen and died and risen again. The (living) population of the planet has been slashed from billions of people down to just millions. When asked how they've been able to stay alive, the only sensible answer these survivors can come up with is, "we got lucky." The question is, how long can their luck last?

My first taste of McKinnon's work came in early 2009. Iain sent me an email telling me that he'd read the *Autumn* books, and that he'd written a zombie novel called *Domain of the Dead*. He offered to send me a copy, and he also happened to mention that he'd had a hand in a couple of short zombie films. He suggested I might like to check them out to get a feel for his work.

That afternoon I sat back and watched *The Dead Walk*, a ten minute movie made from a script by McKinnon. I was surprised more by what the movie *wasn't* rather than what it was. It wasn't like anything I'd seen before. It wasn't your typical, cliched, hackneyed zombie story. There were no desperate groups of survivors trying to flee the infected, no gratuitous scenes of carnage, violence and gore, no attempts to try and show the world falling apart on a shoe-string budget... Instead, the film concentrated on a lone man walking through an eerily empty post-apocalyptic landscape full of sunsets and shadows, listening to the end of civilization through his headphones; snatches of emergency broadcasts, frantic government messages and desperate public service announcements forming the only soundtrack to his lonely journey. It was McKinnon's ability to tell his story and drive it forward with limited action and without any direct dialogue or, indeed, a single conversation between visible characters, that made me sit up and take notice. If you're near a computer right now, head over to YouTube and watch the film yourself to see what I mean.

But if McKinnon surprised me with his short film scripts, then his debut novel, the book you're now holding, surprised me again. It wasn't at all what I was expecting. With an apparently off-the-shelf "...of the Dead" title, all the old zombie cliches immediately sprang to mind, but that's not what this book is about. Reading *Domain* made me think less about Romero's "Dead" films and more about the loud, gruesome, bloody, straight-to-video monster horror flicks of the 1980's and early 90's. Think *Leviathan* or *Deep Star Six* but starring the cast of *Night of the Comet*.

This is a book which achieves exactly what it sets out to do; a quick, violent and exciting adventure that gives you enough explanation and detail whilst still managing to keep you guessing. McKinnon plunges us straight into his nightmare world with a breathless set-up and the pace barely lets up. Mixing the claustrophobia of *Alien* with enough blood, action and reanimated corpses to satisfy hardened gore-fans, I hope you enjoy *Domain of the Dead*.

David

To George, for inspiring the nightmares.

To the crew of The Dead Walk for fueling my obsession.

To Audrey, Dorothy, Emma and Kirsty,
without you this book wouldn't be half of what it is.

To my Mum and Dad for nurturing and loving me.

To Brennus just for being wonderful.

To Alison for soothing the nightmares.

The soundtrack to writing this novel:
Nine Inch Nails, Gary Numan, NFD, Fields of the Nephalim.

For further information visit
www.domain-of-the-dead.com

Ishtar spoke to her father saying,
I will pull down the gates of Hell itself.
Crush the doorposts and flatten the door.
And I will let the dead leave.
And let the dead roam the earth.
And they shall eat the living.
The dead will overwhelm all the living.

—from *The Epic of Gilgamesh*

All the Townsfolk

NATHAN'S EYES FLICKERED A LITTLE as Sarah knelt down beside him, silently retrieving the sealed envelope from the side of his mattress.

"Do you hear that?" she asked, slipping the letter into the pocket of her jeans.

Nathan was too sleepy to register the enthusiasm in her voice. He just let out a sigh and tried to sink deeper into his pillow.

"Listen!" Sarah said sharply as she shook him.

Nathan hadn't opened his eyes. "It's just them," he said, annoyed at Sarah's persistence, and burrowed deeper into his sleeping bag.

"No, listen." Sarah shook him again. "It's something else."

Nathan opened one eye just a crack and mumbled, "Like what?"

"Just listen!"

Scratching his beard, he let out a yawn. "It's another fire."

"No, it's something else I think. It's..." Sarah paused, almost too scared to say it in case she jinxed her hope. "It sounds mechanical, like an engine."

"Seriously?" Nathan's eyes were wide open, the shroud of sleep dispelled.

"Come listen," she beckoned as she quickly made her way to the stairs. From behind she heard the unzipping of a sleeping bag followed by the sounds of a struggle as Nathan tried to hop into his jeans. As she reached the top of the stairs the slap of Nathan's bare feet against the concrete floor echoed ahead of him as he rushed to catch up.

Pushing open the door, Sarah flooded the dim stairwell with the golden rays of morning sunlight. A sharp morning breeze caught hold of the door and tugged at her grip. The air was cold and damp, carrying with it the hint of rain. It was pure clean air carried here from the not too distant ocean. It cleared her nostrils of the stale musty odour of the warehouse below.

The wind's bluster combined its own low moan with those of the undead surrounding the building.

Nathan appeared behind her at the roof door, his stained Nirvana T-shirt half out of his unzipped jeans. The jeans had rips where the wind undoubtedly whistled through, and Nathan's shabby brown leather wristband just added to the shipwrecked persona. As the wind began to bite at his exposed flesh he brought his arms to his chest to conserve heat.

Sarah stepped out onto the flat roof, letting Nathan take the door behind her. She looked up at the azure sky speckled with fast moving clouds. Just a few minutes ago the undersides of those clouds had been tinged pink with the breaking dawn. Sarah stood at the edge like she had just a few minutes ago, but this time she was scanning the sky, looking to where she heard the noise.

Stepping up to the edge of the solar panels to stand level with Sarah, Nathan looked down at the mob filling the street below. Crowded around the galvanised metal fencing were hundreds if not thousands of zombies, their gaping faces staring unerringly at the warehouse.

They all looked the same to Nathan now, grey-blue faces, hair matted and grimy, dirt sodden and tattered clothing. Some had clay-coloured beards where the blood of their long dead victims had dried and stained. If he cared to look closely enough he could pick out clues to the lives they once had: a man wearing a firefighter's thick protective jacket, a girl in a Burger Bar uniform, a children's entertainer in what once must have been a gaudy patchwork shirt, a nurse, a businessman, a police officer. Little remnants of lives lost.

"Are you sure it's not just them?" he said, eyes fixed on the writhing mass of rotten flesh.

Sarah didn't answer.

Nathan looked over at her. Her cheeks, unlike the rest of her milky skin, had a rosy polish to them, undoubtedly from the cold wind. As he watched her, waiting for an answer, a tear blew free from the corner of her eye and forced by the breeze ran down in an arch to the side of her jaw.

For a brief moment Nathan thought to wipe it away for her. His hand had even started to rise before he stopped himself.

The wind changed abruptly, bringing with it the stench of the corpses below. It was like a mixture of fresh dog shit and rotting beef. Nathan looked down at the foul creatures and involuntarily flared his nostrils against the stench. The reanimated corpses jostled and pushed, trying blindly to negotiate their way round the fences that encircled the warehouse, the stronger, less damaged or less weathered barging their more wretched companions out of the way. It formed an unending conveyer belt of festering corpses. A few of the more functional cadavers had spotted Sarah and Nathan on the roof and moaned, stretching out their decaying arms towards them. Like the crowd at a rock concert they reached out with rotten hands as if they were that much closer or that much more prepared to embrace their desire. All aching to get into the warehouse. They never seemed bothered by their smell, or the weather or much else. The only thing they ever showed was anger—or was it frustration, Nathan wondered. The frustration that came from being denied a need. Being denied the chance to devour the survivors they knew were sheltering within this warehouse. Regardless of how maddened they were at the situation, they never went away. Once they stumbled their way here they stayed. Never lost patience. Never just gave up and shambled off. Maybe it was because there were no other people left to devour. Nathan hated coming up here. It always set him off. Locked inside the warehouse below, he didn't have to think about how fucked up the world was. Just how fucked up he and his companions were.

"That way," Sarah said, pointing off into the distance.

Nathan listened but all he could hear was the wailing of the dead.

"I don't hear anything," he said. "It must have been a building collapsing or something." He rubbed his arms, bracing himself against the cold morning air.

Sarah stood motionless, staring out over the decaying town. She was trying to ignore him but she couldn't. The doubt was pushing in on her thoughts. Had she really heard an engine after all this time? Had it just been wishful thinking? Sarah tried to recall the sound she had heard, to replay it in her mind, but it wouldn't come.

"Sarah I don't think... Wait." Nathan craned his head forward as if closing the distance would amplify the sound. "I hear it now."

Sarah thrust her arm out and pointed at a small black speck. "Look, it's a chopper!"

Sarah's yelp brought a wave of moans from the crowd below.

The distant chopper hovered over the abandoned office blocks, occasionally dipping gently or swivelling around like a dragonfly over a pond.

Sarah threw a triumphant punch at Nathan's arm. The blow connected with Nathan's bicep, bringing a wince of discontent from him.

"Yes!" Sarah stifled a shout. "Go wake up Ryan and the others! Quick!"

Nathan turned and ran for the stairs as Sarah stood and watched the speck.

✳ ✳ ✳ ✳ ✳

Ryan stumbled through the roof door closely followed by Nathan. "Do I hear music?" he asked.

Unlike Nathan, Ryan hadn't taken the time to pull his trousers on. He stood there in the boxer shorts and T-shirt he had worn to bed, with only the excitement and a thin smattering of chest hair to keep him warm.

"The music's just started," Sarah answered. She pointed to the street and the shambling mass of decay. "They hear it, too."

Peering over the edge, Ryan and Nathan could see the hordes of undead slowly lumbering their way towards the sound.

"Nathan said there was a chopper?" Ryan added.

"Yeah, it hovered over the insurance building before dropping out of sight. I guess they must have landed in the centre of the business park."

"Yeah, I can hear the blades echoing round the buildings," Ryan said.

"I take it they didn't see you?" Nathan asked Sarah.

"I guess not, but I don't think they're looking for us, though."

The door banged open and the rest of the dishevelled survivors emerged onto the rooftop. There weren't many of them left, but Sarah still thought it a miracle that any of them were alive after so long.

In the warehouse below had been the supplies for their basic needs, but the bare roughcast walls lacked so much. It offered security, but no hope, no reprieve. No freedom.

Sarah stared at the destitute group at the doorway. The clothes downstairs were pristine in their clingwrap plastic covering until the moment they were slipped on. Instantly they seemed to age to match the wearer's level of dejection. The only exception was Jennifer. There was nothing to her; a wiry prepubescent body that had confounded everyone's effort to build her up. Her wide eyes and wider smile forced back their bleak confinement. After all, this was all the eight year-old had ever really known. She had been too young to remember much of the world before. Jennifer had lost her parents and gained this surrogate family: Grandpa George, Uncle Ryan, Uncle Ali and Uncle Ray. For some reason, Elspeth, Nathan and Sarah had missed out on an epithet. Sarah had always assumed that she and Nathan were considered big sister and brother. Elspeth? Well maybe she reminded Jennifer of a long gone nursery teacher or neighbour. Sarah didn't know and she guessed Jennifer didn't know either.

"So what do we do?" Nathan asked, shrugging. "Light a signal fire or something?"

"They might think it was just an accidental fire," Ryan offered.

Nathan looked around the roof for inspiration. "Maybe we could use the solar panels like signal mirrors?"

"They're not looking for us. They're not looking for *anyone*," Sarah said. She turned to Ryan and Nathan. "They're not expecting anyone left alive."

"So what are they here for?" Ray asked. He pushed his glasses back up onto the bridge of his nose. He squinted his eyes and took a good look around the broken skyline.

Sarah noted how he was forever pushing the loose spectacles back into place and squinting to see anything more than a few metres away. It was plain that his eyesight had deteriorated since he bought those glasses. But everything had deteriorated since he had bought his glasses. Ray looked out over the deserted town as if he was trying to spot something he had missed, like a man about to leave his house taking a last look around, checking that he hadn't missed an item.

"If they're scavengers they're shit out of luck," Ray said, pushing his glasses back into place again. "There's nothing left. We've picked this place clean."

"Wasn't much to pick," Nathan grumbled, remembering the fruitless scavenging of last winter.

Ryan shrugged his heavyset shoulders. "So how do we signal them?"

"We don't," Sarah said, folding her arms resolutely. "We go to them."

"*Go to them*, girl?" It was Grandpa George. He shook his head and looked off in the direction of the noise. "We don't even know who they are."

"He's got a point, Sarah," Ryan said. "They could be worse than those things."

"They might shoot us as soon as help us," Elspeth added, her grey hair gusting across her face as she spoke.

"It's been years since we've seen any marauders and none of them were in helicopters. Anyway, they're advertising their presence with the music. It's like they want to cause a commotion—to shake the place up." Sarah slipped her tongue under the stud of her lip piercing, an unconscious habit she had when she was thinking. "No, this has been our only chance of escape in years and it may be our last."

"Sarah, think about it. We're safe in here," George said, to the group as much as to her. "The moment we open the shutters there'll be no turning back. They'll be in here and there won't be no way of stoppin' 'em,"

"How much longer will we be safe in here?" Sarah asked.

No one replied.

She looked at their default quartermaster. "Tell them straight, Ray."

Ray looked nervously around and shrugged apologetically. "I don't know."

"Ray!" Sarah barked.

"Maybe four or five weeks worth of food and that's rationing out even thinner than now."

No one was surprised at Ray's statement. They had begun rationing out their food months before. It wouldn't be long before it was exhausted.

"And Ryan's guzzled the last of the Jack," Nathan grumbled.

"Nathan," Elspeth rebuked.

"What do we do?" It was a rhetorical question Ryan posed. He looked around the group, half hoping to see the spark of an idea in anyone's eyes.

The thin cloth of Nathan's shirt rippled in the cold wind. Goose pimples stood out on his thin arms. "Fuck it. Sarah's right. We have to go to them."

"Hold on."

Everyone turned round to see Ali standing by the water tank. He wasn't one for conversation and the very fact he had spoken without being spoken to demanded everyone's attention.

"You're seriously suggesting we go out there?" Ali nodded in the direction of the sound, his long black beard bobbing with the wind.

"What else would you suggest?" Sarah asked.

Even though Ali had lost a lot of weight from their enforced confinement, he still made for an imposing figure. He'd always looked dangerous, not tough, more strange. He fitted the archetype in Sarah's mind of the creepy unwashed guy behind the till in a sleazy porn shop—not that Sarah had actually been in a sleazy porn shop, but she had been instantly wary of him when they'd met. Ali wasn't pretty to look at. His large nose was lumpy and pointed off at a crooked angle, a sure sign of a violent life, in Sarah's opinion. His complexion was pockmarked and there were patches of paler skin all over his face and neck. His hair, what was left of it, was suspiciously black for someone his age. His mouth would gape open as he watched you and his dark brown eyes looked black under his bushy eyebrows.

As the months had passed, though, Sarah had got to know him in increments. The hair colour was natural, along with the male pattern balding inherited from both his father's and mother's sides of the family. The pockmarks were the result of acne as a teenager, his broken nose the result of a car crash before the days of airbags, and the smattering of light skin was the result of scarring from the broken windshield. The gawping mouth was an indirect result of the accident. His broken nose never healed properly, leaving him unable to breathe through it. The more Sarah had got to know him the less intimidated she felt. The final nail in the coffin for her prejudice had been when she found out he worked for an animal rescue centre.

"You're thinking things are so bad that it justifies going out there?" Ali's eyebrows dipped so low it was impossible to see his eyes.

Sarah looked at Ray. "They will be in a month."

"There are thousands of those pus bags between here and there. One bite, one scratch and that's all it takes to turn you." Ali looked round at the rest of the group's expressions. "You plan on dodging those things long enough to get to a helicopter full of people who are mystery to you?"

Everyone was silent.

Ali continued, "As Elspeth said, they may not be friendly, they may want to shoot us, they may refuse to take us. What then?"

"We don't have time to argue this," Ryan said restlessly. "Who knows how long they'll be there."

"Is it truly worth the risk?" Ali asked. "Do you want to wait here and starve to death or take the chance?"

The congregation on the rooftop started looking at each other.

"I only say that because everyone has to be sure what choice there is," Ali said.

People were looking into each other's eyes, trying to measure what they thought. Slowly everybody started nodding.

Watching the unspoken agreement spread, Sarah decided to take charge. "Okay, leave everything. Only carry a weapon. It's not far to the square but there's a lot of them and we'll have to run the whole way."

She looked at Ryan's toned figure. Unlike the rest of them, he had stuck to a regular workout regime. The lack of fat from the strict diet combined with his improvised weights gave him an athletic appearance. Even then Sarah knew there had been no space for a proper cardiovascular workout. None of them had regularly walked more than the length of the warehouse in years. A mad dash between a thousand infected corpses filled her with dread.

But then so did starving to death.

Adrenaline would have to see them through.

"Nathan, Ryan, get all the Molotov cocktails we have left. Let's try to thin them out," Sarah said, her voice carrying a weight of confidence that surprised even her.

She looked out over the street to the town square. It looked further away than it had just a few minutes ago.

* * * * *

Bates bobbed his head in time to the beat, holding his carbine like a guitar. His gloved left hand held the ribbed heat guard that sheathed the muzzle like it was the neck, whilst his right hand strummed on the collapsible stock. He stood in the midst of this dead town, singing along to a rock track like the last drunk at a student party. His dress didn't match his actions, though; he was clad in a khaki uniform, most of which was obscured beneath protective armour. Overlapping his pristine black leather boots were matt black shin guards. Above them and made of the same dull man-made material were knee protectors. Strapped around his thighs was a holster and various pouches for holding ammunition, all made from the same black synthetic weave material. The tactical vest he wore was replete with ammo pouches and the various laced panels that ensured a tight fit gave the garment a certain fetish chic rather than a military look, sporting a high collar and shoulder protection which came well down past the bicep. The vest had obviously been developed to guard the wearer's vulnerable areas against zombie attack. With the black helmet, elbow pads, gauntlets and his blond shadow of stubble, Bates looked more like a faint-hearted skateboarder than a soldier.

He whipped the stubby black machine gun over and started singing into it like a microphone.

He was used to places like this, familiar with them. In the years since the Rising he had visited a fair number of dead towns like this one. They were all the same lifeless husks. Broken down towns smashed by the panic of the outbreaks, then softened by years of weathering. The smashed shop windows. The abandoned rusting cars. The discarded edifice of life like a singular shoe, a broken pair of glasses or a child's toy. Clumps of moss and grasses clinging impossibly to the stonework of buildings. Nature encroaching on concrete. All of this was commonplace in his life now. Even the skeletons lying bone naked all were mundane.

This was a town like a dozen others he'd visited, like the whole world was like now. Bates was familiar with it, and even though his childish antics said otherwise, he knew he'd never be comfortable with it.

His feet made an amateurish attempt to moonwalk across the cargo net spread over the tarmac beneath. The dance step hadn't been spoiled by the impediment of his armour or the ground underfoot, it was purely Bates' own ineptitude at dancing. He didn't care. The only eyes watching him belonged to the dead and their palsied movement was far more awkward than his own.

Suddenly Bates let out a scream in sync with the track booming out from the battered and duct-tape refurbished stereo. With his weapon taking the place of a mic stand, he stumbled through the off-key lyrics in his impromptu karaoke.

The dead had not been the only ones to watch his juvenile display after all.

A husky east European accent poured over Bates' earpiece, "Don't know what make worst noise—you or the dead."

Bates stopped his singing and looked up across the abandoned car park. Raising a hand to his forehead, he squinted at the rooftop of an abandoned office block. He scanned the rooftops for a glimpse of Angel, the barrel of her gun, a lock of her auburn hair, anything. But she had been trained in the old Soviet mould. Bates knew he wouldn't see her unless she wanted to be seen.

"You come down here and say that, Angel!" Bates shouted in what he thought was her general direction.

"A hui ne myaso!" she taunted back over the radio.

"What you say there?" Bates looked up at the chopper hovering overhead. "What she say there?"

A new voice crackled across the airwaves: "Stay on station, Bates."

Bates scolded, "Angel, speak English!"

"Burak!" Angel cursed.

"Oh, that's it! I know what that one means! I'm coming up there to kick your ass!"

"Bates!" the voice from the chopper cracked. "Stay on station."

Bates cradled the mouthpiece on his radio mic behind his thick leather gauntlets, shielding it from the gusting wind. "Roger that, boss."

Without another word he pointed up at the office block where he suspected Angel was sniping from and mouthed his own obscenity back at her.

"Bait, this is Angel. One Whisky Delta, seven o'clock, one hundred yards out."

"Don't start me!" Bates scolded. "Don't call me bait! You know it makes me jumpy."

"Is your name," Angel answered back, with a tinge of sarcasm in her velvety voice.

"It's Batesssss—you leave out the S on purpose."

"Bates, Angel, this is Lieutenant Cahzalid. You will observe proper radio discipline. Is that clear? No more horseshit!"

Sheepishly Bates replied, "Yes sir, confirm multiple Whisky Deltas one hundred yards out and closing."

"This is Angel, multiple contacts all vectors."

"What's the count, Angel?" Lieutenant Cahzalid asked.

Before she could answer a shot rang out.

"Who fired?!" Cahz demanded, looking out the windows of the cramped helicopter.

"Me sir," Bates replied.

Cahz looked down at Bates through the glass footwell of the helicopter. "What the hell was that for? I didn't see any W.D.'s in your immediate vicinity."

"No, there weren't," Bates said. "Caught one that looked like John Prage a hundred yards out. I just had to pop one in his head."

"Who the fuck is John Prage?" Cahz suddenly realised he'd regret asking that question. "No, forget it. We don't have time. Angel, say again. What are the numbers?"

Bates didn't hear or didn't care that Cahz didn't want to know. "He was this prick I used to work with. If anybody deserved to get bit it was him."

"Shut the fuck up, Bates, or you're on report," Cahz snapped.

Bates had the sense not to cut in.

Cahz repeated his question: "Angel, what's the count?"

"Too many, sir. Suggest we abort and find clearer ground," Angel reported. "There's also smoke. W.D. must have set off something flammable."

Cahz looked over at Idris, the helicopter pilot. "Spin us around to get a look."

"Sure," Idris replied, and the chopper dipped slightly and made a gentle turn.

Looking out over the ruined city, Cahz could see a torrent of grey corpses snaking their way around the derelict cars and other debris to the lure below.

Cahz craned round to talk to the last member of his squad. Cannon almost filled all three seats in the back of the chopper, his muscular square body uncomfortably wedged into the middle seat with his huge heavy machine gun protruding across the other two. Before Cahz could speak, the bear of a man piped up, "There's too many of them, Boss."

"Something must be drawing them in," Cahz said, thinking out loud.

"But what boss?" Cannon asked. "World's been dead a long time."

"I haven't seen this many in one place since that op in Norfolk." Cahz looked through the view port at his feet, at Bates standing on the cargo net below. "It's academic anyway," he said, more to himself than any of his crew.

He flipped the radio on his shoulder to transmit to the two on the ground, "Angel, Bates, we're bugging out. Angel, is your position secure?"

"Yes, Lieutenant," Angel replied with her eastern European pronunciation.

Cahz addressed everyone over his microphone: "Let's move before those W.D.'s and that fire give us cause for concern." He looked out of the window at the rolling black clouds of smoke. "Okay then. Bates, you're first up. Confirm your harness is secure and clean."

Bates spoke into his radio, "Affirmative, Lieutenant. We're good to go."

All the time Cahz watched the pockets of smoke. As he watched, they grew, but they didn't look like a normal fire. The smoke seemed to be concentrated into patches rather than carpeting an area as he would expect. He hadn't seen anything on the way in, and now as he watched, a fifth distinct plume of smoke started to rise up above the buildings. He couldn't see the actual fires behind the ruins and he had no time to investigate.

"Cahz!" Angel hollered over the radio, a tremor in her voice. "We've got live ones!"

Cahz, alert from Angel's exclamation, looked around at the multitude of undead below. "Say again, Angel."

"Multiple humans fighting their way towards Bates. Seven, maybe eight." Angel's voice dropped. "Ah jeez, they just lost one. Coming in on four o'clock."

Cannon lent forward from the back of the chopper. "What do we do, boss?"

His question was serious. In all the years since the outbreak there had never been a straightforward answer. In the early days Cahz had witnessed dozens of people lost in vain on ill-conceived rescue attempts. More people had been lost than had been saved, for the most part.

But Cahz made his decision: "Angel, give them cover fire."

"Be my pleasure, sir."

Angel nuzzled her cheek up against the cherry coloured wooden stock of her sharpshooter's rifle like she was cuddling up to her favourite childhood toy. One eye closed, the other firm up against the sight, she took her finger off the trigger guard and let out a slow exhale. The crack of a rifle shot splintered the moans of the dead city. Angel's target collapsed to the ground, a large part of its head missing. Taking in a slow, measured breath, Angel scanned the mass of zombies for her next target and the process began anew.

Cahz cocked his rifle, placing a round in the chamber. "Bates, clear and hold the LZ. We're coming down."

"*Whoooee!* Lets rock!"

Bates flipped the safety catch off and set his carbine to semi automatic. Butt of the gun against his shoulder, head cocked to peer down the sight, Bates surveyed his surroundings. He slowly turned through three hundred and sixty degrees, assessing the number and proximity of the W.D's. He drew an imaginary perimeter around his position, within which any corpse would be dispatched. The first corpse stepped over his imaginary line and as it did its head exploded. The decapitated body flopped to the ground, black ooze trickling from the stump of its neck.

Turning around again, Bates took stock and waited for his next target to cross the line.

* * * * *

Sarah punched out with the palm of her hand, knocking the cadaver off balance and sending it tumbling into the corpse behind.

She shuddered at the contact. To be so close to the walking dead was horrifying enough. A single scratch could be enough contamination to turn you. The revulsion of the physical contact and the fear of infection pushed Sarah to the verge of breaking down.

13

There was something deeper, more primordial than a phobia that terrified her about becoming one of them.

The creature slumped to the ground, flailing as it went, knocking two others over on its way down. The gap was short lived as a new wave of zombies lunged for their prey.

Sarah knew if she cracked she would freeze up or run the wrong way or something as equally fatal. Her lungs heaved but she couldn't suck in enough air to fuel her muscles. The stitch in her side competed with the burning in her thighs, the cramp in her calves and the numbness of her left arm as she held onto Jennifer.

Sarah had to fight both the macabre creatures swarming the street and the macabre thoughts in her own mind. If she didn't, it wouldn't be just her life that was lost.

Jennifer had her scrawny arms flung around Sarah's neck, her head buried deep in her chest and her legs wrapped tight around her torso. Every time there was a jolt, like a boa constrictor gaining purchase on its prey, Jennifer would grip harder. The young girl's breath was as deep and as rushed as Sarah's. The trembling breaths billowed through her blouse, leaving a hot damp patch above her breast.

Sarah barged though the zombies, the pain of her unfit body drowned out by the fear of the animated corpses, these resurrected husks that had just one instinct. Driven only by their need to infect others, they crowded in on her, arms outstretched, mouths open, ready to bite. Her energy long ago spent, Sarah charged on, fuelled by an explosive mixture of adrenaline and terror.

Something snagged around Sarah's ankle. She stumbled against the obstruction, carried forward by momentum and the extra weight of the child in her arms. Stumbling headlong, legs kicking in an attempt to maintain balance, she crashed face first into a zombie. Its brittle chest cracked from the impact and snapped further when Sarah landed on top of it.

In the fall to the ground the zombie had smashed its skull, fracturing it like an egg shell and causing enough damage to render it permanently inert.

Lying face down in the rotting cadaver's chest, all Sarah could taste was putridity. The taste crawled down the length of her tongue and clogged up her nostrils with its stench. The nauseating mix of decaying flesh, excrement and the musty odour of damp rotting clothes made her retch. Sarah tried to spit out the rank musk but her fear-dried mouth spasmed shut. Choking and gasping, Sarah felt a hand snatch at the back of her blouse. It grabbed a handful of cloth and flesh and pulled hard at her.

"Get up!" Ryan shouted as he hoisted her to her feet.

Before she could thank him for the save, a zombie was at his neck. As it rolled back its lips to bite, there came a tremendous cracking noise and its head flew apart, the explosion sending chunks of scalp spraying into the air.

Neither Sarah or Ryan paused.

Sarah bundled up the young girl she had been carrying and started running again, towards the sound of gunfire.

Ryan looked back at the rest of the survivors. They were getting too strung out. Behind him, Nathan was hauling Elspeth through the melee. The old woman struggled to keep up the pace of her younger companion. In her arms she carried a small bundle close to her bosom. Way behind them was a knot of zombies where Ryan had last seen Ali, Ray, and Grandpa George.

He hollered, "Ray! Ali!"

"Keep going!" Ali's nasal voice cried out.

Ryan didn't keep going. Instead he ran back the way he'd come.

A knot of ghouls pushed their way in front of Nathan and Elspeth. Nathan swung out the fire axe he'd been carrying and the blade imbedded itself into the skull of the first zombie. Nathan's grip sheared as the creature collapsed. The cadaver crumpled to the ground with Nathan's only weapon still wedged firmly in its head.

A second cadaver stretched out its bony fingers for Nathan, clawing and grasping at him. Instinctively he let go of Elspeth so he could fend off the creature with both hands. Elspeth screamed as two zombies grasped at her. For a heartbeat, she stared into the milky eyes of her attackers. Broken teeth bared from behind split, festering lips. Black putrid drool dripped from their rank maws as they lent in to consume their victim.

With a loud whoosh the closest assailant's head disintegrated. The force of the bullet's impact carried the cadaver's body away from Elspeth. A second shot rung out and chunks of flesh and bone erupted from the second zombie's temple. The shot had grazed the side of the cadaver's head, obliterating a wedge of skull and exposing the wet brain matter underneath. Undeterred by the wound, the zombie sunk its reaming teeth into Elspeth's clavicle.

Pain burst through Elspeth's mind. Her legs buckled and she fell to the ground, still clutching the bundle in her arms.

The zombie fell upon her, clawing, scratching and biting.

Nathan shoved the shriveled husk he was wrestling with out of the way and turned to help Elspeth. With one swift kick he dislodged the attacker and dragged Elspeth to her feet.

"Hurry!" Ryan bellowed as he grabbed Elspeth's arm, adding his own strength to Nathan's.

* * * * *

Sarah dodged and barged her way through the shambling corpses. Some of the bodies yielded to her momentum with sickening squelches. Occasionally decaying lumps of flesh would fly free as she shoved past. She could taste the decay halfway down her throat, dry, rasping and musty. It lingered in just the part that made her want to gag.

All the while, shots were ringing out with a steady pulse as if set by a metronome. Sometimes the corpses in front of her would sink to the ground with a round to the head as an unknown marksman cleared a path for her. Like throwing salt on snow, the zombies before her were melting away. But Sarah knew it wasn't enough to hold back the blizzard.

She turned onto the town square and ran hard into a body. A gloved hand steadied her.

"Get to the chopper!" Cahz used his hand around the girl's arm to propel her onwards to the waiting helicopter. He said, "Cannon, watch my six," but knew his old friend would have already anticipated this.

"Sure thing, boss." Cannon positioned himself a few paces away from his commander and readied his huge machine gun.

Cahz raised his carbine and started placing shots into the zombies.

Shot after shot rang out as Cahz, Angel and Bates fired into the horde of undead. Dozens fell only to have their place filled by dozens more. From all over the lifeless city, more and more of its former inhabitants were drawn out by the noise.

Bates swept round, casting his gaze around his imagined borders.

He felt the wind from the chopper's idling blades against his back. His means of escape sat just a few metres away, but he wouldn't let himself become complacent. He focused his attention on the approaching zombies. His line of death was denoted by the corpses he had dispatched, a neat circle around the landing zone.

Bates fired and kept tally as he did. "Twenty-eight. Twenty-nine. Thirty..."

He counted off the last round in the clip. As he reloaded he took stock. His neat circle of corpses was being overwhelmed. The rate at which they crossed the line was increasing as more and more were drawn in by the noise Bates and his companions were making. He knew he couldn't keep the creatures at a distance much longer. Although Cahz and Cannon were now covering half of his original kill zone, the sheer volume of zombies would mean he couldn't shoot them all. Even if he had an infinite amount of ammunition, the time it took to aim at targets coupled with reloading meant that he would eventually be overrun. Bates estimated that at this rate he'd run out of ammo in the next three minutes.

He took a look over his shoulder at the waiting helicopter. It was only a quick jog away. He'd be there in a few seconds. But he still felt uneasy.

He looked back at the encroaching crowd of walking dead. He took aim and dispatched the latest cadaver to cross the line.

* * * * *

Nathan could feel Elspeth becoming heavy. "Come on, Elspeth. We're almost there. We can make it."

The old woman looked deathly pale, like the creatures around her. She looked up at Nathan with sleepy eyes.

Nathan looked down at the bundle in her arms. "Do it for your granddaughter."

Her tired old muscles filled with energy again and Elspeth pushed on.

* * * * *

"Keep going down to the chopper!" Cahz called out to the two men supporting the old woman as they lolloped past.

Cahz looked down the busy street. Hundreds of zombies shambled their way towards him. He peered through the throng, trying to get a glimpse of the other survivors. There was a blur of movement and Cahz spotted a man with a shaggy black beard wielding a metal pipe.

Cahz lent into his rifle butt and started thinning out the zombies in the survivors' position. A break in the mob revealed the dark haired man again. His fist clenched around the pipe as he pounded the zombies around him.

Cahz fired on either side of the man. Through the tunnel view of his sight he could see the man's face sprayed with blood. Pushing the image aside, Cahz continued shooting the zombies.

His scope went black. Cahz pulled back to see just yards in front of him a zombie had stepped into his line of sight. Its arms stretched out, ready to make a grab for him. It was so close that Cahz could read the blanched employee name tag on the shop worker's apron.

Cahz fired and floored the creature.

If its lurching walk hadn't blocked my view, Cahz thought, *I wouldn't have known it was there until it had taken a chunk out of me!*

Cahz was interrupted from his train of thought by a voice over his radio.

"Boss, this is Bates. I'm running dry and there's no let-up."

Cahz toggled his mic. "Angel, have you got eyes on the other survivors?"

The creatures were converging on the town square in the thousands and Cahz realised he could no longer see the other survivors in the mass of zombies.

There was a silent gulf on the radio. "Angel, come in," Cahz said.

"Lieutenant, I have situation," came Angel's belated response.

* * * * *

Behind Angel, on the roof of the office block, there came the sound of splintering wood. The door to the stairwell cracked open, spraying rotten wood onto the gravel. From the darkness of the abandoned building stumbled out a stream of corpses.

"Otyebis!"

Angel whipped round, sending a shower of loose stones tumbling from the rooftop. Incorporating the energy from her twist, Angel leapt to her feet, swinging her sniper rifle over her back as she did. She delved into her holster and pulled out a pistol to take up her new firing position. Leaning forward as if she were about to sprint, Angel aimed her gun.

The zombies' lethargic attention slowly focused on the human. She pulled the trigger, obliterating the lead zombie's skull.

The presence of live prey galvanised the undead and they started shambling towards her.

Angel opened fire in earnest.

Her gun barked with each squeeze of the trigger. Like a drum beat, Angel fired a steady rhythm of deadly shots. Within a few short seconds fifteen zombies lay decapitated.

Angel discarded the empty clip and reloaded her weapon all in one fluid motion. Again she fired until her clip was dry, destroying the next fifteen zombies that stumbled through the door. The bottleneck caused by the locked door dealt with, they were less bunched up now, but there were still too many. Inexorably they shuffled towards her, torn flesh hanging from their outstretched arms and rasping moans surging from their stiff throats.

Again Angel changed her clip with the automatic action ingrained in her muscle memory. She pointed the gun at the closest ghoul but they were emerging from the stairwell faster than she could shoot them.

"Fucking pointless."

She holstered her gun, turned, and threw herself off the building.

Three floors down the line snapped taut against its anchor. Angel's harness jolted against the tension, sending a shockwave juddering through her body. The rope took the force of Angel's sudden stop and, pivoting against the lip of the roof, transferred what was left of her downward force into lateral movement. Stunted by the jolt, Angel could do nothing as her momentum carried her. She swung and bounced hard against the toughened glass of a manager's office. As she hit something snapped. A deluge of pain coursed through her arm. Blackness and nausea pressed in around her consciousness. Light headed, dazed and hurting, she could feel herself slipping into oblivion.

"Pizdets," slipped from her pursed lips as she asserted her will over the pain.

Angel hung suspended by her safety harness, stunned by pain and gently twisting while she cradled her left arm. From the corner of her eye something dark hurtled towards her. She looked up in time to see a hapless zombie plummeting straight down. Angel strained her stomach muscles to give her the tilt she needed to get in tight to the building.

It was too late. Something hard and bony connected with Angel's cheek and raked down her shoulder and back.

A stifled scream of pain forced its way through Angel's gritted teeth.

Her cheek felt raw from the collision. The burning welt from the impact had overwhelmed much of her feeling and she had to know if she was bleeding. If the zombie had broken the skin she knew she would be infected. In absolute terror, she touched her fingertips to the skin on the side of her face.

The skin was tender but dry.

In spite of the pain, Angel felt relief.

She looked up about to give praise to the heavens when she saw the next free falling corpse.

Through its clouded eyes, the plummeting corpse, oblivious to its predicament, lashed out at its target. Having missed, it tumbled downwards, hurtling to the ground. In its retarded mind it had no thought of the impact just moments away. It simply stared up plaintively at the meal it was powerless to obtain.

More zombies stumbled over the edge or were pushed by the eager mass behind them.

Angel's fingers grasped out and found a beam of steelwork to lever herself up with, muscles straining and pain throbbing from her elbow as she kicked down with her feet, righting herself. Twisting round, she pulled herself flat against the grime-coated glass, away from the macabre downpour.

Panting, she hugged tight to the window frame. The stream of bodies was easing off and below her was a heap of rotten flesh. Most of the corpses had been immobilised from their fall but a few splintered carcasses writhed as they tried to move on smashed bones. Occasionally there could be seen a zombie's jaw gnashing in frustration at its spine-shattered paralysis.

Angel's breathing sent plumes of condensation streaking out across the window. She forced herself to take deeper, slower breaths; to calm herself down and sit out the worst of the pain from her arm. From the corner of her eye she saw a dark shape, but this time it wasn't falling from above.

Thump.

The whole window shuddered as a zombie bit down on Angel's face. Angel tensed and in one primordial reaction she had pushed herself away from the building in sheer fright.

The zombie's slavering mouth continued to gnaw down at where Angel's face had been, either unaware or unperturbed by the sheet of glass that separated them. Thick rivers of black saliva trickled down the inside of the glass. The woman's white work blouse had long ago been stained yellow, her shoulder-length brown hair was feral and oily and the ragged and fractured nails that clawed at the glass still had patches of red varnish in places. But the one thing to steal Angel's attention was the eyes. Clouded like a cataract sufferer, they were wide open as she sunk her teeth into the window.

Even a shark rolls its eyes when it bites, Angel thought as she began her descent to the ground.

* * * * *

Cahz looked up at the office block in cold silence. The last of the lemming-like zombies had plunged to their doom and Angel was painfully making her way to the ground before he realised he'd been holding his breath. He knew there was nothing he could have done to help Angel; the cadre sniper always acted alone and away from the team.

That didn't diminish his responsibility or his concern for his comrade. In the few seconds since Angel's radio call, Cahz had been torn between watching out for her and scanning for the survivors lost in the throng of cadavers.

He took in a lungful of rancid air, which peaked his own sense of danger. None of the three men had emerged from the crowd and the mob of undead were now only a few shambling footsteps from his position. He breathed out the rank air, his decision made. Three more casualties among the billions.

"Okay people, time to bug out. Everyone back to the bird."

As he turned to run back to the chopper, Cahz noticed that Angel had stopped one floor from the ground. Below her were half a dozen necrotic arms outstretched, waiting for her.

Before he could order one of his men to help, Angel had unholstered her pistol and dispatched the group. Her shots looked clumsy compared to what Cahz had come to expect. A couple of shots had missed their target before he realised what was wrong. For some reason Angel was firing right handed.

"Cahz, we've a problem," Idris' voice crackled over the radio from the chopper.

Cahz turned round and slapped his buddy, the hulk of a soldier everyone called Cannon, on the shoulder. He nodded and both men jogged back to the chopper.

Around the chopper stood the group of dishevelled survivors. Idris was obviously shouting through the window from the pilot's seat at Bates, but from here the sound of the blades and the music from the ghetto blaster drowned out the conversation. Looking back at the office block, Cahz could see that Angel was down and hobbling towards the landing zone.

"Cannon, go give Angel a hand." Cahz gestured in the sharpshooter's direction.

"You got it." The big man sprinted off with an agility and speed not generally associated with most men his size, let alone for someone carrying a heavy machine gun and a thousand rounds of ammo.

"What's the problem?" Cahz asked as he drew level with the helicopter's open window.

The survivors were in a tight knot around the chopper. The two ragged young men looking anxiously around. The skinny young woman with dirty blond hair bent double and retching, a young girl diligently rubbing her back, and an older woman who was trying unsuccessfully to shush the baby in her arms.

"Are you counting heads?!" Idris shouted above the noise of the engine and the sound of the baby' crying.

Cahz looked at the survivors and then back at the seats in the chopper. "Ah, shit!"

* * * * *

Sarah stepped in front of the man who was obviously in charge. Through raw breaths, cheeks flushed, she panted, "Where are the others?"

"I'm sorry, ma'am. I waited as long as I could," Cahz said in way of an answer.

Sarah knew what he meant. She looked back along the street she and her companions had ran down. There were hundreds of zombies, all walking towards the chopper, but no sign of her missing companions.

Cahz rapped his fingers against the side of the chopper as he thought aloud, "Could we get everyone onboard and try to find somewhere safe to set down?"

"Where?" Idris asked. "Look, we couldn't get airborne with the extra weight even if you could cram everyone in. And if we could take off, where would we get the extra fuel we'd need to get back to Ishtar?"

"What's the problem?" Sarah asked, overhearing part of the discussion.

"Ma'am, the chopper only seats five, maybe six at a squeeze," Cahz explained.

"And there are ten of us," Sarah said, still trying to compose herself.

"Don't suppose the girl and the baby will be a problem. They can sit on someone's knee." Cahz looked around nervously. All the time they stood there the zombies were edging closer. He knew he had to make a decision—and quick—before they were overrun.

Big Cannon trotted up, carrying the sniper's kit with Angel only a few paces behind. Cahz knew her injury must be serious because she never let anyone near her rifle.

Unconcerned by the new arrivals, Sarah continued, "That still leaves us four seats short."

"What's the hold-up boss?" Cannon asked.

"The kids'll fit in fine, but we're pushing the weight limit," Idris chipped in, confirming Cahz's assumption. "We've got enough fuel for the five of us and a few of the pus-bags, but they weigh next to nothing. Even if we do stuff this bird full, we'll be short on fuel. Okay, there's no drag if we don't use the net, but we'll still splash down who knows how short of the ship. And what if the weather turns and we meet a strong headwind? We'll just ditch a whole lot sooner."

Nathan spoke up. "Could some of us get carried in the cargo net?"

"No, we can't take the weight or the drag, son." Idris tried not to sound too annoyed at repeating himself.

"Anyways, you'd die of exposure before we got back to the ship," Bates said. "It's bad enough just getting winched up, but being under that thing for two hundred miles? No way you'd make it."

"No need for a seat for me dear," came Elspeth's soft voice.

Everyone looked round at the unassuming old woman.

"What do you mean?" Sarah asked.

Elspeth pulled her collar loose to reveal a set of teeth marks over her shoulder. The wound wasn't deep, but it had broken the skin and drawn blood.

"No," Sarah wept.

"I'm sorry I couldn't protect her." A tear trickled down Elspeth's cheek as she gazed down at the bundle she cradled in her arms.

Ryan reached over and pulled away a corner of the swaddling. There was a smudge of blood on the yellowed cloth. The child, only a few months old, was crying. Its face was red and its bottom lip quivered as it gasped out wails. Across the baby's face was the drag marks of a zombie's scratch. The welts were puffy and red with infection.

"Oh God no, Elspeth," Sarah gasped.

"Must have happened when I fell," Elspeth sobbed. "I'm so sorry, Ryan."

Ryan stood silent, his fingertips on the baby's cheek. A solo tear trickled from his left eye and Ryan tried to swallow it back down.

"Boss," Bates broke in, "I'm out of ammo and they're close."

"We don't have time for this, Cahz." Big Cannon's deep voice carried more weight than usual.

Cahz looked round at the approaching cadavers and back at the rag-tag group around him.

"Okay, listen up. This isn't an order but we've more of a chance down here than they do." His eyes looked to Bates and Cannon. "I'm giving up my seat."

"Jesus, Cahz, we haven't survived this long to get fucked by a handful of civvies," Cannon protested, loud enough for everyone to hear.

"Like I say, I can't order you to stay," Cahz said.

"You don't give much of an option, Boss. We've stuck together since this shit came down and neither of us would have made it without the other. If you're stayin' I'm stayin'."

Cahz smiled and looked over at Bates.

"I'm taking my seat," Bates said firmly.

"I stay," Angel volunteered.

Ryan stepped up. "No, lady. Your arms busted. I'll stay back."

Sarah started to protest but Ryan cut her off.

"These boys might have the firepower but they don't know the ground," Ryan reasoned. "They've got a better chance with one of us to guide them."

"That's that settled." Cahz grabbed Sarah and lifted her up into the chopper before she could react.

Sarah tried to protest but her voice was drowned out by the noise of the baby crying and the drone of the rotor blades.

Shocked by the sudden pace of events, Sarah peered passed the soldiers at Ryan's steely expression.

Ryan stared down at the swaddled child, gently stroking its cheek. He was so engrossed with the child he was oblivious to the roar of the chopper's engine, the bustling soldiers, and the zombies shambling towards him.

Sarah's view was blocked as Cahz grabbed Jennifer and tossed her on board.

"Soon as you can, get back here and pick us up," Cahz instructed Idris as he ushered Nathan into the middle seat.

Idris nodded. "Keep yourselves safe and give me enough space to land."

Bates was stooped down, gathering up the last of his kit from the cargo net when Cahz stepped up to him. Bates swallowed down a gulp of saliva to lubricate his throat. He straightened up, but before he could speak Cahz stopped him.

"Bates, leave that behind," Cahz instructed.

For a moment Bates was puzzled. He'd expected to be chewed out by his commanding officer for not volunteering his place. He followed Cahz's gaze down to the ghetto blaster.

"How much juice is in those batteries?" Cahz asked.

"Not much, boss. They're rechargeable and they're pre-Zee. If you turn the sound down a bit you might eke out another fifteen, twenty minutes, but I guess about an hour is it."

Cahz nodded. "Okay."

"Boss!" Cannon bellowed.

Cahz and Bates looked round.

"Gettin' a bit close." Cannon, standing with his machine gun at his hip, pointed the barrel at a zombie just a few metres away. Clamping the butt of the gun to his side, he fired a thunderous volley of rounds that shredded the approaching zombie and a few behind it unlucky enough to be in the path of the stray bullets.

"You looking for a decoy?" Bates asked.

"Yep," Cahz said.

Bates smiled and produced a slightly curved, thin green rectangular box from a large pouch on his thigh. Embossed on the inside curve read the words 'Face towards enemy'.

"Set a timer on it for—what—five minutes?" Bates asked.

"Make it twenty," Cahz replied.

When Bates looked puzzled, Cahz explained, "It'll act as a distraction. Maybe pull a few away from us."

Bates quickly set the timer on the claymore mine before grabbing his kit and jumping into the chopper.

"You packin' any more useful toys?" Cahz asked him through the open door of the helicopter.

"Yeah, sure." Bates unclipped his two thigh pouches and tossed out his inventory. "Two more claymores, two flares, a smoke grenade and one MRE."

"Ain't planning on staying long enough to have to eat army rations," Cahz said, holding the pouches like they were a pair of freshly caught rabbits. "Maybe we can tempt those motherfuckers to eat these instead."

Bates gave out a chuckle. "Smear it all over you, then no fucker will want to bite you."

"It's gettin' tight, boss!" Cannon called out.

Cahz shut the door and called over to Idris in the pilot seat, "Get these people out of here!"

Idris gave a solemn nod that was as good as a promise for Cahz.

"Cahz, it's at least an eight hour turnaround!" Angel shouted out from her position in the chopper's front seat.

"Quicker you go the quicker you get back!" Cahz hollered.

"Good luck, Cahz," Angel said as she passed him her sidearm and her last remaining clip of ammo through the small window in her door.

"Are you sure?" Cahz asked, holding the magazine clip with the Cyrillic writing across it.

"I want empties back," Angel warned in a firm tone. "Since Izhmash closed, are bitch to get hold of."

Cahz nodded. He turned and tapped Ryan on the shoulder.

"Okay, we need somewhere high and defendable," he said as he passed Ryan the pistol. "Which way?"

* * * * *

In getting comfortable, the soldier beside Nathan pushed him back into the middle rear seat and blocked his view. He couldn't see which way Ryan had taken the party, only the occasional glimpse of a rotting faces as the zombies pressed closer to the helicopter.

Bates took a wistful look at the battered stereo sitting behind the mine. He grumbled, "Shit, I've got to make up a new mix tape." He sat back in his seat and pushed out a long rush of air, relieved to be in the chopper.

Drawing a breath of his own, Nathan caught the mixture of decay and body odour from the passengers next to him. Nothing unusual, but now it didn't bother him. Now he was escaping it, leaving it behind, not trying to ignore it. Escaping. He pushed his shoulders deep into the back of his seat and let his eyelids fall closed.

"Sarah." Jennifer sounded worried.

Sarah wiped the tears from her eyes and tried to muster a calm tone as she answered, "What is it honey?"

Jennifer looked out the window. "They're getting closer."

Sarah too looked out the window at the approaching zombies.

Nathan opened his eyes, and bobbing his head, looked between Jennifer and Sarah. The zombies were indeed getting close.

"I imagine the pilot has to do things before he can take off," Sarah said, trying to reassure Jennifer without sounding too anxious.

"Shouldn't we be taking off?" Nathan called out nervously.

Idris craned round from his pilot's chair to see his passengers.

"We're going to sit here a bit," he said casually.

"Why?" Nathan asked.

"To give the W.D.'s something to interest them," Idris answered.

Nathan looked at Sarah and then back at the pilot. "What?"

There was a thump at the window and Jennifer screamed.

Sarah looked round to see a decayed face pressed against the pane, a dark grey mass of loose skin and pitted chasms. The dry dead skin raggedly hung around the numerous, deep, ickier filled gashes. As it tried to bite through the glass, streaks of dark saliva were smudged across the window.

"For fuck's sake, take off man!" Nathan bellowed.

"I say when we take off," Idris said, unflustered by the swarm of zombies outside.

Nathan was half out of his seat. "Why the hell are we still sitting here?!"

"Sit down. I'll take off before it gets too dangerous."

Nathan was almost completely out of his seat when an arm reached over and firmly pushed him back down.

Bates pinned Nathan to his seat.

"It looks dangerous enough already!" Nathan complained as he watched a second zombie press up against the glass on the other side of the aircraft.

"Just calm down," Bates said. "This is the closest you'll get to in-flight entertainment."

"So why are we waiting?" Sarah asked.

"I'm playing decoy," Idris said. "The more W.D.'s we entertain, the less Cahz will need to worry about."

"This is fucked up," Nathan said, but he stayed back in his seat nonetheless.

The daylight seemed to fade, sucked in by all the grey-faced cadavers shuffling towards the chopper. The undead now surrounded the aircraft and one by one they were pressing against the windows.

The pounding of dead hands against the skin of the helicopter grew louder as more and more crowded against it. As they reached their goal they squashed their stiff faces against the glass. The chopper began to rock from the force of their pounding hands, and as they pounded the noise grew so loud that it almost enough to drown out the rotor blades.

Sarah held Jennifer in a tight cuddle, repeating calming phrases to her. Nathan sat, his face drained of colour, slumped in his seat as if he were trying to sink out of sight of the insatiable zombies.

Sarah noticed that the pilot and the two soldiers onboard were sitting quite placid and silent.

"All right," the pilot said as he flicked a switch on the dashboard. "This is your Captain speaking. We're getting the hell out of here."

With that, he pushed forward on his stick and the faces around the windows started to drop away.

The chopper rose into the morning sky with ease, unhindered by the mob that had surrounded it. Its pilot watched from his vantage point as the three men and one woman ploughed through the throng of corpses at the far end of the square. Beneath the chopper there still stood a multitude of zombies futilely clawing at the empty air.

He turned the stick in the direction of home and within moments his view of those left behind was lost, obscured by the broken skyline.

With the chopper gone, the zombies stopped groping for the sky and ambled their aphasic way around the town square, some lured by the music from the ghetto blaster, more still drawn towards the people fleeing on foot.

The Queen of Heaven

FOR THE LONGEST TIME THERE WAS SILENCE in the chopper. Everyone had donned headsets with attached mic's which muffled the sound of the engine and allowed them to talk, but as they passed over the devastated land there seemed to be little to talk about. Beneath them was the husk of a world long gone. The motorways were clogged with the rusting carcases of automobiles. Where the road wasn't clogged it was often washed out or carpeted in a blanket of green where nature had started to reclaim what was hers. Spindly saplings forced a home in parking lots and moss coated those roofs that hadn't collapsed or been gutted by fire.

It was a rotten world made all the more rotten by the aimless wanderings of the zombies that inhabited it. It seemed to Sarah that the dead had fashioned a derelict realm over which only they had domain. A dead world populated by dead people. She kept her gaze out of the window so no one could see her tears. She felt ashamed for crying. She had lost everyone close to her during the Rising and she had cried for them. Today she had lost all but two of her friends, but this time their deaths were her fault.

Broken rail tracks and toppled power lines punctuated the feral pastures until a strip of lonely beach heralded the boundary between the land and the ocean. A finger of fresh water bled into the ocean, its lighter shade of blue pushing out against the overwhelming power of the sea.

As the land disappeared behind them, the occupants' attention turned away from the windows.

Sarah felt Jennifer's breathing relax as the young girl drifted off to sleep. It felt comforting to have this young child asleep on her lap. At least Jennifer had survived. Running a hand over the child's hair, smoothing it down in a long stroke, Sarah wrapped her arm around her. Closing her own eyes, Sarah tried to drift off. She felt exhausted. Now that the adrenaline had worn off, her legs ached from the mad dash carrying Jennifer.

In the darkness behind her eyelids, sleep wouldn't come. All Sarah could see were the faces of the people she'd left behind. Ryan's stoic visage as he stroked his infected daughter's cheek. Elspeth's apologetic eyes pouring out regret for her failure to protect Ryan and Sam's child. Even though she had been bitten defending the baby, Elspeth had shown no concern of her own plight. Then there were the others. Ali, Ray and George. All left behind, lost in a sea of decay. A very small part of Sarah threw out a modicum of hope. She hadn't seen them die. Them might have fought their way free and met up with the soldiers; they all might be safe back at the warehouse waiting for rescue.

It was just a wishful thought and Sarah knew it.

Nathan was the first to break the silence. "I'm Nathan. This is Sarah and Jennifer."

"Shit yeah," Bates said in way of an apology. "Kind of got caught up. I'm Bates. Gideon Bates." Bates lent forward and placed his hands on the seat in front of him. "And this is Angelika Chernov—or *Angel* as we like to call her, our team sharpshooter." Bates drummed his fingers on Angel's seat. "Expert shot and poker player, both because she never blinks."

"And you never shut up, Bates!" Angel retorted.

Bates continued, his enthusiasm unabated, "And your pilot for this flight is Idris Hayder."

Idris raised his hand and gave a slight nod of acknowledgment at the introduction.

"So what's happening to the rest of the world?" Nathan asked.

"How long you been out of the loop?" Bates said.

"We stopped picking up radio broadcasts, what, about three years ago? Things were in bad shape when they went off air."

"Yeah, it's the same all over, W.D.'s all over the place," Bates answered, rubbing his cheek. The straps from his helmet had obviously irritated him but not enough for him to remove his protective Kevlar helmet until the helicopter was safely away from the infected mainland. He ran a hand through his cropped blond hair, rubbing the spots matted flat by the pressure.

"*Double-you dee's*?" Nathan asked.

"Whisky Deltas." When Nathan stared back at him blankly, Bates elaborated, "Walking Dead."

"Ah," Nathan nodded.

"The dead fucks have taken over the planet. Nowhere's safe," Bates said.

"Well, almost nowhere," Idris chipped in.

Nathan lent forward, more to show interest than to hear better. The noise in the cabin would have been overpowering if it weren't for the headsets. "So what's left?"

"There are a few places, mainly islands like Ascension, Hawaii, the Falklands," Bates said.

Idris' matter-of-fact voice cut over Nathan's headphones, "I hear Greenland is nice this time of year."

Again Bates filled in some of the blanks. "Yeah, lots of places in the arctic circle are still safe. The Scandinavians are doing better than most."

"Why's that?" Nathan asked before thinking.

"W.D.'s don't like the cold," Angel said. "They freeze solid."

"Of course." He remembered back to the winters where they had gone foraging in the comparative safety of the frozen city. "So where did you guys spring from? You seem well equipped, well organised..."

Bates jumped in, all too happy to pass the time with small talk. "We're assigned to Ishtar."

"What's an Ishtar?"

Bates smiled. "Ishtar is a research ship. Got some fancy scientists on board lookin' for a cure."

"So is that government funded?" Nathan asked.

"Ain't no government," Angel added, her Russian lilt rolling over the words.

"No social security cheques either," Idris said.

"Well, there's a government of sorts," Bates corrected. "Whole world—or at least the bits we have left—is under martial law." He paused, thinking. "So how did you guys last so long on the mainland?"

Nathan was about to answer when Sarah spoke up. "We got lucky."

Surprised that Sarah was awake and listening, Nathan shrugged in grudging agreement. True, they had worked hard, but he had to admit much of their success was down to good fortune.

"Suppose we did," he said. "I mean if Sarah hadn't been up on the roof when you flew past, we might never have heard you." He smiled over at Sarah. "Yeah, lucky. I take it you couldn't sleep and went for a wander?"

Sarah nodded. "Yeah."

She turned and looked out the window to hide her face. She didn't know if Nathan would spot the lie but she didn't want him to question her. She didn't want to explain the real reason for her being there, standing on the ledge looking out, her mind full of the urge to step off.

What made her cry as she looked out over the ocean was the cruelty of it all. Bereft of hope a few hours ago, she had been about to kill herself. She put her fingers into the pocket of her jeans and felt the now crumpled corner of her suicide note—the note she had left at Nathan's bedside before she went to watch one last sunrise.

Nathan could see Sarah was crying from the way the silent sobs rolled across her shoulders.

Bates was still looking at him, waiting for the rest of Nathan's story.

Nathan decided not to press Sarah. After all, they were both upset at losing their friends. He turned back to Bates and explained, "A few of us found our way to a groceries warehouse. We met up by accident in the first few weeks."

"How'd you keep em out?" Angel asked.

Nathan tried to sum up the last few years for his saviours. "Luckily..." he heard himself start. He ticked off a mental note that he had agreed with Sarah and they had just been lucky. He continued, "Luckily for us the warehouse was in a bad neighbourhood. Place was built like Fort Knox. When we got there the place was still buttoned up tight. We broke through the main gates and Sarah suggested we barricade them after us so that we didn't meet any surprises on the way out." He looked across at Sarah to see if he could pull her back into the conversation, but she was still staring out of the window. "We got into the main building looking to scavenge what we could. The place was a goldmine, far more than we could haul away in the van. It was Sarah who saw the potential. She suggested we clear it out and stay."

"And you've been there ever since," Idris chipped in. "That explains why there were so many W.D.'s in the area. You must have been pulling them in for miles."

"It wasn't bad to start with. The fences were strong enough to keep 'em out, so we just ignored them to start with, no point going out and getting them all agitated. When the world got quiet and they started to swarm, we decided to try and thin them out. More out of frustration than anything else. I mean we were doing something, taking some of it out on them. Occasionally in the dry weather we'd go up onto the roof and throw petrol bombs. You can vent a lot of anger doing that, but generally we tried not to leave the warehouse much cause of the smell an' all."

"Those fuckers smell bad enough without barbequing 'em," Bates agreed.

"Damn straight," Nathan said. "But we had it pretty good for a while. Set up a rain butt to collect fresh water. We even had electricity."

Bates was genuinely interested, "Yeah? How? A generator?"

"To start with, yeah, but when the fuel ran out we used solar power and then wind generators. What was that kids name?" Nathan gently elbowed Sarah.

"Gabriel," she replied, annoyed at Nathan for his lack of reverence towards a deceased companion.

"Yeah, Gabe," Nathan said, missing or ignoring Sarah's implicit chastisement. "Smart kid. He wired up a whole bunch of those solar powered lawn lights to some car batteries. On a sunny day we could cook stuff up in the microwave." He turned back to Sarah. "How old was he?"

Sarah couldn't remember and she felt hypocritical for her failing. A lot had happened since those early days; a lot of companions had died. How much had slipped from her memory? She shook her head slightly and guessed, "Twelve? Thirteen?"

Nathan beamed, recalling some of the excitement he had felt at the boy's achievements. "He set up solar heating. Well, he designed it. Ryan and Grandpa George did most of the work. Set it up on the roof, gave us hot showers and it took the chill out of the winter that first year."

"Cool," Bates said, soaking in some of Nathan's excitement.

"He died." Sarah's harsh statement chilled the conversation. She was angry. She had survived when others hadn't and she felt responsible for that, angry at herself for exposing her friends to the monsters outside the warehouse. But she was also angry at herself for what she had forgotten. Gabriel wasn't with them long but he had deserved to be remembered. Now Sarah couldn't even recall his last name. She had let that die.

Bates gave a knowing frown. He asked, "Got bit?"

"No." Sarah's face went blank as her memory retrieved the boy's death. This she recalled in piercing detail; she hadn't forgotten that. She remembered the blue tinge to his lips, the pallor of his skin, the hard rasping breaths that finally surrendered. Except for the lack of a fever, Gabriel's death was almost identical to one of the infected.

"Asthma attack," Sarah said, recalling Gabriel's futile puffs on his long exhausted inhaler.

Nathan scowled his thin lips, sucking in stifling remorse. "His puffer ran out."

"Shit..." The shock made Bates' jaw drop.

"I remember finding a couple of unopened ones in a bathroom cabinet that winter when we went foraging," Nathan said. "The apartment was just a five minute walk from the warehouse." He shrugged. "No way we could have saved him, not with those things crowding round us like they were."

"Harsh, man," was all Bates could muster.

There was silence again in the cabin.

Feeling uneasy with the quiet, Nathan decided to break it. "There must be all manner of shortages like medicines and fuel and stuff?"

"We got plenty of gas," Idris said, pointing up as if to connect the chopper's rotors with his comment.

Bates nodded. "Yeah, no fossil fuel crisis anymore."

"Why's that?" Nathan asked.

"Oil rigs were the first things the military moved to protect," Bates answered. "W.D.'s ain't no good at climbing and they proved just as hard for panicked civvies to crack. Kind of like castles, just pull up the drawbridge." Bates smirked. "Well, ladders in this case."

Idris elaborated, "And those things are hell of a tricky to land a bird on unless you know what you're doing." He made a thumbing motion in Bates' direction. "Just need a couple of grunts like him with a machine gun to discourage any unwanted company."

"I miss beef," Angel said suddenly, breaking her silence from quietly enduring her pain.

"Christ, when was the last time any of us had a steak?" Bates complained.

"We had steak last Wednesday," Idris said.

"Proper red meat." Bates lent forward and prodded Idris in the shoulder. "Tuna doesn't count."

"Ah, what's the difference?" Idris asked.

"If you'd been raised in the south and fed proper food you'd know," Bates said. "Everything your momma made for you came out of a can swimming in tomato sauce."

"Bates," Angel interrupted, "Everyone eat out of cans now."

Laughter filled the cabin but the good cheer grated at Sarah. Her thoughts were still with Gabriel and Elspeth and George and all the others not able to share in the joke. She cocked her head around Jennifer, who was fast asleep.

Nathan asked, "So what were you doing this morning anyway? I saw a cargo net. Were you looking for supplies?"

"No, it wasn't a supply run," Bates said. "We get most of ours from Cape Verde."

Angel corrected him, "Was supply run of sorts."

Bates sniggered in agreement. "I suppose."

The blank looks of the awake survivors begged clarification.

"We were specimen collecting. Every few months we get sent out to round up some W.D.'s."

"Why?" Sarah's tone was almost shocked.

"The scientists need them," Bates said.

"What for?"

"Oh, number of reasons." Bates scratched his head as he tried to retrieve all the uses the zombies were put to. "Well, they monitor how quickly they're decomposing..."

"They're trying to work out how long before they crumble to dust," Sarah guessed.

"Yeah that's right."

"How long then?"

"How long what?" Bates stumbled before he married the train of thought. "Oh, I see. Um, I don't know. Guess it must be a while, 'cause if it were good news they'd tell us."

Sarah restated her original question: "So what else do they do with them?"

"They experiment on them. Mainly trying to find out what will kill them."

"I can tell you that," Nathan grunted. "Nothing except turning their brains to pulp."

"Do they know what caused it?" Sarah asked.

Bates shrugged. "If they do they ain't telling us. Some talk of viruses, but if you ask me they don't know dick."

The chopper dipped down through a layer of feathery clouds, bringing into view a dreary pallet of green and blue.

"There she is, folks," Idris declared. "The Ishtar."

Beneath them in the roll of teal surf was a scruffy cargo vessel, her paint blistered and her seams tinged with rust. On her cargo deck was an empty square with the letter H in bold yellow paint. None of this caught the survivors' attention as they craned for a better view from their approach. What mesmerised them were the people. On deck and in the bridge there could be seen a myriad of living human beings. None of the people were apparently interested in such a mundane thing as a helicopter.

A smile broke out on Sarah's face as the skids of the chopper touched down on the deck. For the first time in years she felt safe.

✳ ✳ ✳ ✳ ✳

A whistle pierced the noise of the rotor blades winding down.

A thick set marine shouted out, "Hey Bates, where's the rest of the crew?!"

"Still in country!" Bates called back.

At the side of the landing pad stood two marines. Unlike Bates, they wore green uniforms and soft peaked caps. Sarah didn't know much about the military but the one who shouted had a couple of stripes and an anchor insignia patch on his arm.

The lead marine bellowed, "Who the fuck are these civvies?!"

"Survivors, French," came Bates' curt reply.

"What, Cahz and Cannon are still on the mainland and you found room for some useless civvies?!" French blustered.

"Was his idea, so don't go blowing your shit, Lawrence," Angel said.

The second marine spoke up. "Looks like you got a promotion."

"No one's got any promotion just as soon as this bird is refuelled. Idris is heading back for them," Bates said, giving a reluctant Angel a hand getting out of the chopper.

The door to the deck opened and through it came striding the executive officer. Like the rest of the ship's crew, Commander Patterson wore a version of the soldier's uniform excluding the armour and webbing, but unsurprisingly the garment was a navy blue. His blue peaked baseball style cap was clutched in his right hand to prevent the down draft of the dawdling rotor blades from blowing it away. The same wasn't true of his thinning blond hair; the combover flapped in the wind like a tattered flag on a forgotten battlefield. The tints on his round gold-framed glasses had turned opaque in the strong afternoon light, obscuring his over magnified grey-blue eyes.

"Private Bates! Private Chernov!" Patterson hollered as if he were chastising children.

"Yes sir!" the pair barked back.

"Captain wants debriefed immediately!" Patterson thumbed his free hand in the direction of the bridge.

Bates was still helping Angel out of the chopper. Her injured arm had swollen up and a suffusion of purples and reds had spread out from her elbow.

Bates shouldered Angel's rifle. "Sure I'll just stow—"

"Just nothing, Bates," Patterson scolded, maintaining his schoolmaster persona. "NOW!"

"Yes, sir," Bates sneered while giving Patterson a limp salute.

As they passed him, Patterson stopped Angel. "What's up with you soldier?"

Angel, clutching her arm, looked down at her injury and then back up at the executive officer. "Women's troubles, sir."

Without looking back she walked off.

As quickly as the wind changed the position of his combover, Patterson's demeanour also changed. As Sarah stepped out of the aircraft, he stretched out his hand to help her and her young ward onto the landing platform.

"Ma'am, I am Commander Patterson," he said, utterly unphased by the insubordination displayed by Bates and Angel. "And you are?"

"I'm Sarah, this is Nathan."

"Hi," Nathan said.

Patterson knelt down to bring himself eye level with the third survivor. He pealed off his glasses and asked, "And who might you be, young lady?"

Jennifer looked up at Sarah. It wasn't a look for permission; Jennifer had grown up in a world devoid of stranger danger and parents fretting over child abduction. Jennifer was looking to Sarah for reassurance that it was worthwhile getting to know the man.

Sarah's smile was the security she needed.

"Jennifer," the girl said as she extended her hand.

Patterson swapped his cap and his glasses into his left hand. He smiled and simultaneously shook her hand, saying, "Pleasure to make your acquaintance, Jennifer." He stood back up. "I had a niece about her age before..."

He didn't need to finish the sentence. The people in Patterson's world had seemed to become closer since the Rising. It wasn't just the banding together for protection or the shared experience of survival. Everyone had been in the same situation. Everyone had lost people and it meant that everyone could connect empathically, instantly.

He broke off from his train of thought and back to the task at hand. "If you and your party care to follow me, we'll have our medical staff check you over."

"Thanks," Sarah said, holding a hand out for Jennifer to follow.

"I'm sorry, what do we call you?" Nathan asked.

"Only the sailors and the soldiers need address me as *Sir*. You guys being civilians can call me whatever you feel appropriate."

Nathan didn't look any the wiser.

"Mr. Patterson would do fine," he added.

He looked at the three. They had the slender look of starvation on them. No curves, only points where the bones threatened to pierce their paper-thin skin. "Lets see about getting you people a hot meal. I can't begin to imagine what it must be like on the mainland."

* * * * *

Sarah stopped at the bottom of the steps from the helipad and arched her back. The confined flight and the strains and contusions from their exodus had combined to numb her muscles. She stretched her neck up high and tried to drop her shoulders before walking away from the landing pad. The sun was bright and although the wind took the warmth out of the day she didn't mind. The salt air brought with it a sense of cleansing. It was a pure unfetid smell. Occasionally there was the whiff of grease or gasoline, but it wasn't the terrifying smell of a wildfire consuming and corrupting the air or the stench of rotting flesh. It was clean and uncontaminated. The view around her was less threatening, too. Nothing but open ocean. No derelict buildings with unknown dangers inside. No hoards of the undead hemming them in. Just the calm sea, a smattering of clouds and the odd seagull trailing the ship for scraps.

The shadow of the bridge blocked out the sunlight on the last few paces into the ship. From the seemingly infinite space of the deck, Sarah found herself being funnelled into the comparatively cramped corridors that ran through the ship's interior.

The ship had looked small as the chopper came in to land, but now Sarah realised the Ishtar was a sizeable vessel. She stepped over the bottom lip of the hatch into the thin corridor. Steering from behind, Patterson called directions as they travelled deeper into the hull.

Sarah felt overwhelmed by the sheer number of new faces. Seemingly unconcerned by the new people, they went about their duties. Occasionally one of the curious would strain their neck to watch the new arrivals as they squeezed through the narrow corridors.

"How many people are there?" Sarah asked.

"On the ship or in the world?" Patterson replied.

Nathan's voice was quick with excitement, "Both!"

"On the ship there are thirty-two seamen, fifteen marines and soldiers and an assortment of others, making fifty in total," Patterson informed them.

"And the rest of the world?" Sarah asked.

"About fifteen million," Patterson answered. "Give or take."

"Only fifteen million?"

"Lowest human population since before the last ice age, we're told," Patterson replied. "Kind of knocked the whole overpopulation fear on the head, wouldn't you say?"

"Fifteen million," Sarah said, trying to get her head around the figures.

Patterson waved his arm, instructing them which turning to take. "Experts say once the W.D. problem is solved we can repopulate the world in just a couple of hundred years and the eugenicists are saying we'll be better for it."

"What do you mean?" Sarah asked.

"Well, it's the survival of the fittest, quite literally," Patterson replied. "Since the Rising you don't get any fat American tourists anymore."

Sarah smirked. "Darwinism in action."

"You have to be fit, smart and lucky these days. All the chaff has been weeded out. Or so the eugenics folks say." Patterson smiled. "Personally I think it's mostly down to luck."

"Seems like one hell of a big boat for just fifty people," Nathan commented.

"Ishtar used to be a cargo ship before it was requisitioned." Patterson was more than happy to chat about his favourite subject. "Even then it only takes a crew of about twenty to get her to where she's going. There was a lot of automation fitted back in the late eighties, early nineties. Before all that, a ship like this would have needed three times the crew."

"So what's the cargo?" Nathan asked.

Patterson let out a wistful sigh. "Oh, no cargo. Those days are long gone. Nothing but supplies in her holds now." He gave a passing bulkhead a couple of slaps with his palm as if he were patting a faithful dog. "We don't make port. A supply ship rendezvous with us each month and brings in fresh provisions. They give us cans of sweet corn and we give them hard copies of the research work."

Sarah started to tune out of Nathan and Patterson's conversation. In the confined space of what was obviously a busy ship, the rich and sometimes pungent odours were a welcome pleasure. It took Sarah quite some time to work out why she was so transfixed. It wasn't the presence of an odour she was enjoying, it was the absence of a particular one: The smell of putrefaction—which had been ever-present since the Rising began—had been whisked away by sea breezes. The smell was nonexistent here.

Sarah realised the source of her delight had been the unlocking of her past, a time before all the hardship and loss.

"I'm sure you'll have a chance to speak to Doctor Robertson about the research conducted onboard." Patterson raised his voice. "It's just this door on the right."

Sarah was dragged back from her daydreaming. Next to her was a plain grey door with the word INFIRMARY stencilled at eye level.

"Just inside there if you wouldn't mind." Patterson ushered the group into the room.

"These will be the new arrivals, Mr. Patterson?" the woman standing in the infirmary surmised. She wore a white lab coat with a light blue checked blouse underneath and a dark knee-length pencil skirt. Her hair was a deep brown and worn loose around her shoulders. Sarah guessed she was in her mid thirties but would never voice her guess openly. She knew how the Rising could add years. She tried to imagine how she herself looked, gaunt and drawn from the lack of food and the stress of being imprisoned by masses of rotting flesh.

How much older than twenty-four must I look? Sarah wondered.

"I'm Dr. Robertson. The Captain asked that I give you a look over. I hear you've been on the mainland all this time. That can't be true, can it?"

"It is," Nathan said.

"I'll leave you people to it and I'll pop back down in say..." Patterson studied his watch as if he were waiting for the second hand to reset so he could synchronise his timing. "Forty minutes?"

"That would be fine," Doctor Robertson said. "Well, you look in good shape but there are a few tests I'd like to perform to see—"

"To see if we're infected?" Nathan cut in.

Doctor Robertson frowned. "I was going to say to see if you've suffered any effects of malnutrition. But yes I will also be checking you for infection."

She went to one of the cupboards on the wall and started laying out the medical equipment she needed. "I'll be running a full blood work to check for a variety of communicable diseases such as Typhoid, Tuberculosis, HIV, Hepatitis, and of course the big Zee."

Sarah gave Nathan a warm smile and nodded her head in silent solidarity with him. It had been a paranoid question Nathan had asked but she could understand why he was feeling uneasy. Yes they were safer than they had ever been in that warehouse, but this was an unfamiliar environment for them, populated by strangers they didn't know if they could trust. Couple that with the day's events and it was easy to empathise with Nathan's wariness. Things had moved too fast to be comfortable yet.

"Okay, lets start. Who wants to go first?" Dr. Robertson asked, an empty syringe in hand.

Sarah stepped up to the examination couch. Dr. Robertson motioned for her to sit down.

"Do you have any pre-existing conditions I should know about? Pregnancy, diabetes..." Dr. Robertson stopped herself. "Of course not. Any insulin would have gone off by now." She stared off into space for a moment. "I don't suppose that even if you are pregnant you'd know for sure at this point either?"

Sarah felt her hand against her emaciated belly and realised she'd unconsciously placed it there. There was no chance she was pregnant but the doctor's comments had made her think of Sam. The excitement of a child being born had galvanised the survivors cooped up in that warehouse. It had filled them all with a new vigour as everyone rallied around Samantha and Ryan. It had turned all too quickly to horror. Clutching her own stomach, Sarah remembered her friend, baby in her arms, as she lay on the warehouse floor and bled to death.

"You know it's been years since I last had to do a physical."

Doctor Robertson's voice jerked Sarah back.

"But it's still ingrained. Like I was still..." Doctor Robertson sighed. "Well, that was a lifetime ago." She assembled the syringe. "Do you have any symptoms or ailments I should be made aware of?" Without waiting for an answer she placed a stand on the workbench, ready to accept the vial.

"No, not really," Sarah said hesitantly. There were a number of health issues, but she felt none of them were serious enough to disclose. Nothing that mattered.

"Someone mentioned this was a research ship?" Nathan said.

Dr. Robertson rubbed antiseptic on the nap of Sarah's elbow. "That's right. Professor Cutler and I are investigating the walking death." She took the protective sheath off of the needle. "You'll feel a small scratch."

"Walking death? Is that what it's called?" Sarah asked. She knew placing a name on it would dispel the supernatural associations. If it could be analysed and categorised and labelled, Sarah told herself, it could be fought. It could no longer be the wrath or God or the work of the devil or any of those evangelistic reasons that were so prevalent at the beginning. The sanitization of the condition brought her comfort, but it couldn't dispel the menace.

Dr. Robertson looked up at the ceiling and made a soft humming noise. "*Ambulatio mortuus.*" She shook her head. "No, it would be *Mors*. Ambulatio Mors." She tutted and went back to Sarah's arm. "Doesn't have much of a ring to it, but no it doesn't have an official name yet. Hasn't been catalogued."

"So you haven't worked out its taxomity?" Sarah asked.

"No, it's been illusive. We think it might be a satellite RNA virus that pairs a yeast, but it's been impossible to positively identify and group it."

"What does that taxi thing mean?" Jennifer asked.

"It means they can't name it until they know which family it belongs to," Sarah explained.

"Like Ryan and Sam's baby?" Jennifer asked.

Sarah was startled by Jennifer's simile.

Jennifer elaborated, "The baby didn't have a name because they didn't know who its family was?"

"No, it's different." Sarah thought to stop there but she knew Jennifer's curiosity would elicit more questions. She decided not to condescend to the young girl. "No, that's different. We knew who the baby's family was. It's just that Ryan was too sad to give the baby a name after Sam's death."

Jennifer's surrogate brother, Nathan, stepped alongside Jennifer and placed a hand on her shoulder.

Doctor Robertson waited for an appropriate break in the conversation before giving Sarah a slight nod and placing the needle in her arm.

Sarah watched as the tip of the needle pushed against her skin until its sharp point poked through.

"What have you found out?" Sarah asked.

"Oh, quite a bit." Dr Robertson smiled as she pulled back the core of the syringe. "Where would you like me to start?"

Sarah was transfixed by how red the freshly drawn blood appeared behind the plastic of the syringe. Her mind went back to Sam. She remembered her blood being darker, almost black.

Nathan ushered Jennifer to a small plastic seat before leaning against a workbench, arms folded across his chest.

"What's causing it?" he asked as if he were the grand master of an inquisition.

"The contagion has proven difficult to pin down. It has a number of unique properties which has meant we have had to study it indirectly," Dr. Robertson said as she labelled the vial of blood.

Jennifer swung her legs as she perched on the edge of the plastic chair. Bored by the conversation that excluded her, she intently watched her red and white trainers as they swung in and out of view behind her knees. Peeking her head further out and clutching the sides of the chair, she could just about see her feet swing through the full arc. Slipping forward, she decided to test her dexterity. She brought her trainers as close to the ground as possible without touching. Tongue between her teeth in concentration, Jennifer tried to trail the lopsided lace on her left trainer along the floor without scuffing the sole.

Dr. Robertson took the freshly drawn blood and placed it on the work station.

Jennifer hopped out of her chair and rushed up to the workbench intrigued, by what Dr. Robertson was doing.

"Careful honey," Dr. Robertson said as Jennifer peered at the ruby liquid clinging to the sides of the vial.

Jennifer looked in awe at the container of blood.

"Have you never seen blood before?" Dr. Robertson asked.

"Not like that," Jennifer said, her eyes fixed.

"It has always looked like that," Nathan said.

"No," Jennifer said, frowning at him. "In jars."

"Do you want to be a doctor when you grow up, honey?" Dr. Robertson asked.

Jennifer looked at her with a blank expression. "Um..."

Dr. Robertson tried to tease an answer from her. "You know, when you're older? What job would you like to do?"

Jennifer looked back over at Sarah as if she needed translation.

Sarah let out a gentle huff. "It's just..."

"Just what?" Dr. Robertson asked.

"We never spoke about things like that," Sarah said, shaking her head. "There wasn't that kind of talk in the warehouse. We were shut in. Surviving, that's all. We didn't think we'd be rescued. We didn't dream anything like real life was left."

Dr. Robertson cast an eye over Sarah and Nathan. She said, "Oh, I see. Well, you should start thinking about it soon. If you don't focus on a job then they'll draft you into the forces like your new friend Bates was. You'd better start looking at your C.V.'s. If you don't have a specialty they can use, it'll be manual labour for you. Or worse: the *army*."

"Who's they?" Sarah asked.

"What do you mean the army?" Nathan asked.

"Oh, I'm sorry," Dr. Robertson said. "I didn't mean to scare you. You see, what's left of the world is under martial law. It's complicated. The world's governed by a mixture of sovereign nations and military overlords. It's kind of like the UN, but with teeth." Trying to continue with the medical, Dr. Robertson fastened a blood pressure cuff around Sarah's arm. "It's not that bad. Most of the western powers have kept their military in check. There are a few warlords who've carved out their own island territories, but they're kept in line by the nuclear powers."

"You mean they've actually threatened to use the bomb?" Sarah was appalled that after all that had happened, people were still willing to kill each other.

"It's no threat," Dr. Robertson said.

"What do you mean?" Nathan asked, though he had already guessed the answer.

"When the shit hit the fan, nuclear power plants started blowing like popcorn," Dr. Robertson said, taking note of Sarah's high blood pressure but deciding to ignore it given the events of her rescue. She unhitched the black fabric cuff. "Add to that the bombs China dropped on her own cities, no one's concerned about the environmental damage a couple more Nagasaki's or Hiroshima's will make."

"The government would actually do that?" Sarah asked.

Dr. Robertson lowered her voice, almost as if she were afraid of being overheard. "Look, there was this strike in Russia a year or so after the Rising. There was this copper mine middle of nowhere in the Arctic circle. The miners wanted better conditions." She scoffed and huffed under her breath, "*Better conditions*. As if there *were* better conditions." Then she continued, "There was a riot when the local military tried to force them back to work. Things got out of hand real quick."

"They were massacred!" Sarah gasped.

"Worse," Dr. Robertson said. "They won. They took over the whole town."

"Did they get nuked?"

"No, the copper mine was too valuable. No, the military council assembled a multinational force. Unlike the UN where they'd get a few countries to participate, they got soldiers from every military left on the planet. Remember how they used to say on MTV how the revolution would be televised?"

Sarah and Nathan nodded.

"We found out the suppression would be too. Every man, woman and child were made an example of. Seven thousand people and it felt like you saw every one of them die."

"That's horrific," Sarah whispered.

"All for the survival of humanity," Dr. Robertson said, "The government sent a message. Everyone plays their part."

"Or else," Sarah added.

"The supply ship gets here next week, so you'll need to have had some thoughts as to what you want to do, or what you can do by the time it arrives," Dr. Robertson said.

Sarah and Nathan looked shocked.

"It's not that bad really. It's no worse than working for a faceless corporation nine to five. If you've got some practical skill they need you'll get your pick of posting."

"And what if we don't?" Nathan asked.

"Then you'll be assessed for a suitable manufacturing, agricultural or military role." Dr. Robertson saw how worried the pair looked. "You know, like working in a factory or a farm or something like that. Look, I'm sorry if I've panicked you. It's really not that bad. All the work people do now is geared toward preserving mankind. Whatever you end up doing, it's all in aid of our survival."

Neither Sarah or Nathan looked convinced.

"All of that's a way off." Doctor Robertson turned her attention back to Sarah's physical.

"So what do people do?" Nathan asked.

"For the war effort? They produce the raw materials to keep us going. Food, steel, oil, concrete. Things like that. The military acts like police and enforce quarantine to protect the general population from infection. They're also used to secure infected territory, like foraging for supplies on the mainland or clearing islands of the walking dead."

"That all I got?" Nathan said bitterly. "Serving fries, pumping gas or joining the army?"

"Well, there are specialist roles like the research onboard the Ishtar," Dr. Robertson said.

"Hell, end of the world happens and my career prospects are the same as they've ever been," Nathan joked.

"We got sidetracked," Sarah interjected. "What's causing the walking death?"

"It looks like a virus," Dr. Robertson answered.

Sarah caught her gaze, "What do you mean by *looks like*?"

"It's all bit technical," Dr. Robertson said dismissively.

"Humour me," Sarah said.

"Okay. Well, it has all the appearance of an enveloped virus, but we haven't been able to extract any of the genome, only the host's."

"Won't DNA tell you where it comes from, like the AIDs and monkey thing?" Nathan asked.

"Well, not quite," Dr. Robertson responded. "If we can sequence it, it won't tell us anything for sure, just narrow down the search."

"What do you mean it has the appearance of an enveloped virus?" Sarah asked.

"It doesn't lysed its host cell it—"

"You what?" Nathan butted in.

Sarah turned to him and explained, "It means it doesn't destroy the host cell. Most viruses pop the cell they invade like a balloon, spreading copies of themselves in the process."

"I'm impressed," Dr. Robertson said. "You obviously have a good grasp of biology. Were you a nurse?"

Sarah gave the tiniest of smiles. "I was studying at university before..."

"Medicine?" Dr. Robertson's voice held a note of excitement.

"Inorganic Chemistry," Sarah said.

"Oh." The excitement was lower but Dr. Robertson was still interested. "Well, maybe you'd like to assist Professor Cutler and me."

"I don't know," Sarah said.

Dr. Robertson nodded. "No, I understand it's been a busy day for you all, I dare—"

A loud crash drew their attention to the corner of the room as a metal lid thundered its way off the workbench onto the floor. Now open, a silver container bubbled a cloud of steam down its sides and onto the desk. Beside it, Jennifer stood, looking panicked.

With a calm, slow voice and an unblinking gaze, Dr. Robertson addressed the girl. "Back up slowly to Nathan now, Jennifer."

Hearing the doctor's measured voice, Jennifer shot a scared look at Sarah.

Gently, Sarah simply nodded.

As Jennifer backed into Nathan's arms, Dr. Robertson opened a drawer and donned a thick, flame retardant glove. She retrieved the lid and secured it back onto the container.

"I'm sorry," Jennifer said, with a tremor in her voice and a sheepish look on her face.

"It's okay honey, just don't go touching stuff in here," Dr. Robertson said, replacing the glove.

"What is it?" Sarah asked.

"Just liquid nitrogen," Dr. Robertson said. "Nut if she had spilt it on herself..."

"That's that stuff you see on science programs where they dip a flower in and it shatters like glass," Nathan blurted enthusiastically, keen to show his education included something other than shooting squirrel.

Bending down to eye level, Dr. Robertson spoke to Jennifer. "How would you like to go next?"

Jennifer nodded slowly, unable to refuse after her mishap.

"All this balloon popping," Nathan began as he lifted Jennifer onto the gurney, "does that tell you how it started?"

Dr. Robertson looked at Sarah, who was wearing an apologetic smile. "Well, it reproduces using the host cell and sending out copies of itself cocooned in parcels of the cell membrane." She looked at Nathan. "It's kind of like wearing a space suit because the virus can't survive outside the body." Happy Nathan had grasped the analogy, she returned her focus to Sarah.

Sarah took her glance as in invitation for another question: "So it is dormant outside a host unlike a bacteria?"

"Well, here's an interesting thing, Sarah," Dr. Robertson explained. "Its envelop gives it a short window outside the body, no more than a few hours, but after that it dies. Some viruses can lie dormant almost indefinitely, but not this one." She attached an automated blood pressure cuff on Jennifer without breaking stride. "This will go tight on your arm for a moment." Looking back up at Sarah, she continued, "The virus appears to need to colonise the body to survive."

The machine whirred as a motorised pump inflated the cuff.

"So if it doesn't survive outside the body, are we the natural reservoir?" Sarah asked.

"No," Dr. Robertson said as she unhooked Jennifer from the blood pressure monitor. "I don't think so. It's too destructive, too contagious and too quick. If it had been in humans before it would have surfaced—"

"Doctor Robertson," a man in the crisp blue uniform said as he stepped into the examination room. Suddenly the cabin felt cramped.

The man was old but energetic, with a complexion that looked as weathered as his ship. He reminded Sarah of her great uncle. His stride was confident and his face reflected a hard fought life, no scars just well worn with rough and sagging skin. The man's hat looked old in comparison to his uniform, as old perhaps as his thin translucent skin, but its millered perfection outshone the baseball style caps the rest of the crew wore.

"Captain Warden, let me introduce our guests." Dr. Robertson gestured with her hand. "This is Sarah, Nathan and Jennifer."

"Let me extend my sympathies," Captain Warden said. "I hear from Private Bates and Private Chernov that you lost companions this morning."

"We did," Sarah said. Both she and Nathan dropped their gaze at the thought. Sarah composed herself. "Thank you, Captain. I don't know what we would have done if your men hadn't come along."

"You're lucky they did," Dr. Robertson said as she labelled Jennifer's sample. "I'm surprised you had the strength to make it to the helicopter." She turned her head to face the captain as she worked on the samples. "Captain, both Sarah and Nathan are malnourished. Another few weeks and I don't think they could have made it. I'll give them all vitamin shots, but other than that it's just a matter of diet."

"Good." Captain Warden looked around the small medical bay as if he were looking for some lost item. "I've asked Commander Patterson to arrange some quarters." Unable to locate the imagined object, he addressed Sarah. "Once you've had time to get cleaned up, I'd like to invite you to the Captain's table for supper. I'm sure we all have a lot of questions."

Sarah and Nathan thanked him.

"Doctor Robertson, where *is* Professor Cutler?"

"He's working on an important culture right now," Dr. Robertson said, her voice flat and clipped.

"Wasting more specimens?" Captain Warden said.

Doctor Robertson put down what she was working with, turned and folded her arms. "No, he's working on cultures. Those are the small round dishes."

Captain Warden's face flushed red as he jabbed a nicotine-stained finger in Dr. Robertson's direction. "Don't…" He lowered his hand and took an audible breath. He cast his eyes over the survivors before steeling his gaze once more on Dr. Robertson. "This is a conversation for later. In the meantime you have another patient to attend to." Captain Warden called into the corridor, "Private Chernov."

"Yes, sir," Angel replied in her creamy Russian lilt.

She came to the door, but didn't enter, unwilling to add to the already crowded room. Instead she stood in the corridor supporting her injured arm with her good one.

"What seems to be the matter?" Dr. Robertson asked.

Captain Warden stepped out of the line of view so that the doctor could see the deep purple bruise emanating from Angel's elbow.

A disembodied voice billowed down the corridor, "Is the Captain with you?"

"Yes, Commander," Angel spat out the harsh K like it was an insult.

"Ah, Commander Patterson," Captain Warden said as Patterson popped into view from round the door. "Would you show our guests to their quarters? They've had quite a day and I'm sure they'd like to freshen up."

"Certainly, sir. This way please." Patterson beckoned the survivors out into the corridor.

Doctor Robertson called after the trio, "Before you go, we'll need to monitor you for a few months. I won't know for sure until I've run a few more tests, but it's a good bet you've suffered liver damage. I'd recommend no alcohol until we've had a good few weeks of recovery."

Sarah and Nathan nodded.

As they squeezed into the corridor, Patterson stepped past them back into the medical room. He reported, "Sir, we've have a weather update from the Azores. Hurricane Emily has changed course and is heading north. The leading edge should we with us in about six hours."

"Damn!" The broken capillaries on the Captain's face flared red again. "What's the rating?"

"It's a category three, which means we're in no danger we can simply hove to, but..."

"But we can't land the chopper in a storm," Warden surmised.

"Idris has already refuelled and started pre-flight checks."

"On whose orders?" Captain Warden asked.

"No one's, sir."

"Does he know about the storm?"

Patterson nodded.

"The times don't add up, Mister Patterson. He'd never beat the storm back."

"I agree, sir," Patterson said.

"Very well. Tell Idris to stand down on the rescue mission." Captain Warden covered his mouth with his hand and gently pinched his nose as if he were about to clear his cyanosis.

"Aye, aye, sir," Patterson acknowledged as he exited. He nodded to Sarah and Nathan. "If you'll come this way..."

"Now I've got two of my best men stranded on the mainland with no hope of a rescue until this storm passes," Warden snarled out the last of his livid breath with, "All because of you!"

"What do you mean because of *me*?" Doctor Robertson said indignantly.

"You and your damn specimens!" Captain Warden looked ready to draw an angry fist along the row of blood-filled test tubes. "I've lost eight people because of your insane experiments, Doctor."

"Losses are a regrettable part of—"

"If you and Frankenstein would stop wasting specimens..." Warden butted in. He shuddered and swallowed down his rage, standing contemplating for a moment, before speaking again. "Private Chernov, give me and the Doctor a few moments alone, please."

"Aye, sir." Angel turned and stepped down the corridor, still cradling her wounded arm.

Captain Warden closed the door to the medical bay. "Anything I should know about?"

"What do you mean?"

"The survivors!" Warden snapped.

"If you mean bite or scratch marks, then the answer's no."

"Any sign of the contagion?"

"No." Dr. Robertson knew where the Captain's questioning was leading. "If it does use a carrier I doubt any of them are it."

"You'll run the blood testing regardless."

"Of course I will, but we've never found a symptomless carrier and I don't think we ever will. It's just too damned invasive." Dr. Robertson could see the Captain's jaw twitch. "And before you ask your next question, *no* it has not gone airborne on the mainland."

"How can you be so sure?" Captain Warden demanded.

Dr. Robertson despaired at the Captain's lack of scientific knowledge. She pulled her hand from her lab coat pocket and gestured in the direction the survivors had been led. "For one, these people wouldn't have lasted this long if it had gone airborne. Secondly, I doubt there are any more survivors on the mainland to get infected. The contagion has effectively stopped spreading because there is no one left to spread it to. That means less chance for it to interact and less opportunity for it to mutate."

Teeth clenched to hold back some of his anger, Captain Warden growled, "You said it yourself, *less of a chance*."

"There is always a margin for error in science," Dr. Robertson said unapologetically, "but it's almost impossible."

"Just as impossible as the dead attacking the living!" Captain Warden bellowed.

Dr. Robertson felt chastised. "That's unfair, Captain, and you know—"

"Unfair or not I have to weigh every possibility. If I just had my crew to worry about then the scales would have tipped against you and your arrogant boyfriend long ago, but I don't just have the responsibility of this crew on my hands, so you'll have to excuse me if I'm cautious." His brow furrowed as he remembered what had angered him in the first place. "Anyway, where is Dr. Frankenstein? I gave orders for both of you to examine the survivors."

"*Professor Cutler,*" Doctor Robertson stressed the pronunciation of his name, "is in his lab and he doesn't appreciate it when people call him that."

Captain Warden violently brought his fist down on the work surface. The thump set the vials of blood shuddering in their stand. "Appreciate it or not, I gave orders for both of you to conduct the examination."

Dr. Robertson's jaw fell slightly open. "Professor Cutler was at a crucial point in his research and didn't think it necessary to—"

"Necessary!" the Captain shouted.

Dr. Robertson flinched at the ferocity of the Captain's bark.

"I've had it with him disobeying my orders. You tell him I want a report on his crucial research by nineteen hundred hours tonight."

"The supply ship's not due to pick up our research for another seven—"

"I said I want it on my desk tonight!"

Although stunned by the Captain's aggression, Dr. Robertson was now angry at both the captain for being so disrespectful and at herself for taking it. She snapped, "Tell him yourself! I don't take orders from you!"

To demonstrate her indignity she stepped past the Captain and opened the door to let him out. As she pulled the door open, Captain Warden took a grip of her arm. Dr. Robertson looked down at the rough hand squeezing her bicep. The grip was forceful and tight enough to cut off the circulation. Her first thought was to say *you're hurting me* but she didn't want to give him the satisfaction. He stared deep into her eyes. His were watery and pale, like the blue had been leeched from them by years of harsh weather. They sat in eyeballs the colour of parchment as if tainted by the nicotine of his habitual smoking. Trails of red blood vessels threaded their way over the tarnished white.

"As long as this is my ship," Captain Warden hissed, "you and everyone on it follow my orders."

"Or what?" Her defiance wasn't past her lips before she regretted it. Warden could be dangerous but Dr. Robertson had faith that her special status would protect her. Her regret was that her lapsed restraint would bring down a tirade of complaining.

"I have the authority to destroy this ship and everyone onboard if I deem it necessary. You, me, your boyfriend, everyone. What makes you think I'd be any less willing to kill any one of you? Hell, you give me a reason to execute the both of you and this pleasure cruise is over." He let go of her arm, subconsciously emphasising his point. "Me and the crew could sail straight back to St Helena for some R & R. There's not a soul onboard who would say no to that."

"And risk getting posted to the South Island?" Doctor Robertson pointed out. "You wouldn't."

"No?" Warden challenged.

Suddenly it dawned on Dr. Robertson that this might not be an idle threat. Maybe the years out on the open water had drained him of more than his eye colour. She said defensively, "You wouldn't. You know how important our work is here."

"Important?!" Captain Warden snapped back. "You could kill us all! What little is left of humanity could die if you fuck up! Christ, it's hard enough losing good men to your work, and today's foray may well have added to the death toll you and Frankenstein have inflicted."

Dr. Robertson changed tack. "It's still better than the risk you'd be taking clearing out W.D.'s in New—"

"You work out this risk Doctor," Captain Warden broke in. "You and your twisted boyfriend better start showing me some results and some respect starting with that report, nineteen hundred hours tonight!" He stepped out of the medical bay. "Or the things tied up in your lab will be the least of your worries."

He turned and barged past Angel.

Dr. Robertson placed her palm to her forehead and let out a long breath of exasperation. She quivered slightly as the last of the air slipped out. There was a slight pause before she composed herself and started breathing normally again.

A Russian voice shook her from her introversion.

"We have term in Russia for people like him," Angel said as she entered the room. "Zasranec." Angel judged by her expression that Dr. Robertson's grasp of Russian wasn't sufficient enough for a translation. "It means asshole."

Dr. Robertson let a smile rise on her exasperated face.

Angel smiled back. "Now would you look at my arm?"

Gathering Storm

A GREY HAND FLEXED over the clean linen. With shattered nails it rasped its mummified fingers over the cloth. A patch of grime showed where the hand had been clawing.

Professor Cutler turned the valve on the cannula protruding from the pawing hand and flicked a switch. Whirring to life, a pump started sucking half congealed vitriol from the corpse. The white tape that secured the tubing to the pallid flesh was in stark contrast to the dark brown fluid that oozed out. The cadaverous gunk trickled into a beaker at the side of the gurney.

With milky eyes, the unwilling subject followed its tormentor around the lab. The zombie would like nothing more than to sink its teeth into the flesh of its captor but the thick leather straps held it firmly down. The creature tried to give out a moan but the ball gag in its mouth stifled its plaintive call to a soggy gurgle.

Before the Rising, Professor Cutler had likened many of his contemporaries to zombies, dull minded and slavish creatures. Again and again his maverick ideas had been dismissed by the hierarchy of academia. Time and time again, Professor Cutler's work had stood up to his peers' scrutiny. Eventually the establishment had been forced to acknowledge this young genius. Now he was the world's leading expert on Virology. Professor Cutler liked to think that it was in spite of most of his former colleagues being turned into actual zombies.

Satisfied that he had enough of the brown sludge, Professor Cutler twisted the valve closed with his latex-clad fingers and walked across to his workbench. He sat down on the high wooden stool beside the microscope and placed his macabre sample in front of him. Turning round, he walked past a second, empty, gurney. It had been set up to receive one of the fresh specimens from the mainland that never arrived. He made a mental note that he should tidy it away as he drew up to the lab's fridge. On the front was a notice in his own handwriting: 'Medical samples only. No food or drink.'

He had originally written, 'No consumables,' but Amy, (Doctor Robertson as he called her in public,) argued the need for such a sign since no one used the lab other than them.

Professor Cutler felt he eloquently argued the hypothetical merits of his protocol. Whether Amy had finally seen his point or simply grown bored of a fruitless debate, she had relented. As a parting shot, though, she had sunk his original sign by pointing out the rest of the crew wouldn't know what *consumables* meant.

Professor Cutler pulled on the chrome handle and looked inside. On the top shelf at the front was a carousel neatly cradling a dozen vials on two levels. An ideogram in yellow lettering and swirling black tendrils adorned the container: 'Danger - Biohazard'

Cutler plucked one of the vials free. Another label in Professor Cutler's handwriting was stuck on the Perspex. It simply read 'S-117a'.

Upon shutting the fridge door, there was a sharp click and the compressor hummed to life, the appliance determined to compensate for the intruding warmth of the lab.

The zombie strapped to the gurney writhed as it watched the human pace the room, its unwavering gaze fixed on its prey. The Professor ignored its dissent with the same mundane disregard he held for the humming fridge.

Setting the vial down next to the microscope, he opened up one of the many cupboards and pulled out a syringe and a line of plastic hose.

Like a junkie, Professor Cutler bound up his arm with the plastic tubing and sunk the needle into the most promising-looking vein. The nape of his elbow looked like a reconnaissance photo from some bombing campaign, pockmarked and scabbed in pinpricked increments. He drew yet another syringe full and taped a plaster over the leak.

The last item for the impending experiment was a fresh petri dish. He lined his equipment up in a neat row to the right of the microscope: the syringe of fresh blood, the empty petri dish, the vial of serum and finally the beaker of fluid from the cadaver. All the pieces in place, he pulled two new pipettes from a drawer in the desk and unwrapped them from their sterile casing. The wadded-up wrappers were squashed into a ball and tossed across the room towards a waste paper bin in the far corner. It hit the wall above the bucket and tumbled down onto the rim of the bin. Hitting the edge, it bounced and fell unsuccessfully onto the tiled floor.

Professor Cutler gave a huff of disgust. He flicked on the computer attached to the underside of the desk. It was an old beige thing, yet another symbol of the under-resourcing he'd had to deal with. The hard drive churned and clunked as the cooling fan gathered speed to a steady purr. Light emitting diodes blinked red and yellow and green as the relic wheezed to life. The only modern looking thing about Professor Cutler's computer equipment was the large black box that housed the uninterrupted power supply. Like the beige box it sat beside, it too was signaling with bursts of traffic sequence lights. The ship's erratic diesel engines and the decades old wiring competed to short out Professor Cutler's hard drives, hence the necessity for an emergency power supply.

A sharp beep drew Professor Cutler's attention to the monitor as it flickered on, revealing bright white lines of bootup prompts against the black.

Sometimes the computer would just freeze up at this point, usually in hot weather or if it had crashed after a prolonged amount of use. The screen jumped again, this time showing the operating system's front window. A ribbon of rainbow colours softly paraded below the company logo. Content the machine was working, he ambled over to the bin to retrieve the wayward rubbish.

With his long fingers, he scooped up the packaging and dunked it into its rightful place in the bin.

Cutler's tall, thin physique would have made him most people's first choice for their basketball team, but the truth was his academic work had always taken precedence. At school he had excelled in all his subjects including sports, but as soon as the opportunity arose he had abandoned everything that didn't support his love of biology. He still had the same mop of chocolate brown hair he had when he left school some twenty years ago. What's more, his exodus at age seventeen to university and the seclusion of a laboratory had protected his skin from the ravages of natural light. Other than losing the acne, he had retained a youthful appearance. Unlike most other people, the Rising hadn't drained him. Cutler knew he didn't look his age. Part of him hoped it was his boyish looks that had attracted Amy to him, but he knew it had more to do with the lack of men with an I.Q. above one hundred onboard ship. The pragmatist he was saw no point in worrying about Amy's reasons; just accept it and enjoy it.

With the Rising, his dogged obsession in all things microscopic had become one of the greatest assets in mankind's arsenal. Professor Cutler liked that, not that it hadn't always been true, but at least now the world knew it.

Well, what's left of the world.

And with no intellectual equals within two thousand miles, he'd got the girl as well. Professor Cutler also liked that. Recognition and a healthy sex life. Had there ever been any other research professor in the history of mankind who could boast that? For one person, at least, the global catastrophe had worked out just fine.

Cutler sat back down, content with the thought as to how fortunate he was, regardless of how well deserved it may be.

He pinched the first pipette between thumb and finger and corrected the angle by a fraction of a degree. Satisfied all was regimented to perfection, he leaned back and stared at the computer screen, willing it to life. Eventually the screen lit up, accompanied by a soft chord of strings. Professor Cutler took no time to bring up the program that interfaced with the microscope. On the screen a glowing white blur appeared. Contented everything was in place, he launched the recording software.

"Test serum one-one-seven," he said into the microphone beside the monitor.

He picked up the syringe and squirted some of the still warm blood into the petri dish. Setting it aside, he picked up the vial, and despite the lack of purchase from his latex gloves, he twisted off its cap with ease. Reaching across the table he picked up the first pipette, dipped it into the container and drew up a drop of serum. The droplet was added to the pool of blood and Cutler used the tip of the pipette to stir the elixir in. Happy that it was thoroughly mixed, he placed the petri dish under the microscope and dropped the used instrument into the bright yellow medical waste bin beside his workbench.

The screen flooded with a view of corpulent red blood cells and the room took on a pink hue as the computer monitor turned crimson. Professor Cutler adjusted the focus to see the blood cells before picking up the second pipette.

He sucked up a small amount of ooze from the container holding the loathsome zombie bile and brought it over the dish with his blood.

His hand hesitated, hovering over the petri dish as if he were waiting for the light to turn green or a starter's whistle to sound its shrill call.

A little mantra, (a *prayer* would be the correct term if Professor Cutler were religious,) circled in his mind.

"This will work this will work this will work."

Slowly he lowered the virus laden fluid into the blood.

* * * * *

Nathan emerged from the bathroom, face clean-shaven with red, leopard spot nicks. He rolled up the very corner of his towel and wedged the point into his ear. Swirling the tip frantically as he did reminded Sarah of a dog scratching an itch.

Standing in front of her with just the towel in his hand and the one around his waist, Sarah was struck by how skinny he was. She hadn't seen him in this state of undress for such a long time. His muscles were well defined, but instead of looking toned he just looked gaunt.

She looked down at Jennifer on the bed beside her. She too was thin, but it was more due to the growth spurt she'd had in the last few months than malnourishment. When Ray had come to Sarah at the end of February with the stock take, they had all cut their rations even further, with the exception of Jennifer's.

Nathan took the towel out of his ear. "This is the weirdest thing to feel. Like..." He paused, searching for the right words.

"Like things are normal," Sarah said as she stroked a brush through Jennifer's damp hair.

"Yeah," Nathan agreed. He walked over to the dresser, rubbing the towel to his head, giving his damp hair a final rubbing. Hanging from the side of the unit was his drying Nirvana T-shirt. The faded shirt looked newer, the water sodden fabric making the colours appear darker than usual.

Nathan threw the towel he'd been using for his hair over the back of the room's solitary chair. He reached onto the dresser and picked up his leather wristband. There was an almost imperceptible tan line across his forearm where he wore it and the brown leather of the band was scuffed and cracked, but the distressed look had been in fashion before the Rising and Nathan had said it added character. As he fastened the leather strap by its plain silver buckle, Nathan caught a glimpse of his arm.

"Jeez, would you look at that," he said, displaying the underside of his arm to Sarah and Jennifer.

Around the grey square of residual glue left from a sticking plaster was the puncture mark from where Doctor Robertson had taken blood. Around the small red hole was a coin-sized bruise, bright purple and angry.

"That looks sore," Jennifer said.

Nathan prodded at the bruise, gently to start with, then deeper. "Nah, its fine."

"I thought Doctor Robertson told us to keep the plaster on for twenty-four hours," Sarah said.

"She did. Must have fallen off in the shower," Nathan said, continuing to poke at the discoloration.

"You'd better go and get it. I don't want to find a used plaster stuck to my toothbrush." Sarah screwed up her face and made an *ewww* sound as she stuck her tongue out at Jennifer. Jennifer giggled and joined the chorus.

"I'll look for it in a minute," Nathan said as he felt his T-shirt. Feeling the garment was still wet, he turned back to Sarah. "Is there an iron in here?"

"An iron? No I don't think so," Sarah answered. "What do you want that for?"

"Take some of the dampness out of my shirt," Nathan replied.

"Why not get some clothes from the ship's stores?" Sarah asked, looking at the shabby T-shirt. Rather than trying to launder out the grime and viscera of their rescue, Sarah had settled for a pair of jeans and a military style green shirt.

Nathan feigned shock. "And lose my identity along with everything else?"

"They'll clean it and hand it back," Sarah said. "You'll be missing it for a day or so. That's what I did."

"I don't like other people doing my laundry. They always do it wrong. Like when Elspeth put in that fabric softener that brought me out in a rash."

"That was only once," Sarah countered, "and she felt guilty for months after."

"I wish Elspeth were here," Jennifer said in a quiet voice.

Sarah paused from brushing the young girl's hair. "I know, we all do."

"Will she have turned by now?" Jennifer asked.

Nathan looked at Sarah, his face blank in shock at the question.

Jennifer hadn't been her normal boisterous self and Sarah now realised that she'd been too busy with her own grief to think about Jennifer's.

When Sarah didn't answer, all Nathan could let out was a dumb *ummm* sound.

"That would depend on the infection," Sarah said. "Some people last longer if they're stronger or if there wasn't much infection."

The simple explanation called up dozens of faces for Sarah. The faces of the people she had seen turn. The first one had been her flatmate.

Sarah had awoken to the sound of pounding coming from the landing outside. There was a jingling noise and as Sarah drew closer to the door, a whimpering sound like an injured dog came from behind it. Through the spyhole, Sarah could see light and shade twist through the glass as someone or something scratched and thumped outside. Just as she was about to turn the lock, the door flew open and in stumbled her flatmate Tricia. Her face was pale with wide, raw eyes staring out at Sarah. She lurched forward, almost collapsing as Sarah reached out to steady her.

"Lock it!" Tricia screeched as she slumped down the wall. It was only then that Sarah noticed a glistening trail of blood had followed her in.

Seeing the blood, Sarah had knelt down to help her friend.

"The door! Get the friggin' door," Tricia hissed.

Tricia's keys were still in the door and around the barrel of the lock were gouges where the keys had scratched into the paintwork. A scream echoed up the landing and Sarah thought she saw figures in the hall below. She didn't wait to get a good look. Instead, she had yanked the keys free and shut the door.

"What happened? Are you okay?" Sarah blurted out.

"No, I'm not okay!" Tricia sobbed, tears streaming down her face. "Some fucker attacked me! There's a riot goin' on!"

Upon Tricia saying that, Sarah had become more attuned to the sounds from outside: breaking glass, shouts and screams all punctuated by distant sirens.

This had been Sarah's induction into the Rising and Tricia was only the first person Sarah would lose to it.

"Will the soldiers shoot her when she turns?" Jennifer asked.

Sensing Sarah's mood darken, Nathan tried to shut down the conversation. "Let's not talk about this just now."

"I'd want to be shot," Jennifer added. "I don't think it would be nice to come back. I wish we were all here."

"I wish that too, Jennifer." Sarah said hugging her close. Tears started rolling down her cheeks and onto the little girl's hair. "I wish they were here, too."

Nathan sat down on the bed next to Jennifer and put an arm around both girls. "You made the right decision, Sarah," he said, trying to comfort her. "You made the *only* decision."

"What about the rest of them, Nathan?" Sarah asked, more tears in her eyes. This morning the last of her hope, exhausted by melancholy and the chorus of moans outside, she had decided to die. Now that disregard for her own life had brought the reckless deaths of her friends. "It wasn't the right decision for *them.*"

"Ryan's with those Marines. He'll be all right," Nathan said, feebly trying to placate her.

"It's my fault," Sarah sobbed. "If we'd just have stayed put, maybe signalled the helicopter or something, rather than running for it…"

Nathan squeezed his fingers gently into Sarah's shoulder. Her soft warm skin had an addictive quality to it. Her vulnerability just made him long to be close to her. He said, "If we'd have stayed, we would all have died of hunger, or been overrun trying to get food." He squeezed her shoulder again and stroked his palm down her arm. "Remember the Hanson brothers. And if we'd have signalled the chopper there's no telling if they would have seen it and we would still have had to gone outside. No, you made a good call and we all agreed with you. No one argued against it because we knew it was our only hope."

"It's just so wrong, it's all so wrong," Sarah protested at the injustice.

Nathan reached over and kissed her tenderly on the cheek. "We're safe now."

"Nathan don't," Sarah snapped and pulled back.

Nathan let his embrace slip and he sat back.

"Don't what?" Nathan rubbed at his eyebrows with his thumb and forefinger. "I mean, I'm just... We're only..."

Not for the first time, Nathan couldn't find the words. He stood up, grabbing his jeans and his wet T-shirt.

"Fuck it. I'm going to find an iron," he said, discarding his towel as he hopped into his jeans.

"Nathan," Sarah reluctantly called out in a weak voice.

Nathan ignored her, and barefoot he padded out of the cabin, clutching his wet T-shirt.

✳ ✳ ✳ ✳ ✳

The door to the laboratory burst open and Doctor Robertson stomped in. Cutler smiled without looking up from his work. When Amy got into a mood like this it reminded him of little girls pretending to be grown up, chastising dolls with stern looks and wagging fingers while they clomped around in mummy's shoes. A snort came from behind him.

"The Captain just threatened to have us executed!" Doctor Robertson exclaimed.

"Just in time with the liquid nitrogen. I want to preserve some of these samples." Professor Cutler held out a petri dish, gaze still firm on the computer screen.

Doctor Robertson thumped the flask of liquid nitrogen onto the workbench and snatched the sample out of his hand.

"Aren't you listening to me?!" Doctor Robertson placed a forceful hand on Cutler's shoulder and spun him round to face her. "He's threatening to kill us if we don't start producing results and bowing down to his orders!"

"Amy my dear, you know he can't do that." Professor Cutler clasped her free hand in both of his. "What would Ascension Command have to say if he came back without us—and more importantly, without our research? Hmmm..."

Doctor Robertson pulled her hand away from his light grip. "He's got two people left on the mainland and he's looking for an excuse to blame us."

"Well, that's terrible, but I think these latest findings will placate him." Cutler let a smile grow on his thin lips. "The resequencing worked this time."

He clicked on the mouse and zoomed in on the blood sample, bringing the cells into sharp focus.

Doctor Robertson's face dropped in disbelief. She bent down to stare at the screen.

"Look, the pathogen isn't affecting the sample," Cutler said as he moved out of her way.

"That's amazing!" Doctor Robertson gasped.

"The tissue immunised with the modified agent shows normal cell function," Professor Cutler said, trying not to sound boastful.

"Which one?" she asked.

"One-one-seven-A," Cutler replied.

"This is a huge leap forward," Doctor Robertson said, still stunned by what she saw on the screen. A wave of excitement rushed up within her. After four years of dead ends and failed experiments, here was the first tangible breakthrough. She turned round to face Professor Cutler, and grabbing him by the lapels of his lab coat she pulled him in, planting a huge open-mouthed kiss on his lips.

When Amy finally pulled away, Cutler was short of breath, grinning and very turned on. He caught his breath and let his pragmatism take hold.

"It's just a blood sample," he said. "We won't know if it works until we test it on a living human being."

"But we'd need to immunise them, then deliberately infect them," Doctor Robertson said, still flushed from the kiss.

"I know, it's unethical. But we don't have to deliberately infect anyone. We can immunise the collection party," Professor Cutler reasoned. "I mean, what's their attrition rate at the moment? One in ten? Okay, the study will take longer, but—"

"No, no, no," Doctor Robertson said, tapping a finger against the desk as she thought. "It would never work. The Captain wants results now, and he's not willing to risk any more men. We have to think of a quicker way of proving it. Still, it's a tremendous breakthrough."

Cutler nodded in agreement. "And for once, something the Captain can understand."

* * * * *

Bates stomped towards the ship's makeshift gym to work out some of the frustration boiling inside him. For the second time today Patterson had interrogated him over what had happened on the mainland. Annoying though this was, what really pissed the marine off was the news that the rescue operation had been postponed. Bates figured that battering hell out of the bench press was preferable to battering hell out of the executive officer—or battering hell out of Lawrence French for his remarks about promotion through attrition. Bates knew that if anyone could survive on the mainland it would be Cahz. But he also knew the longer he stayed there the higher the likelihood that something would go wrong.

The gym was the best idea. If he struck a superior officer it would exclude him from the rescue operation. Patterson and Bates didn't get along and the executive officer would use any excuse to put him back in the brig.

As he marched past the open armoury door he spotted Idris with a trolley of stacked ammunition.

"Where you going with that?" Bates asked.

"Just loading the bird up," Idris answered, a nervous smile on his face. "You know, prep for the rescue mission."

Bates folded his arms. "Patterson's just told me the op's been scratched due to the storm."

"Yeah, it was," Idris said, trying to push past Bates. "I'm just getting organised to take off when the weather clears."

"You know it's against regs to store ammo in the chopper if it's being tied down for a storm." Bates lent against the bulkhead, deliberately blocking Idris' way. "Hey, wait a minute..."

"Bates..." Idris looked around checking to see if Bates was the only one within earshot.

"What?" Bates said, trying to keep his smile from detracting from his innocent tone.

Idris placed a finger up to his lips.

"Ahh," Bates said as he mimed zipping his mouth shut.

Idris took one last look around before continuing to load up the trolley. He asked, "How the hell does someone so dumb live so long?"

Bates took the ammo box Idris was struggling with and stacked it on top of the rest. He replied, "I stay alive by avoiding doing stupid things like flying out to the mainland in a storm!"

"Storm's four hours away," Idris said. He lent in closer to Bates. "That gives me time to find Cahz and the rest before it hits."

"But that chopper won't fly in a storm," Bates pointed out. "Even if it does, you can't land it back on the ship with thirty foot waves."

Idris shook his head, "I ain't coming straight back."

"The ammo!" Bates twigged. "You're planning on landing and sitting out the storm!"

Idris nodded. "It might never make landfall, and even if it does, with just me and the ammo on the way out we've got enough fuel to fly inland if we have to."

"So you weren't planning on inviting me along?" Bates said, pushing the trolley out of the armoury. The cart was heavy with munitions and it took a heave to get it rolling.

"No way, man," Idris said, laughing. "How else you gonna stay alive?"

Bates took a glance over his shoulder at Idris as he followed behind. "Look, you sure you want to do this? I mean, you've not been in country more than thirty minutes since the world died and even then you've never left the chopper." The trolley veered to the right and Bates had to push hard to compensate for his oversteering. "Hell, you even piss in a bottle rather than setting down."

"I'm not leaving my friends out there," Idris said. His voice held a weight of conviction Bates seldom heard.

"This isn't just a rescue op for you, is it?" Bates said.

"I learnt to piss in a bottle when we were evacuating Richmond." Idris squinted in the bright sunshine as the pair of them emerged onto the deck. "I logged a hundred and sixteen hours flight time that week; only slept when they were refuelling the bird. I was one of the last choppers out, and yes I saw the compound being overrun."

Bates grunted as he shoved the trolley up the shallow incline to the landing pad. "Where do you want these?" he asked as he wheeled the crates level with the chopper.

"Best put them in the back seats in case things are hot when I arrive," Idris replied.

They started loading the ammunition.

"Richmond was a cluster fuck," Bates said as he loaded the first crate.

"Navy air had it down tight," Idris replied. "We ran like clockwork. We even got the abort over the radio a couple of miles out. Ops centre had an eye in the sky. Whole thing was on fifty-eight inch plasma screens on the command deck of the Defender."

Idris paused for a moment. Bates wasn't sure if it was the memory or the weight of the crate that caused him to stop.

"I kept going anyway," Idris continued. "I guessed there must be somewhere to land, a clear rooftop or something, but there wasn't. They were everywhere. You could hear the screams over the sound of the rotors. There were people reaching out for me, begging for me to land but the place was crawling with W.D.'s. Even then I might have tried a landing if it hadn't been for the comm chatter. The chopper ahead had landed despite receiving the abort. Something must have jammed his comms open, 'cause after the screams had stopped you could hear him being eaten. Don't know why, but I shone my lights where he'd landed. The blades were still spinning but that was all."

Bates placed the last ammunition box in the back of the chopper. He turned back and shook his head. "Those sort of things can haunt you."

"I don't think that part of the op ever bothered me," Idris said, shrugging. "Guess it was too much. That much carnage kind of overwhelms you to the point of being numb. No, what stays with me was the route out. That's what stops me from sleeping at night." Idris paused and shuffled uncomfortably, looking around as if he were nervous about who might overhear. When settled down, he locked eye contact with Bates. "We flew over a lot of fucked-up country. Same route every time to make search and rescue easier if a pilot went down." Idris felt he needed to explain. He knew Bates wasn't as dumb as he led people to believe, but he didn't assume he knew the intricacies of air traffic control. "It keeps stuff moving in air corridors, too. You also knew you weren't going to fly headlong into another chopper. The route took us past an electricity pylon; one of the big metal ones carrying power into the city. On the second day of the op, I spotted a group of W.D.'s at the base of one of them. It was their outstretched arms that drew my attention. They had spotted something they wanted to get to."

A deck hand walked passed and nodded at Bates and Idris as they stood by the chopper. Once he had passed, Idris continued, "Sitting among the struts, out of reach, was a family. Grandpa, Dad, couple of kids and a baby held in mommy's arms. They saw me fly out and waved like hell, but I was heading back to the carrier with a full load of brass. Few hours later I was on my way back out and flew past them again. They waved like hell again but by now the base of the pylon was heaving with corpses. Even if I could have landed there was no way they could have got to me."

"Couldn't you have winched them up?" Bates asked.

Idris shook his head. "Not a chance. The power was still on at that point. Would have fried us all if I'd have tried. I lost count how many times I flew past them that week but every time I flew past there were hundreds more of those things gathered round the base of the pylon. Every time I flew past, the family waved furiously and every time I felt worse that I was abandoning them." Idris' eyes glistened as they started to fill up with tears. "God, it wrenches me to think of what they were going through, the hope that this time they'd be rescued, then the dismay as I would fly off. Then the weather took a turn. Nothing severe. We kept flying, but it rained so hard that on my next trip that I couldn't see them."

Idris looked out across the ocean. Bates followed his gaze to see that the clouds rolling in from the horizon were a dark grey.

Idris swallowed and went on, "The next day it had cleared enough for me to see that Granddad and mom hadn't made it through the storm. The dad was sitting there with the baby and the two kids huddled around him."

Bates whispered, "Jeez..."

"On my last flight out, there was only one of the boys left. I flew close enough to see he was crying—not sobbing—but howling, red faced, eyes screwed shut."

A tear escaped Idris' eye and trickled down his cheek.

Bates placed his hand on Idris' shoulder, "Wasn't your fault, man."

Idris sniffed back the emotion. "It doesn't help when you sit in the dark sick with guilt. You can try and tell me I did all I could, that the people I was ferrying out were worth saving, but none of that counts for shit. I did everything by the book. I filed a report my first flight back. When I pushed for a rescue op I was told civilians weren't mission critical. They threatened me with a psych evaluation if I didn't drop it. But I should have done something. But I didn't. That's my memory from the Exodus and that's why I have to go back and get Cahz now. The longer they're on the mainland the less chance I have of rescuing them. And that's why I'm ignoring Patterson's orders."

Bates slapped Idris hard on the shoulder. He said, "God speed."

* * * * *

Nathan's mind was still back in the cabin with Sarah as he wandered through the ship. He walked aimlessly with his head down, feeling dejected. Each step he took sent an ache of fatigue through the muscles in his thighs and calves.

It wasn't the pain that was weighing on his mood. It seemed to him that every time he tried to show compassion to Sarah she shot him down. Nothing he could do was right.

He trudged down the corridor, head hung low. As he turned a corner a figure loomed in front of him.

Nathan gasped and jumped back.

"Watch where you are going," Angel ordered. She stood shoulder on to Nathan, her good arm protecting her injured one.

"Sorry," Nathan said.

Angel's sour expression lifted. "You need be more careful," she said, moving her good arm from its guard position. She studied Nathan from head to toe. He was standing in a pair of threadbare jeans and nothing else. His chest bare, he clutched a damp rag in his left hand. Her eyes focused on his naked toes. "Could be anything round corner. You run into ammo trolley it break your foot."

His eyes drawn to the fresh white plaster cast, Nathan asked, "How's the arm?"

As he finished he looked at Angel's face. She was quite pretty, he thought, despite the swollen red welt down her temple. Her soft alabaster skin was framed by auburn hair that had natural hues of red running through it. She was also tall, he realised now that he stood eye to eye with her. She had appeared shorter when he'd seen her next to the other soldiers.

"...and the face," Nathan stuttered, realising she'd caught him staring at her.

"Elbow is broken." Angel shook her head. "Will be unable to use it for months, Doctor says. No more trips in country for me for a while. The *face*..." She paused. "I get by on charm alone for now." A mischievous smile materialised over her normally stoic features. "Still will give me time to make bullets."

"Are things that bad you have to make your own?" Nathan asked.

Angel laughed. "No, I measure out the powder more accurately than that mass produced factory govno."

"Is that important?"

"The bullet travel different trajectory with different amounts of cordite. I measure out each bullet's powder so I know they all fly the same. Means I need to calculate one less thing when I take shot."

"Well it obviously works," Nathan complimented. "I don't know what we would have done if it hadn't been for you and the others."

"You would have been eaten," Angel said in way of an acknowledgment. "You walk around ship almost naked... Is there a reason for this?"

"Oh..." Nathan held the damp T-shirt in front of him and looked at it like he'd been caught red-handed with the cookie jar. "I was looking for an iron."

"I not have one," Angel said sternly.

Nathan stared at her awkwardly. He'd never suspected she would carry one, but her answer threw him. Finally he put her answer to one side, convinced it must have been down to some misinterpretation of translation.

"Do you know where I could find one?" he asked.

"Laundry room," Angel replied. "Is three decks down towards the prow of the ship." When Nathan looked back blankly at her, she nodded in the direction. "Towards pointy end of boat."

"Okay, thanks," Nathan said as he walked off in the direction Angel had indicated.

Nathan now felt strangely exposed. Walking through the confined corridors was much like the warehouse, but back there he'd never have worried about wandering about half dressed. He suddenly felt self-conscious about his semi-nudity.

He sniggered out loud. It had been a while since he'd felt like he'd had anything to conform with.

He reached the laundry room door with a wide smile on his face, knocked and stepped in.

The room was hot and noisy. Two short skinny men with jet-black hair laboured away with piles of laundry.

"Excuse me," Nathan said.

"Hi!" One of the men replied in an overly aggressive manner.

Nathan nervously held out the wet T-shirt. "Um, I'm trying to get this dried?"

The man simply nodded towards an open drier and got back to his work.

Nathan stepped over to the appliance and tossed his shirt inside. Squatting on his haunches, he peered at the settings on the dial.

"Excuse!" a voice said from behind in an accent that said that English wasn't their first language.

"Sure," Nathan said, moving out of the way.

The man bundled in an armful of wet clothing before shutting the door and setting the machine.

The two men chattered away in what Nathan guessed was some Asian dialect. Excluded from their conversation, he watched as his T-shirt made periodic appearances in the drier's window.

He eventually found a corner of the cramped laundry room where he could avoid being shooed on from and stood counting the times his top came into view.

Finally the drier stopped and one of the men opened the door, handing Nathan the warm and crumbled item of clothing.

"Thanks," Nathan said, pulling it over his head. He slipped his arms through the sleeves and pulled the cloth flat at his sides. He started walking to the door. "Thanks again."

Behind him the two men exchanged a few words.

"You Nathan?" one of the men called after him.

"Yeah."

The man who'd called him stood holding an old pair of jeans in one hand and a creased envelope in the other.

He passed the letter over. On the front of it was Nathan's name.

* * * * *

With the meticulous precision he always worked to, Professor Cutler scrutinised the implements on the tray before him. The items were laid out from left to right in the order they were to be used: antiseptic wipe, syringe and needle still in their protective packaging, and one last but vital item. On the side of the small glass container on a white sticky label, written in a neat hand was 'S117a'.

Professor Cutler started the computer recording. As he spoke he rolled up his lab coat sleeve.

"Because the contagion does not affect other life forms, my research has been understandably stymied. The use of human cell cultures has obvious limitations to the speed and accuracy of my research."

He took the antiseptic cloth and wiped his forearm liberally.

"The sample tested by myself earlier today has proven resistant to the contagion. I have therefore succeeded through my sheer genius to create a vaccine."

Careful not to rest his forearm on the table, Cutler opened and assembled the syringe.

"It is proven to prevent the spread of the contagion in the cultures and so the next stage before a field test is to innoculate a test subject."

Like a tattoo artist at work, he dipped the needle point into the serum. He pulled back the plunger and sucked up a few millilitres of clear fluid.

"To facilitate the cooperation of the military personnel..."

Pointing the needle skyward, Professor Cutler squeezed the plunger back a fraction, causing a stream of serum to be discharged.

"I have decided to innoculate myself with the first batch of the modified contagion."

Lysed

SARAH PLACED HER FORK DOWN on the gold-rimmed china plate. The metal and china gave a sharp tinkle as they met. The plate in front of her was empty save for a few crumbs of bread and a smattering of white sauce which formed an arch where she had mopped it up with her roll. The full stomach forced her to take in shallow breaths as her digestive system worked to make room. She sat back to ease the pressure on her stomach and hoped there would be a long pause before dessert.

"This is delicious," Nathan proclaimed as he saluted the Captain with his half empty beer bottle.

Even in the modest surroundings of the captain's dining room Nathan's lack of refinement shone out. Although he was freshly shaven, his scraggy hair, the napkin tucked into his hastily laundered Nirvana T-shirt, and his abandoned gusto marked him out as uncouth.

Sarah wondered if there was still room for etiquette. In a world of the dead it didn't seem to matter much.

Wiping his mouth clean of escaped sauce, Nathan declared, "I'd forgotten just how good being clean and being full felt."

Sarah had to agree. "Yes, this is amazing. I don't remember when I last had fresh fish."

Captain Warden lent back in his chair. "You have Commander Patterson to thank for the menu suggestion." He dabbed his lips with his napkin. "I have to confess, the rest of the crew are sick of fish, but I see it as one of the perks of this posting."

"It's not fine French cuisine, but it's palatable," Doctor Robertson said.

"Huh!" Captain Warden snorted. "I'm glad it's not French, otherwise it would be glowing bright green!"

He gave out a loud snigger at his own joke, but the rest of the diners remained quiet.

"I don't get it, old man," Jennifer said cheerily.

"Jennifer!" Sarah chastised.

"But I don't," she replied.

Captain Warden laughed, "From the mouths of babes." He looked Jennifer in the eye and smiled. "Have you been listening to sea dogs?"

"Yes, old man," she said.

"Jennifer, that's rude," Sarah said.

"It's a touch disrespectful, but I won't make you walk the plank this time, young lady," Captain Warden said. He smiled and turned to Sarah. "You see, the Captain of a ship is referred to as the Old Man. It's a term of endearment really, but you shouldn't address me as such." He turned back to Jennifer. "It is a bit rude, I suppose. No, you should call me Captain."

"But I still don't get the joke, Captain," Jennifer said, keen to use the proper title.

"No, I suppose you wouldn't. You see, there were a lot of nuclear power stations in France but with no one to look after them..." Captain Warden made a whooshing noise and then a loud rumbling sound from his throat, all accompanied with the raising and parting of his hands. "They blew up."

"Oh," Jennifer said, still none the wiser.

Sarah simplified the concept for Jennifer: "You see, nuclear power stations use radioactive material and that glows green."

"It feels like we're being treated like royalty, Captain!" Nathan exclaimed, then stifled a burp. "This is the first beer I've had in years that wasn't stale."

"Nathan, don't you think you should go easy on those?" Sarah said.

Nathan ignored her and continued speaking to the Captain. "Not that it isn't bad, I mean it's great."

Captain Warden held up his hand to halt Nathan's embarrassed rambling. "That's okay, son. Compliment accepted."

"It's obvious that the world is still run by men," Sarah quipped shaking her head. "Everything has fallen apart, but one priority for getting civilisation going again is beer."

"On the contrary, beer may not be a priority but it is a byproduct of bread making," Warden said. "I have a contact who gets me a case now and again. It isn't contraband as such, just that its manufacture isn't encouraged by the government." The Captain looked back over to Nathan. "God knows where they get the hops or even where it's brewed. Some warlord on a private island somewhere I'll wager."

"Well, I'm very grateful for your hospitality," Nathan said, holding up his drink in salute.

Warden smiled and deep wrinkles spread across his face. "Frozen veg and canned meat are taken for granted onboard ship. Most of the crew moan at the lack of variety in their diet. I guess your arrival has helped the crew to realise just how lucky they are."

He cast a glance to Doctor Robertson.

Robertson ignored the inference and changed the topic. "How did you managed to survive so long? The last reports of survivors we had would have been more than a year ago."

"Just lucky I guess," Sarah said.

"Well, it was more than that," Nathan said, casting a glance over at Sarah. "Sarah pretty much kept us all together. When the shit came down, no one knew what was happening or why or anything like that. Sarah, she kept her head. Got a few folk organised, rescued a few others like me."

"How many of you were there?" Captain Warden asked.

"Twenty-seven of us when we found that warehouse," Sarah said. The math stood out at her. Twenty-seven minus three equalled twenty-four dead. Sarah, in a small burst of hope, corrected the figure—maybe Ryan was okay with the marines on the mainland.

"We cleared the dead fucks out of the place," Nathan said, furrowing his eyebrows. "What did your guys call 'em?"

The question took Captain Warden by surprise. "Um... Oh, the marines call them Whisky Deltas. W.D.'s."

Nathan nodded in recollection. "Yeah we didn't have much stuff with us. Just one gun and some tire irons, a few makeshift bludgeons and the like. Originally we were just there to try and raid some supplies, but when we got in..." Nathan shot a smile at Sarah. "You called it, what, an Aladdin's cave?"

Sarah smiled back. "Yeah, the place was stocked to the roof."

"We blocked the gate after we'd got in just so we didn't meet any surprises on the way out," Nathan explained. "Sarah suggested that we could hold up for a while, so she got us to barricade the entrances and check out the warehouse in groups."

"We lost Mr. Aslam that day and the guy from the supermarket to a bite a few days after that," Sarah said.

"Jeez, I'd forgotten about him," Nathan said. "Never could remember his name. Had to keep looking at his name tag. Seems like such a long time ago."

"It must have been hard for you all," Dr. Robertson said, unintentionally shifting her gaze onto Jennifer.

"My mommy and daddy died," Jennifer said.

"It was tough on us all," Sarah added as she put an arm around the young girl.

Nathan sat back in his chair while pushing his plate away. "A few folk went stir crazy. We had a couple of suicides early on. Just couldn't hack the moaning outside and the claustrophobia inside."

Sarah's thoughts were wrenched back to the roof of the warehouse. It was only this morning but yet that too felt like a lifetime ago. She closed her eyes and felt an almost imperceptible shaking of her head. Her emotions were in turmoil. She hated herself because she had decided not to go on. It hadn't been a snap decision, a moment of madness brought on by the oppressive conditions. Sarah had measured it out in her mind. She had weighed the difference between the possible enjoyment and misery her life had to offer. She had decided that what scant moments of pleasure she could scrape from her existence would be vastly outweighed by the misery. When Ray had come to her with his appraisal of the food supplies, the balance tipped still further. Now there was a timescale to the futility. Now she knew how long it would last and that that time would inflict more hardship. It seemed pointless to endure it for a few extra weeks. Now there was even a positive side to her death. Now Sarah could add nobility to her suicide. One less mouth to feed would mean more food for those trapped inside.

Sarah suddenly realised it wasn't the fact she had planned to kill herself that she found disturbing, it was the clinical way in which she had weighed the worth of her life.

"It's sad when people die," Jennifer said.

"Yes it is," Sarah agreed. She lent over and gave Jennifer a full-blown hug. Sarah needed the contact, the reminder of what was good about life. She paused for a moment, soaking up the affection from this young girl and felt guilty for ever wanting to abandon her.

Nathan went on, "Then the Hanson brothers decided that they were going to take their chances, try and get help. Hell, even the radio had been dead for months by that point, but a good few folk said they'd rather risk it than stay locked up inside. You know, even though the radio had been dead for years we always knew we weren't the only people left in the world."

"Oh, how did you know that?" Captain Warden asked.

"Was it just the hope?" Doctor Robertson asked romantically.

"We needed to keep our morale up, but it was more logic than faith," Sarah said.

"Yeah, one night Ray and Sarah got out these marker pens and flip charts and started..." Nathan paused, searching for the right words. "What did Ray call it? Brain dumping?"

"Brain storming," Sarah corrected.

"How did that work?" Doctor Robertson asked.

"There we were a couple dozen people bunkered up in that warehouse," Sarah said. "Ray and I guessed that if we could do it, other people would have, too. We came together by chance and got lucky with the warehouse, but as Ryan pointed out, there were much more prepared people and places."

"Yeah," Nathan chimed. "Hell, you were always seeing something on the news about some nutter in the hills with like a million rounds of ammo and a personal nuclear bunker."

"And leaving those apocalypse survivalists to one side, we knew governments all over the world were a thousand times more prepared. I mean, statistically it was impossible to think we were the only ones left alive out of seven billion..."

Nathan butted in, "Ray did that calculation about the lottery tickets." Leaning over the table with a slightly drunken lurch, his face lit up. "Ray said that the chances of us being the only people left alive was the same as winning the lottery every draw for a year."

"Well, he was right," Doctor Robertson said. "I think it worked out at one in four hundred survived."

"That's horrendous," Sarah said.

"High command estimate there are between twelve and seventeen million left," Captain Warden said. "And if you ask me, that's a fair number."

Doctor Robertson added, "We're not on the endangered species list yet."

"Seven billion is a lot of walking dead though," Nathan said.

"No, it didn't work out that way, although I follow your logic," Doctor Robertson said. "You see, the majority of deaths didn't come from bites."

Nathan and Sarah looked surprised.

"Most people died of disease or starvation. More people died from civil unrest than were infected. In Los Angeles I saw more gunshot wounds than bites."

"Christ, that's fucked up," Nathan said.

"In the first few days after the panic hit, I found myself in a supermarket," Sarah said. Her head hung low. "I saw this frail old man punched to the floor for the loaf of bread he was holding."

Doctor Robertson, sensing her guilt, reached out her hand across the table. "There was nothing you could have done, Sarah."

"His nose was busted up and bleeding and his wife was half kneeling on the floor holding him and crying. I know I couldn't have stopped that thug," Sarah said, pre-empting Doctor Robertson's platitudes. "But I could have stopped to help that old man and his wife. Instead I grabbed what I could off the shelves and ran."

"Nothing more inhumane than man," Captain Warden said as if reciting a quote. "We've all seen and done things that were unpalatable."

At that he shot a look over at Doctor Robertson.

"It may be unpalatable, but there's nothing inhumane about our work, Captain Warden," Doctor Robertson protested. "We only work on cultures and infected cadavers. We don't even conduct vivisection."

"I still find what you and Dr. Frankenstein do distasteful, not to mention dangerous," Warden replied. "Besides, I don't see the point in your work. All we need do is keep out of their way until they rot away to nothing, rather than wasting our time tinkering away with the corpses in your lab."

"What's to say that will be the end of it?" Doctor Robertson demanded. "What if it lies dormant or re-emerges from its reservoir!" Her voice took on a belittling tone. "The risks involved in our tinkering are minimal and the gains substantial."

"To you maybe, but what about the collection team!" Warden retorted.

Dr. Robertson felt her jaw clamp shut. She had been thinking about the likelihood of something going wrong in the lab without even considering the soldiers sent out to collect their specimens. Technically they weren't her responsibility, but it was her work that necessitated the dangerous incursions.

Ever conciliatory Sarah stepped in. "We're very grateful that your helicopter landed so close to us," she said.

"Yes, you were very fortunate our marines chose to set down where they did," Captain Warden said.

"It was very lucky," Nathan agreed and looked over at Sarah again. "If you hadn't been up on the roof so early we might never have known you were there. Very lucky—'cause you had no reason being up there at that time."

"We do get the collection teams to set down in different areas," Warden said. "It helps us build up a better picture of how things are playing out on the mainland."

Having failed to elicit a response from Sarah, Nathan turned in his chair, arm over the back and faced the Captain. He said, "You said they were collecting specimens. I've got to admit having those things downstairs—"

"Below decks," Jennifer corrected.

"What? Oh, right." Nathan stumbled before continuing, "Having those things below decks would creep me out."

"The whole purpose of this ship being here is to research the contagion," Doctor Robertson reiterated, more for the Captain's benefit than the guests'. "We experiment on the cadavers and from time to time we collect new specimens either because we have exhausted the ones we have or if we want to track the rate of decay."

"And anyway," Captain Warden spoke up, "we don't have more than three or four onboard at one time. That was one security protocol I insisted on in spite of our resident researchers' protests. I believe there is only one at the moment, isn't that correct, Doctor Robertson?"

Doctor Robertson nodded. The Captain's regulation hadn't added to the safety of the crew, only the perception of safety. Fewer specimens may have reduced the risk of an accident onboard, but it had necessitated more trips to the mainland which in turn had added to the attrition rate of the extraction teams.

"That's right, Captain," Doctor Robertson said. "That's why we had to send the marines out on a roundup."

Doctor Robertson didn't know what had made her say that. Placing any blame back at Warden wasn't going to make her situation any better.

"So what sort of experimentation do you do?" Sarah asked, sensing the rising tension.

Doctor Robertson replied, reiterating her mandate, "We research the contagion. We're authorised by Ascension Command to explore any area that will be of benefit. The cause, its life cycle, its transmissibility."

Sarah leaned closer. "You didn't mention in the infirmary where you think it comes from. What causes it?"

"We don't know," Doctor Robertson admitted.

"I heard," Nathan butted in, "it was a plague from space brought back by some probe or something."

"That would seem unlikely," Doctor Robertson countered.

"Why?" Nathan asked.

"It's unlikely it could have survived the high temperatures of re-entry," Doctor Robertson explained.

"Or the freezing in outer space," Nathan chipped in, eager to prove he had a grasp of something scientific.

"But wasn't there some biological samples that survived when that shuttle crashed a few years back?" Sarah asked.

Doctor Robertson smiled. "It's debatable whether or not that was contamination as a result of the crash."

Sarah looked Doctor Robertson in the eye. "So it *is* possible?"

"It's not *im*possible." Doctor Robertson looked across at Nathan. "Both the cold of space and the heat of re-entry would likely kill off any active agents."

"I sense a *but* in that," Sarah said.

"There would have to be a whole chain of suppositions. We've already shown in the lab that it doesn't survive lower than minus one hundred degrees. But I suppose if the contaminate were deep inside an asteroid or comet, although freezing it could be possible to get enough energy to keep it viable. Then suppose it were to fall to Earth and if it were deep enough inside the meteorite to insulate it. That's just too farfetched."

"As farfetched as the dead coming back to life?" Captain Warden threw in.

"Dead is a misconception clearly addressed in our reports," Doctor Robertson admonished.

Sarah lent forward, excited by what the Doctor had just said. "What do you mean? Are they dead or aren't they?"

"The person dies but the body is colonised, for want of a better term. Even though the person's brain is starved of oxygen, the contamination keeps some of the simplest of functions going as a means of propagating itself. These people are dead as we would understand it, but their resurrection it isn't some kind of supernatural force. It's biology. Some organism is killing then hijacking their host."

"That sounds like something from outer space to me," Nathan said.

"Saying it's from outer space when there's no evidence to support that theory is just as misleading as claiming it's God's wrath," Doctor Robertson objected.

"So how come it all sparked off at once?" Nathan asked, waving his fingers as he wafted his hands over his dinner plate. "That's explained by a spacecraft burning up in the atmosphere. All those germs wafting down on the planet below."

"No, it just appears to have flared up all at once," Doctor Robertson said. "Remember when SARS flared up in Hong Kong? Toronto saw cases a matter of days later. The disease spread so quickly because it was easy for people to travel. A businessman from Kowloon catches the virus and in the few hours it takes for it to incubate he's across the Pacific and in an office in Canada. Couple that with the fact that so many of the initial reports were miscategorised and we have a far more plausible scenario than bugs from outer space."

"But it's not impossible," Nathan said.

Doctor Robertson rolled her eyes with frustration. "It's not impossible but it's so improbable that it's not even worth calculating the odds, let alone investigating it."

"And there it is again, Doctor," Captain Warden huffed.

Doctor Robertson was brought back to their conversation in the infirmary and the Captain's exasperation at the lack of any tangible progress. But now there was something he could understand and Doctor Robertson had to use every ounce of her willpower to keep quiet. She couldn't steal Professor Cutler's thunder. She wanted to see the look on that sour face when they presented him with the scientific breakthrough of the century.

She kept her eyes down, loading her fork with another mouthful of dinner.

"What do you mean by that, Captain?" she asked, talking into her plate.

"We've been on this boat for years and what do we have to show for it?" Captain Warden said.

Doctor Robertson raised her head and addressed the Captain. "On the contrary, Captain Warden, we have advanced our knowledge of this condition quite considerably." Waving her fork at the Captain, Doctor Robertson's pride grew into defiance. "You well know Professor Cutler and I have produced as much research as all of the other facilities combined!"

"That, my good Doctor, is due to the fact that we haven't been overrun!" Warden replied venomously. "In no small part due to my safety protocols!"

Sensing the full-blown argument was about to spoil her dinner, Sarah spoke up. "Doctor Robertson, you got sidetracked on where the virus comes from."

Both Doctor Robertson and Captain Warden looked round at her. Captain Warden ceased his rancour out of an atavistic politeness for his table guests.

Doctor Robertson saw what Sarah was trying to do straight away and was more than happy to break off from yet another pointless argument.

"Of course, you have more than a passing interest in science," Doctor Robertson said, turning to the Captain. "Sarah here was at university studying Chemistry."

"Is that so?" Captain Warden said, not knowing where Doctor Robertson was going with this line of conversation. Anticipating an ambush, he kept his response polite but neutral.

A smile spread across Doctor Robertson's face. "I'm hoping she will accept my invite and help us with our research."

Sarah shook her head. "I doubt if I could be any use. I was only a second year."

"As you can probably tell, there is a skills shortage at the moment. A second year student is a whole lot better than anyone else can boast on this boat."

"We were speaking in the infirmary about what caused the outbreak. You never got round to answering the question," Sarah said, trying to turn the attention away from herself.

"That's a difficult question," Doctor Robertson said. "We've never been able to isolate the contagion."

"I don't understand."

"Neither do we," Doctor Robertson admitted. "We can see the effects but none of the agent. It acts like a virus in its propagation but seems to derive energy like yeast. The lack of aerobic action—"

Nathan laughed, "Does that mean it can't dance?"

Jennifer's snigger encouraged Nathan to laugh more.

"That's the scientific term for breathing," Sarah interpreted. "You were saying...?"

"The lack of aerobic activity is perplexing." Doctor Robertson shook her head and pursed her lips, obviously still puzzled by the conundrum. "It was Professor Cutler who pushed us beyond that impasse."

"Go on, Doctor," Sarah pushed.

"Well, he had an interest in Psychology. He's a bit of a polymath. You see, in psychology there is the situation where you can't isolate the parts of the brain which determine behaviour. Instead theories are advanced on their external features, not the internal working."

"I'm lost again," Nathan said, laughing. "You'll need to slow down. I just attended school, I didn't pay any attention."

"Psychologists often look at a list of symptoms and make a diagnosis on what is manifested because they can't go around sawing open people's heads," Doctor Robertson explained. "Professor Cutler did the same thing. He said if we can't find the cause lets look at the symptoms and see if we can address that."

"He skipped the identification and started looking for a cure?" Sarah asked.

"A cure?" Doctor Robertson shook her head. "I don't think that will ever be achievable."

"Huh, makes me wonder why the hell we're still out here," Captain Warden blustered.

Doctor Robertson shot a look at Captain Warden. "We're here looking for information that will prove useful. I thought the military axiom *know your enemy* would be enough justification for our work? Ascension Command certainly thinks so."

Captain Warden folded his arms across his chest and sat back in his chair.

"To start with, we looked at what the contagion could and couldn't do," Doctor Robertson went on, addressing Sarah specifically. "We examined its effects. In every way it resembles toxic shock. It's toxic to all vertebrates, killing them within a few hours. Plants, fungi, algae, even colony creatures like the Portuguese Man-of-war weren't affected. And here's another curiosity: all the animals we've tested instinctively know not to eat the resurrected flesh. Not even the carrion eaters."

"Does that explain why they don't just rot?" Sarah asked.

"Partially. The normal bacterial activity that happens when we die is retarded in the infected. The contagion overwhelm the bacteria and destroy them, preventing normal decomposition. But the contagion seems to have a preservative effect as well. Like mummification or pickling." Doctor Robertson picked up her wine glass and swirled the dark liquid around the sides for emphasis. "We've detected trace amounts of esters and ethanol which would imply an amount of alcohol production within the host cell. This could be the energy source that keeps the W.D.'s going. We also suspect that this chemical change is detected somehow by animals which is what warns them off from eating the infected."

"Is that why they don't attack each other?" Nathan asked. "Do they smell the difference?"

"That's a distinct possibility. They could also act on things like temperature, movement and noise." Doctor Robertson relished the chance to demonstrate her knowledge. "The neurons in the nose that detect smell die off and don't regenerate as they would do in a living person. That means that although they could use smell as an identifier they would gradually loose that ability over a matter of just a few months. Walking dead over five years old have been examined and they still react to the presence of a living human, so they must be using more than just their sense of smell. I believe they use their senses in concert and that the information is still being processed, although on a rudimentary level."

"So are you looking for ways to destroy it?" Sarah asked.

"No," Doctor Robertson replied. "Well, not at the moment. In the early days we did. We've frozen it with liquid nitrogen to as close to absolute zero as we can get and yes that destroys it. Boiling has the same effect. High concentrated acid or alkaline, but antibiotics have no effect. Oxygen kills it."

"But isn't there oxygen in your blood?" Nathan asked. "Surely that would kill it."

"That's true, but in the blood stream it's bound up by the red blood cells. When it infects you through the blood stream it can't infect the red blood cells because they have no nucleus to usurp. Also the oxygen in the red blood cells kills off the infection but they are poisoned in the process and eventually collapse. It's that toxicity of oxygen that means it can't live outside the body. But even then, if it's outside the body your skin is an ample barrier against infection."

"Does that mean you can't catch it from blood?" Nathan asked.

"You can't catch it from red blood cells, but there are a whole host of other constituents in blood that the infection can use to multiply." Doctor Robertson took a swig of her wine and looked at the red liquid as if it were a sample. "We've found out lots of useful things about the contagion, but very little we can implement in the field. At that point we stopped trying to simply eradicate it and switched to mapping the parameters of its abilities."

"A wholly unproductive approach," Warden criticized.

Doctor Robertson set her glass down on the table. "The approach is a sound one. If we know how it works, we'll have a better idea of how to stop it."

"How does it work?" Sarah asked.

"The infected cells metabolise like a yeast. We know that it provides some protection to the cells that they inhabit, probably as a way of securing its survivability which is most obvious in freezing."

"The ethanol," Sarah said.

Doctor Robertson nodded. "Most probably."

"Yeah, each winter those things would freeze solid," Nathan said. "We used to leave the warehouse and gather up supplies when that happened." He nudged Jennifer. "Remember all those Christmases we would go out with the baseball bats and smash their heads in?"

Nathan pretended his fork was a miniature bat which he swung at his beer bottle in lieu of a demonstration. The bottle reverberated with a low clunk as the metal fork struck. Jennifer giggled at both Nathan's actions and the fun they'd had during their winter respite.

"No matter how many we destroyed, when the thaw came more would come," Sarah added.

"Yes, we have frozen cells down to minus eighty and when they were thawed they were still viable carriers of the contagion," Doctor Robertson said. "Whatever it is it stops the cell from bursting, so yes, come thaw the infected just start moving again."

"It does sound like a space plague to me!" Nathan pushed.

"Some say it was a genetically engineered weapon," Captain Warden added.

"A plague from space, the wrath of God. Some mad scientist's demented solution to overpopulation or CO_2 emissions. Take your pick. In the early days, Doctors Moody and Greatshell even proposed it was a panacea gone wrong." Doctor Robertson shook her head and snorted.

"What's a panacea?" Jennifer asked.

Sarah could see that Nathan was as keen on an answer as Jennifer.

"A cure all, like penicillin plus. The way that the contagion breathes life into the lifeless and maintains the cell integrity."

"Could it have been man made?" Sarah asked.

"Definitely not," Doctor Robertson replied, adamantly. "If it were, then it would be a manipulation of known agents. Since we can't isolate the contagion to analyse it then it would be inconceivable that it could have been produced in a lab. After all, if we can't isolate it, how would the people who created it have been able to work with it? The whole idea is ludicrous. My personal opinion? I believe that the virus is a recent mutation. Something which doesn't have its regular reservoir in man."

"What do you mean, like the flu?" Sarah said.

"One hell of a cold," Captain Warden commented.

The door to the dining room opened and in came three ratings. The Captain nodded to them and they began to clear away the empty dishes.

"Yes, like the flu," Doctor Robertson answered over the sound of crockery. "The natural population for the flu virus is in birds, but if it mutates it can cross species sometimes with truly catastrophic effects."

"The nineteen eighteen virus killed millions," Sarah said, glancing across at Doctor Robertson for conformation. "It's like Aids or E-bola. They started in primates and jumped to humans."

"But the flu doesn't make corpses walk around biting folk!" Captain Warden protested.

Doctor Robertson did well to keep Warden's glibness from riling her. "No, that's very true and again an interesting effect of the contagion. Only humans are resurrected, not even our cousins the great apes. Gorillas, Chimpanzees, Bonobos, Orang-utans... all of them just die. For years I was an antivivisectionist—even supported PETA—but when the shit hit the fan we slaughtered thousands of animals trying to find answers. God knows we killed a lot of apes in the early days, trying to find out why it only propagated in humans." She leaned into the table to draw closer to Sarah. "You see, most contagions and parasites have a life cycle which promotes or even controls their propagation. Some, like this one, even control their host."

Captain Warden looked at Nathan and then back at Doctor Robertson, "Now, Doctor, I think you've lost all of us."

The point hadn't been lost on Sarah, though. "You mean like toxoplasmosis," she said.

"Yes, that's a very good example," Doctor Robertson replied, the high note in her tone giving away how impressed she was with the new arrival. Seeing that the rest of her audience did not share Sarah's level of astuteness, she explained, "Toxoplasma gondii needs to jump species as part of its life cycle. It needs to get into a cat's intestines to reproduce. The disease is picked up from cat faeces and can affect mammals or birds. It used to be thought that the disease was harmless to all but the most vulnerable; the elderly, pregnant women and people with a suppressed immune system. But what we found out was that it increases dopamine production and reduces reaction times. The end result is that animals like rats or mice take more risks, are slower to act and are easier for cats to catch."

"That means that the cat catches the toxic..." Jennifer struggled with the new word.

"Toxoplasmosis," Sarah said.

"Exactly. Thereby continuing the Toxoplasma gondii," Doctor Robertson added.

Captain Warden objected, "That's nonsense, Doctor, and even if it were true, it wouldn't affect a higher life form like us!"

A dry smile broke out on Doctor Robertson's lips. She had cornered him. "Wouldn't it? A study before the Rising showed that seventy percent of people killed in traffic accidents in North America had the Toxoplasma gondii in their bloodstream."
She sat back in her chair, savouring her intellectual victory over the pigheaded Captain.

"So the virus makes the dead person wander about biting?" Nathan's voice held both scepticism and curiosity.

"In a nutshell, yes. The change in the host's cells function coupled with the lack of aerobic action gives them the energy to move. Animals don't eat the corpses and bacterial action is retarded, so really only weather wears them down, meaning they could remain active for decades."

"But if they're dead how do they know to bite, and if they know that much why not other things, like who they are?" Captain Warden countered.

"Even normally there is brain activity for up to a month after death," Doctor Robertson elaborated. "Not cognition. Not thought you understand. The reanimates only show the crudest of intelligence."

Nathan added his thoughts: "Too right. I stood on the other side of a chain link fence once and at least a dozen W.D.'s walked up to it and just stood there clawing the air even though it was only twenty yards long. They could have walked round and got me if they'd had any sense. Dumb as chickens, the lot of them."

"And there's the point, Nathan," Doctor Robertson said. "These reanimates only possess the most rudimentary intelligence. Only the innate—not the learnt."

"Like chickens?" Nathan asked, surprised that he had grasped the concept.

"When a baby is born, if you support it up by its armpits it will try to walk. When it sees its mother it will stretch its arms out to grasp on. When it is presented with the breast it latches on. None of these are learnt behaviours; all of them we are born with. Like the reanimates, all they retain is the primordial drives."

"To bite people," Nathan said.

"Exactly," Doctor Robertson replied.

"So where is the walking death's natural reservoir?" Sarah asked.

Dr. Robertson pushed a short puff of breath out of her nostrils and her eyelashes fluttered as if she were embarrassed. "That I don't know. We just don't have the resources to pursue that avenue at the moment. I doubt it's in mammals, because in every one of our studies they died from the infection. It can't be anything humans have regular contact with, because if it were we would have seen similar types of infection before."

"If we don't know where it comes from, how are we to eradicate it?" Sarah asked.

Dr. Robertson started to answer, but at that moment the door flew open, almost knocking the crockery from a seaman's hands.

The whole table looked round to see who had entered with such gusto. Standing in the doorway in an immaculate dark blue suit was Professor Cutler. The deep blue was contrasted by his crisp white shirt and complimented by a maroon satin tie.

Sarah suddenly felt underdressed in the jeans and shirt that had been found for her in the ship's stores.

"Professor Cutler, so glad you could finally join us," Captain Warden said with a bitter edge.

Again Doctor Robertson tried to deflect the Captain's antagonism. "Sarah here is one of the survivors I was telling you about," she said. "She was just asking how we could eliminate the contagion's reservoir."

Professor Cutler took a couple of long strides and pulled out his chair. "What we do is we find a vaccine," he said. As he sat down he tossed the folder across the table. When they landed with a thump, he explained, "Captain, the report you asked for."

"A vaccination?" the Captain said, without even touching the report so indignantly delivered to him.

Professor Cutler lent back, tipping his chair onto two legs. "Garçon," he demanded, snapping his fingers at one of the ensigns clearing the plates. "I'll have what they had. It smelt divine." He was oblivious to the cutting look from the Captain. "Oh, and see if you can't find a medium white wine." He looked across the table at the little girl opposite him. "Red wine with fish and a white sauce?" He clicked his tongue and shook his head.

"This was the crucial work that Professor Cutler was working on this morning," Doctor Robertson said. She wondered if the reminder of this afternoon's altercation with the Captain would placate or infuriate him.

Captain Warden waved his hand over the abandoned report. "What does this mean, in real terms?"

Sarah's eyes were wide as the curiosity and excitement grasped her. She blurted, "Does this mean that if you've had the vaccination you won't turn into one of them?"

"Exactly!" Professor Cutler answered.

Dr. Robertson was quick to add, "That's the theory. We've yet to run human trials, but the results from the cultures indicate that—"

Professor Cutler placed a hand on Dr. Robertson's shoulder. "Doctor Robertson is both cautious and modest. There is no reason to suppose this won't work outside the lab. In real terms, Captain, if your men were to be inoculated, then wounds sustained from the infected would no longer be fatal. You would treat bite wounds as you would any other. Furthermore, the contagion would be prevented from spreading."

"It's not the cure we were sent out to research, but it's a start," Captain Warden said.

"Start?!" Professor Cutler slammed both his fists onto the table. "Start?! You imbecile, you have in your hands the most important medical breakthrough in the history of mankind and you treat it like a common headache tablet!" He stood up, pushing his chair over. "My work could very well be the salvation of humanity!"

Dr. Robertson took hold of Cutler's hand and stood up more sedately than her colleague.

"Pearls before swine, Captain!" Professor Cutler spat out.

"Professor Cutler," Doctor Robertson said in a soft, appeasing tone, "let's just give the Captain time to absorb the significance of this. In the meantime, let's go back to the lab and work on synthesizing the vaccine."

Again the door to the dining room burst open and in rushed Commander Patterson.

"Captain!" Patterson announced. "Idris has just commandeered the helicopter!"

"What?!"

"Get in here, marine," Patterson said.

Into the room came a sheepish-looking Bates.

"Bates says he was going back to the mainland for the rest of the team," Patterson explained.

"Did no one tell him there's a storm coming?" the Captain asked.

"I informed him myself, sir," Patterson said. "Told him to stand down on the op until the storm had passed."

"And how do you know where he's going, Private Bates?" Captain Warden asked.

"He told me, sir," Bates admitted.

Captain Warden lent forward. "He told you?!"

"Yes, sir," Bates replied, trying to sound meek.

"And *what*," Warden bellowed, "did you do about it, Private Bates?!"

"Nothing, sir?" Bates replied.

Patterson interjected, "One of the deck dogs saw the two of them loading the chopper."

"Nothing?" Captain Warden asked again, this time more inquisitively. The question had changed from *why didn't you stop him* to *why did you help him*.

"Well, almost nothing," Bates said in way of a defence. "I just helped him carry some ammo, sir."

"Did you try at all to stop him?"

"Well, not really, sir."

"Not really? Not really?! You just gave him a hand and waved him goodbye?! What the hell were you thinking?!" Warden slapped his hand down on the table, making it jump.

"He plans to wait out the storm on the mainland," Bates said. "I thought it was a good idea."

Warden shook his head. "You're not paid to think!"

"I'm not paid at all," Bates replied.

"What?!" Captain Warden bawled.

"Shit. Shouldn't have said that," Bates whispered into his collar.

"Good God, Bates." The broken capillary's in Warden's cheeks flared crimson and an angry flash of red rushed across his forehead. "Surely not even you are dumb enough to think that's a good plan! We're going to lose him and the rest of your squad!"

"I did—"

"You don't even know when to shut up!" Warden screamed. "Patterson."

"Yes, sir?" Patterson barked.

Captain Warden started pinching the bridge of his nose in an attempt to alleviate the headache that was spreading. "Put Bates in the brig until I decide what level of punishment his insubordination and stupidity deserves."

"Yes, sir!" Patterson barked again. He grabbed Bates by the collar in a symbolic gesture of power. Although Bates could have easily overpowered Patterson, he decided not to make things worse and allowed himself to be dragged from the officers' mess.

Professor Cutler still stood by his place at the table, his grand exit ruined by what had just happened.

"If you'll excuse me," Captain Warden said, throwing his napkin onto the table, "I appear to have lost my appetite."

At that he pushed past Cutler and exited the room.

Cutler seemed lost for a moment. After all, there was no one left in the room to rile at. Without a word he turned and left.

"Um..." Dr. Robertson voiced as she considered what to do. Finally she decided Professor Cutler needed her attention more. "I should really..." She didn't exactly know what she should do, but she did know Cutler needed her more than the dinner guests. The sentence, having fumbled to a petering end, she too left.

A perplexed ensign stood with the last of the crockery to be cleared away. He finally came out of his stupor and inquired, "Apple crumble with custard, anyone?"

* * * * *

"With people like him in charge, no wonder the world's gone to shit," Professor Cutler raged. "Short-sighted, moronic, unappreciative..."

Dr. Robertson opened the door to the lab where they had been working. The red wine during the meal had been a pleasant indulgence. The sailors on board regularly drank homemade hooch, but wine was an infrequent luxury. Dr. Robertson hadn't drank for some time and the alcohol had taken the edge off the day.

The lab was dimly lit by a collection of standby lights on equipment and the warm red glow of the computer screen, still showing the Professor's blood sample. It didn't feel unnatural entering the gloomy lab; the pair of them had worked so many late nights here over the years.

Doctor Robertson pulled the still fuming Professor over the threshold, into the lab.

"Well, *someone* appreciates your work," she said, dragging him deeper into the room. She grabbed a dustsheet from the unused gurney and threw it over the struggling zombie strapped to the second one.

"Thank you," Professor Cutler started, oblivious to his colleague's intentions. "At least you realise the importance of—"

Dr. Robertson flung her arms around his neck. "That wasn't the work I had in mind," she said.

With a tipsy stumble she pushed Professor Cutler onto the vacant gurney.

Dr. Robertson quickly unfastened her blouse and skirt, discarding them to the floor. Professor Cutler hurriedly unbuckled his belt and kicked off his shoes.

Under the hastily deposited sheet, the immobilized zombie tugged at its restraints. It tried to raise its head to see past the sheet hastily tossed there, but the strap around its neck held firm. The creature curled its lips back to moan, but the ball gag silenced all but the slightest noise. The sheet over its desiccated body did nothing to reduce the sounds from across the room—the soft moaning, the drip-like noise of moist lips kissing, the rhythmic groans and creaks of the adjacent gurney.

The zombie used what feeble strength it had to try to force itself loose, to free itself and gorge on the living flesh so tantalizingly close. But it was futile. Its bonds were too strong and its flesh was too weak.

The lovers, lost in their passion, were oblivious to the futile writhing of the tethered zombie.

None of the room's occupants noticed as the light in the room slowly began to change. The warm red glow softly darkened. One by one, the corpulent cells on the computer monitor shrivelled and blackened.

Lull

CAPTAIN WARDEN TOOK A LONG first draw on his cigarette. The orange glow reflecting off the window could easily have been mistaken for the lights of a distant ship. With an exhale of smoke, he visibly relaxed, the tough muscles in his neck and shoulders sinking down as the tension was blown away in a puff of tobacco.

There were three places a sailor could smoke on board: your own cabin, on the poop deck, and the officers' mess. Etiquette from an older generation had prevented Captain Warden smoking in the mess in the company of his guests. He appreciated that it could put others off their food, but now that he was back on his bridge the need for a post repast draw was overwhelming.

Taking a second long draw, Warden knew none of the bridge crew were paying the least attention to his smoking. The privilege of being the captain meant that he never broke the rules because he could just amend them. He had occasionally smoked on the bridge before, but only in times of stress. It struck him that now was one of those times.

He and his crew had weathered storms more ferocious than the approaching hurricane Emily. They would be at the edge of the storm's force, and barring engine failure, Warden knew the Ishtar could handle it. As long as she wasn't swamped by a freak wave, on its own the weather was no cause for concern.

A gust of wind hurled a sheet of rain against the bridge window as if summoned by his fear. He could sense the increase in the decks roll.

95

"Seas getting up," he said calmly as he drew his second puff.

"That she is, Captain," he heard Patterson say in his usual crisp, obedient tone. Warden realised he'd been so lost in thought that he'd forgotten Patterson was even on the bridge.

Patterson had always been a capable officer. He knew he wasn't a well-liked man onboard, but as the second in command that was to be expected. He'd always been amiable and acceptable company in Wardens opinion, not charismatic or quick-witted, but trustworthy and decent. He was the Captain's enforcer, the man who carried out orders and imposed order. Warden acknowledged to himself that the discipline Patterson imposed on the crew made his life easier and kept things running smoothly.

But even with Patterson's indispensable service, things were not running smoothly today.

Warden drew the cigarette from his lips and with his free hand he stroked his brow. He looked down at the skinny rollup he held between his thumb and forefinger.

The smoke was more paper than tobacco; short and thin to eke out what he had left. It mirrored the way the ship ran. Everything rationed, nothing wasted.

The only thing that wasn't rationed was the constant annoyance from the ship's resident scientists. Warden had considered that maybe he was part of some perverted experiment to find his breaking point. All that Professor Cutler and Doctor Robertson were doing was inventing more ways to piss him off.

That thought led Warden to his second frustration.

Being at sea when the outbreak had happened meant Warden hadn't been witness to the hysteria and chaos as society broke down. It also meant he'd only ever seen a zombie in the lab or when the chopper returned, capture net squirming with them.

It made Warden tense enough to encounter them in these relatively safe environments, but it chilled him to think what it must be like on the mainland.

Disturbing as it was that he had two men stranded on the mainland, the predicament was exacerbated by his pilot's reckless rescue attempt. Warden felt qualms of unease at the thought of three men missing in action with no means of getting any of them back.

Warden turned to face his first mate. "Commander Patterson."

"Captain," Patterson acknowledged.

Warden held out the brown manila folder Professor Cutler had delivered to him over dinner. "Get this in the twenty four hundred hours report."

"Will do, sir."

"I'll be in my cabin." Warden looked down at his watch. "I've got just over three hours to summarise the events of the day."

* * * * *

Nathan sat up in a flash. He threw the covers off and dived for the bathroom door.

It frightened Sarah, but she didn't want to alarm Jennifer. She softly called out, "Nathan?"

Then Sarah heard it: A deep guttural bark followed by a tremendous splash. The gushing sound was still in full flow when she reached the bathroom door. As she swung the door open and flicked on the light, the spewing trickled to a stop.

Nathan knelt in front of the toilet, crying and gasping for air. He turned and looked up at Sarah, his mouth dripping with fresh bile. Sloshing around the toilet bowl were recognizable chunks of dinner churned up by the ship's motion. The acrid smell of vomit had started to fill the cabin, making Sarah feel queasy too.

Nathan whipped back and convulsed from the floor up. His face twisted in pain as his stomach spasmed. A pitiful dry retch brought up a trickle of fluid.

Sarah knelt down next to him and gently rubbed his back.

After pulling his breath back, he sat spitting into the bowl, mucus dripping from his nose.

Sarah pulled free a wad of toilet paper and passed it to him.

"Is Nathan okay?" Jennifer asked, standing in the doorway.

"He's just feeling sick," Sarah answered. "Would you go pour him a glass of water, honey?"

Jennifer nodded and hurried off.

Nathan groaned. The harsh florescent light above made the green hue to his skin look even more deathly.

By the time Jennifer arrived with a glass of water, Nathan was leant against the tiled wall, looking exhausted.

"Thanks, Jen," he said as the glass was passed down to him. He took a swig and rinsed out his mouth, spitting the yellow-tinged slew in to the toilet.

He breathed a heavy sigh. "That was shitty."

"You okay?" Sarah asked.

Nathan lifted the glass to take a swig. "Yeah, I think so."

"Just take sips," Sarah advised. "You don't want to set your stomach off again."

Nathan nodded.

"What do you reckon made you sick?"

"Oh... don't know." he took another sip of water. "Sea sickness and over-eating, I guess." He looked down at the contents of his stomach swimming around the bowl. "Ship's rocking must be getting to me."

Sarah looked back into the cabin at the rain-smeared porthole. "Yeah, the storm is getting up."

"You did have a lot of beer," Jennifer added helpfully.

"Thanks for that, Jennier. You think they'll have sea sickness tablets on board?"

"They may. If not, ginger is good at stopping you feeling nauseous," Sarah offered.

"Did you learn that in chemistry class?" Nathan asked.

"No, Elspeth told me when Sam had morning sickness."

"Ah," Nathan said. "That explains where the last of the ginger beer went." He struggled to his feet using the sink for purchase. "I'm going to see if the doc can give me anything."

"Do you want me to come with you?" Sarah asked.

Nathan had squeezed a lump of toothpaste onto his finger. "Nah, I'll be okay. You keep Jennifer company." He sucked up the white lump off his finger and drew it through his teeth a few times before spitting.

- -

The corridors felt quiet with the lights turned low. Nathan had checked the time out of curiosity before leaving the cabin; it was just before midnight but it felt later. Lying awake in bed for the past two hours gradually feeling worse and worse had distorted his sense of time. To Nathan it felt that he'd been awake all night.

He found walking awkward as his centre of gravity kept shifting. He put a hand against the wall to steady himself as he went.

Bracing himself and at his plodding pace, he eventually reached the door to the stairwell. Unlike the cabin doors, this was a heavy metal thing with latches and an intricate collection of levers to secure the door shut. He pulled on the handle and opened the heavy metal door. It screeched far too loudly for this time of night. As he stepped through, the ship caught a wave and the door was wrenched from his grasp. Nathan practically jumped back, pulling his trailing leg through the hatch. The door skiffed his foot and banged hard against the frame. The noise bounced off the steel walls of the stairwell, and before the echo had faded the door rocked open again. He grabbed the handle and using the next swell, he shut and secured the door. Lesson learnt, Nathan placed a hand on each of the guide rails and cautiously walked down the stairs. Two steps from the bottom he had to pause as the ship rocked violently again. The pendulous motion subsided, but Nathan remained on the stairs taking slow deep breaths, desperately trying to suppress a swell of his own. His stomach knotted and what little liquid there could be left felt like it was bubbling. His methodical breathing began to quell the churning. He was just coming off the steps when the steel door in front of him opened.

Commander Patterson looked at Nathan and then up at the top of the landing. "Was that you making all that racket?"

Nathan nodded.

"Oh, okay," Patterson said and ducked back round the door.

"Just a minute," Nathan said as he followed Patterson through the open hatchway. It had suddenly dawned on him that although he knew the way to the infirmary, it was highly unlikely anyone would be in it at this time of night.

Patterson was already across the hall at an open door. Static and tinny voices emanated from the room.

"Mr. Patterson," Nathan said, half worried that he should really have said commander.

Patterson raised a hand, which Nathan read as a signal to wait.

"Can you confirm our transmission was received and verified?" Patterson asked.

Nathan peered round to look into the room. It wasn't much bigger than a broom closet; just enough room for a table and chair. A seaman was sitting facing a panel of dials and screens. He wore a pair of headphones Nathan was more familiar with on DJs than sailors. There was, however, a microphone on a stalk from one of the ears.

The sailor turned round. "Aye, aye, sir," he said. "The Russian sub *Pskov* has confirmed our twenty four hundred hours sitrep."

"Thank you, Ensign. I sleep better knowing our sitrep is through." Patterson turned back to Nathan. "Can I help you? You don't look too good."

"No I feel half dead... keep throwing up," Nathan replied.

Patterson gave a wry smile. "Not found your sea legs yet, eh?"

Nathan nodded.

"Best thing to do is go down one level to Doctor Robertson's cabin." Patterson threw a paternal arm around Nathan's shoulder and started walking him back to the stairwell. "I'm sure she can give you a shot for the nausea."

"Thanks," Nathan said. "Which one is it?"

"Turn right out of the stairwell," Patterson said, gesturing. "It's the third cabin along. You can't miss it; her name's on the door."

✳ ✳ ✳ ✳ ✳

Doctor Robertson slipped out of the lab. She finished buttoning up her blouse and made her way down the swaying corridor. A loud metal clang in the distance had finally made her decide to head back to her own cabin. The uncomfortable gurney and the twitching cadaver next to her hadn't been the impetus to make her leave. Those irritations had been relegated by the pounding in her head and the cramps in her stomach. Before creeping out on her lover she had quietly swallowed a couple of anti-nausea tablets. Now on the short trip back to her own bed, she cursed herself for having sex on a full stomach and for drinking too much wine before a storm.

A futile hope came to mind as she totterd down the moving corridor. *If only the swaying of the ship and my spinning head would fall into sync then I would feel fine.*

As she thought this, she heard her name being called. There was a dull knocking and again her name was gently spoken. She turned the corner to her room and saw Nathan rapping on her door.

"Doctor Robertson, are you in there?" Nathan asked at the door.

"No, I'm not," she said from behind him.

Nathan spun round to see Doctor Robertson coming towards him. There was a light smattering of perspiration on her forehead and neck and she looked tired and drawn.

"You gave me a fright there," Nathan admitted. "Commander Patterson said you could help me with my sea sickness."

"Oh yes, certainly. There's something for that in the lab. I've just come from there." Doctor Robertson nodded and made an about turn.

Nathan followed her up the corridor. "I'm not used to this," he said. "I went out on a ferry one day as part of a school trip. Haven't been on a boat since."

"You get used to it, I guess," Doctor Robertson said. "Though saying that, I feel a little nauseous too. Could be dinner disagreeing with us."

"Speaking of disagreements at dinner, the captain seemed a little tetchy," Nathan said.

Doctor Robertson gave a lopsided smile. "None of us were picked for our temperaments. David..." She paused when she saw that Nathan hadn't recognised the name. "Professor Cutler and the Captain don't get along. David's work here could save mankind, but the Captain's first concern is for his crew."

"I take it that your work is dangerous?"

"Everything is dangerous," Doctor Robertson admitted. "Especially since the Rising."

"You worried one of those things could get loose on board?" Nathan asked.

"No, worse than that. The top brass are worried the contagion will mutate and become airborne." Doctor Robertson placed a hand on the wall to steady herself from her spinning head and the lurching of the ship. "That's the fear that fuels the animosity between the two of them. It doesn't help that Professor Cutler is a risk taker and Warden... well, he plays it by the book." Doctor Robertson shrugged. "Fire and water."

"More like fire and gasoline," Nathan corrected.

"Just a moment," Doctor Robertson said as they reached the door to the laboratory. "I'm not sure if Professor Cutler had finished what he was working on," she lied, fearful that Nathan might spot the signs of their tryst. "I'll quickly pop in."

Doctor Robertson slipped into the lab. It was dark inside and she had automatically went for the light switch. A soft moan emanated from the gurney Professor Cutler lay on. By the tight shaft of light from the door, it looked like he was rousing.

Doctor Robertson moved her finger away from the light switch. He had been dead to the world when she had left him and she didn't want to wake him unnecessarily. "I'm just getting some Scopolamine, David. Both Nathan and me are feeling a bit queasy," she whispered apologetically.

Another grumble came from the direction of the gurney.

"I'm going to go back to my cabin to sleep it off," Doctor Robertson said as she removed the container from where she had left it five minutes ago.

Professor Cutler let out a mournful groan.

"I'm sorry, David. I'm not feeling great. I think I'll be better of in my own bed." She stopped for a moment and clasped the white plastic pill tub with both hands. She took half a step forward, about to kiss her lover goodnight when a tight cramp seized her gut. She winced against the discomfort.

"I'll see you in the morning," she said before she turned and left the lab.

The door clicked shut, leaving the room in darkness again. In awkward puppet-like movements, Professor Cutler made his clumsy way off the gurney. He slipped, pushing the gurney away from under him and landed heavily on his knees, his left arm flailing out until it found the purchase of the second gurney. His hand grasped around the arm of the tethered zombie. The creature simply lay there motionless. Unlike before, it didn't try to lash out at the other occupant in the room. It simply lay there unconcerned.

Professor Cutler pulled himself up and shuffled stiffly to the door. He bumped into the closed hatch and stood there motionless, stymied by the barrier in front of him.

Frustrated by the obstacle, he let out a low, asthmatic sigh of breath.

On the gurney behind him, the bound zombie struggled, trying to join in.

* * * * *

Doctor Robertson popped open the lid of the tub. She dipped in her fingers and pulled out two of the pastel pink tablets. She squeezed the lid back on and handed the container over to Nathan, keeping the ones she had removed in her fist.

"Take one of those with a small amount of water as soon as you get back to your cabin," she warned. "Just take the one. These are very strong. You shouldn't need to take any more for at least six hours." She paused and screwed up her eyes as a cramp took hold of her stomach.

Nathan held out a hand to steady her. "You okay, Doctor?"

She nodded. "This doesn't feel like sea sickness. I thing we might have food poisoning."

"Sarah and Jennifer looked fine when I left them."

"Well, hopefully it's just us." Doctor Robertson straightened up and stepped away from Nathan's supporting hand. "Now, you can only take three of these a day..."

"Three a day, tops," Nathan acknowledged, nodding.

"If Sarah and Jennifer get sick, let me know straight away. If they do, then chances are we've all got food poisoning and the Captain will need to know."

"Okay."

"If Sarah does take ill you can give her a pill, but not Jennifer. She's too young. If she does fall ill, come fetch me."

"Sure."

Doctor Robertson had reached her cabin door. "Now this isn't like before; we can't just hop down to the local pharmacy and get some more, so if you don't use them all or if they don't work, bring the rest back to me."

Nathan looked down at the precious white plastic tub. "Yeah, sure thing."

* * * * *

Again an icy torrent of water found its way into Patterson's waterproofs. He felt his clothes cling to his body, tugging against his every move. The cold water drew yet more heat away from his skin. This was a part of the Navy he'd never liked. He didn't like being wet. In Patterson's experience, if you were wet in the Navy something had gone wrong. Tonight just reaffirmed that belief. He peered over the top of his rain-splashed glasses to get a better look at the broken supports. A barrel had come loose and been tossed into the raised deck of the helicopter landing pad. Three of the four supports on the side it had struck were damaged; one knocked free, the other two smashed. The barrel was lodged under the platform by some of the debris it had carried with it.

Patterson looked up. The ship's carpenter was pointing the beam of his torch at the damage and behind him stood two equally drenched deck dogs.

Patterson shook his head. "Ah, shit."

"What do you say, sir? Lash it down and fix it after the storm?" the carpenter said hopefully.

"Sorry, Kelly," Patterson said as he straightened himself up. "Normally I'd say yes, but with Idris out on a rescue op we've got no idea when he'll be coming back. We might not have the time and he might not have the fuel to wait for us to fix it."

"Aye, aye, sir," Kelly said reluctantly.

Patterson heard the disappointment in the man's voice. He knew this wasn't a choice job, but he knew they couldn't risk not fixing it. He also knew he would have to chip in. Not that his men weren't capable, but because he had to be seen to endure the same hardships as those he commanded. "Get what you need from Stores, Kelly. We'll try to free the barrel."

Kelly nodded and trudged down the deck, through the spray, towards the hatchway.

Patterson addressed his two helpers: "Okay, we need to get a rope secured to this. One of us under the platform guiding it out, the other two at this side pulling—"

His planning was interrupted by a scream in the direction of the poop deck. Looking round, he saw the door hatch wide open and Kelly slumped in the corridor.

Patterson ran as best he could across the tilting deck. Waves rocked the ship so that the door swung open and shut with each swell, shut obscuring Patterson's view of the stricken joiner.

The door slammed shut just as he reached it. Grabbing the handle, Patterson heaved it open, bracing himself against the roll of the boat.

"Hold this!" he shouted to the first deck hand to reach him.

Patterson jumped inside.

"Mah' fuckin' hand!" Kelly cursed, sitting against a bulkhead with his arms folded in as if to conserve warmth.

"Let me see," Patterson said calmly.

Kelly unfolded his arms and held out a shaking hand. The tip of his right index finger was missing. Remarkably there was very little blood, just a flap of skin and some raw pulp.

"What happened?"

Kelly nodded towards the door. "Blew shut on me."

Patterson looked round to see a pink and red blob by the door. It sloshed back and forward with the waves. "You'd better wake Doctor Robertson," he said. "You okay to make your own way down?"

"Yeah, sure. What about the platform?"

"We'll handle that. Just you get yourself fixed up."

* * * * *

A moan of twisting metal shuddered down the whole length of the ship as she pushed through the storm. Again Doctor Robertson convulsed. The cramps had whipped their way through her whole body like tendrils. Frail gasps of pain withered out of her arid mouth and into the languid silence of her empty cabin. Beads of perspiration bathed her pallid skin. Her frozen joints were torn between shivering muscles and even the shallow pants she took scorched her lungs. A cough clawed its way out of her reluctant chest, wracking her with pain from her diaphragm to her lips. She spluttered out a final breath of red frothy droplets. This time she didn't take an inhalation. A few drops of pink, foamy saliva crawled their way down her cheek onto the sweat-soiled pillowcase.

A knock came at the door.

Doctor Robertson's eyes shot open.

"Look, I'm coming in so you'd better be decent," the anxious voice said.

Doctor Robertson cocked her stiff neck and began to raise herself from the bed.

Again the knocking came at the door. "Look, I've lost the top off my finger, lady. I can hear you moving about in there."

Out of her bed and shuffling towards the door, Doctor Robertson gave out an excited moan.

The door handle started to turn. "I'm coming in. I don't care what you and Frankenstein are up to."

A shaft of light spilled into the dark room from the doorway. Kelly lent into the room, blinking as his eyes tried to adjust to the darkness. Out of the gloom he could make out the shape of Doctor Robertson coming towards him.

She stretched out her hands and grabbed Kelly's head.

"What are you... Shit!" Kelly screamed as Doctor Robertson stepped into the light. He saw her face: Her lips cracked and broken, trails of blood across her chin and those milky eyes bereft of life.

Off balance, leaning half through the doorway, Kelly couldn't find the purchase to pull away.

Doctor Robertson lunged in and started biting.

Squall

SARAH PANTED. Her chest burnt with each breath. The sound of her trainers slapping against the tarmac cascaded around the alleyway. An agitated moan echoed after her, but in front of her she could see daylight in the street ahead.

A silhouette shambled across her exit. Sarah skidded to a halt. More moans; their attention drawn by the noise. More shapes congregated at the end of the alley. Looking round, Sarah could see her pursuers lethargically ambling towards her. Frantically she looked around for an escape route. She threw herself against unyielding doors and with every failure the groaning crowd grew closer.

Seizing an assortment of boxes and trashcans, Sarah started piling all that she could find under a fire escape. A gust of wind blew down the tight walls of the alley, bringing with it the stench of rotting flesh.

The zombies were too close now to do anything else. Sarah flung herself at her pyramid of garbage. Her weight made her sink into the loosely packed material. Her hands and knees sunk down, pulled in by the mire. In slow motion-like movements, Sarah clambered up. Something swiped at her legs but missed its grasp. She kicked out harder, dislodging some of the structure beneath her. She pushed up, her left hand scrabbling at the rough brick wall for purchase, her right hand stretched out and clawing for the bottom rung of the ladder. Hands grabbed at her feet and legs.

Sarah pushed off with all her strength. She felt the pile disintegrate and collapse beneath her. Her hand grasped out and clenched around the first rung of the ladder. Now with her full weight tugging on the rust-pitted rung, a squeal of metal dragging against metal sounded round the alley. Slowly the ladder started to pull down and as it slid further down she to sank deeper into the pile of trash and closer to the dead hands clawing at her. Before the ladder had time to trundle to a stop, Sarah threw her left hand onto the second rung and started to climb. The escape ladder sunk down to the ground and she climbed. Each thrust upwards did nothing more than keep her stationary. With a metallic clunk the ladder met its full extension and stopped moving. Kicking wildly against the grabbing hands, Sarah finally hauled herself beyond the reach of the ghouls. Gasping for air, she sat on the first landing. Beneath her the alleyway swarmed with the living dead, rotting arms outstretched for her.

Sarah picked herself up, and finding the fire exits barred, she started walking along the ledge around the building. Her body flat against the wall, she cautiously edged her way along the alley towards the daylight and the street beyond. As she shuffled along she came to a window. Inside looked like the living room of a small apartment. As she picked her way around she noticed a pair of legs in the doorway between this room and the next. She continued shuffling along the ledge until she encountered the next window. Inside, lying on the kitchen floor, was a body. The girl on the floor was crouched over by a ravenous zombie, eviscerating its victim.

This flat was familiar, but somehow out of context. In a flicker of insight, Sarah recognised the place.

This was the flat she had shared with Tricia.

Sarah took a second look at the victim. Behind the sandy blond hair and the blood splatters, it was her—the body on the floor was Sarah.

She let out a gasp at the realisation.

The zombie looked up from its feast. Its chin dripping with blood, its eyes dead and cold. Sarah expected to see her long dead flatmate, but it wasn't. It was Sarah's face that stared back at her with death's gaze. Both the corpse and the zombie were her.

Before Sarah had time to absorb any of this, the zombie picked itself up and with none of the familiar stiffness it charged at the window.

Sarah stood there on the window ledge in disbelief as the glass shattered and the zombie doppelganger burst through. The impact knocked Sarah from the ledge and tumbling towards the sea of outstretched cadaverous arms.

She kicked and screamed as she fell, propelling the bed covers across the cabin.

"Fuck!" Nathan bellowed as he too sat bolt upright.

Jennifer gave out a shrill scream as the ruckus woke her too.

"It's okay," Sarah gasped as she regained her bearings. "I had a nightmare. That's all."

"You scared the shit out of me," Nathan complained.

"Me too," Jennifer added.

"I'm sorry," Sarah said. "Let's go back to sleep."

The trio started settling back in.

"How are you feeling anyway, Nathan?" Sarah asked.

"Still shitty. Been lying here dozing." Nathan rolled over to face Sarah from his bed. "I'm hungry but I'm too scared to eat any—"

"Wait!" Sarah cut in. "Quiet!"

Nathan and Jennifer lay there, silent and still. The ship was making low groans as she ploughed her way against the storm. The rain and the waves showered the porthole of their cabin while the wind found tight nooks and taut lines from which to whistle.

Nathan shook his head, but kept quiet.

After waiting fruitlessly for a repetition, Sarah finally explained, "I'm sure I heard a scream."

"I hate to say this," Nathan said, "but could it just have been the wind?"

"No, something doesn't feel right," Sarah replied.

"Look, it's our first night on a boat and we're in the middle of a storm," Nathan reasoned, rubbing his upset stomach. "Of course nothing feels right."

Sarah sat up and slipped her feet into her shoes.

"Where are you going?" Jennifer asked.

Sarah picked up the shirt she'd worn to dinner and slipped it over the baggy white vest and boxer shorts she'd worn to bed. "I'm going to take a look."

Jennifer looked worried.

Sarah bent down and kissed her on the forehead. "It's probably nothing, but if I don't check I'll be up all night worrying about it."

"If it was something serious, don't you think they'd have a warning siren or something?" Nathan's voice had reflected his own insecurity. It was more of a question than an attempt to allay anyone's fears. After a moment he grumbled and tossed off his covers. "Ah, hell. I'm coming, too. Wasn't getting any sleep anyways." He pulled on his jeans and slipped on his trainers.

"Can I come?" Jennifer asked.

"No point in us all losing sleep, honey," Nathan said. "You wait here."

Sarah opened the door to the hallway. "Best lock the door, honey, and don't open it until we get back."

Jennifer nodded.

* * * * *

The hallway was on night time lighting, with only half the lights illuminated. It felt deserted. Even the constant drone of the engine was lost to the noise of the storm outside.

"Sarah," Nathan said softly, getting her attention. "Why were you on the roof this morning?"

"What?" Sarah asked, taken by surprise.

"What were you doing up on the warehouse roof so early?"

"Like I said, I couldn't sleep," Sarah said.

"No, I said that," Nathan corrected. "I don't recall you saying anything."

"What are you getting at?"

"Why wouldn't you talk to me?"

"Nathan, you're not making sense."

Nathan slipped his hand into the back pocket of his jeans and pulled out the envelope he'd been passed that afternoon. He held it out for Sarah. "You forgot to clear your pockets out when your stuff was taken to the laundry."

Sarah slowly reached out and took the letter from Nathan's grasp. "I don't know what to say, Nathan."

"Obviously not, otherwise you'd have spoken to me before you wrote this," Nathan replied. "We would have thought of something even if these guys hadn't shown up."

Sarah stood there, head bowed low.

"Sarah, I... I wouldn't want..." Nathan stopped, unable to say what he wanted.

"Nathan, I never wanted to hurt anyone..."

"But you would have."

Sarah let out a puff of breath that juddered with the beginning of a sob.

Nathan broke in, "Any idea where we're going?"

"I was hoping I'd hear something," Sarah confessed.

Nathan waited a moment, hoping Sarah would become inspired. Finally he said, "Patterson and a guy were in the radio room downstairs. We could check there first. Maybe they heard something."

Sarah let a shallow smile grow on her lips and placed a hand on Nathan's arm. "Thank you."

"Watch the doors on the way down," Nathan warned. "One of them swung back and almost took my leg off."

When they reached the radio room the door was shut.

Nathan knocked on the door. "Anyone there?"

"I can hear something," Sarah said.

"Yeah, I suppose it's the radio," Nathan guessed. "You can hear beeps like what's it... Morse code?"

"Would they leave the radio on if no one was listening to it?" Sarah asked. She didn't expect an answer from Nathan but it felt suspicious to her.

Nathan gave his usual shrug. "Don't know, they might. I used to leave my PC on all the time 'cause it was easier than booting it up. Maybe it's a similar thing here."

"Maybe."

"There's nothing going on," Nathan said. "Now can I try and get some sleep?"

Grudgingly, Sarah said, "I suppose."

Nathan was already opening the hatch to the stairwell when Sarah stepped in, closely followed by Nathan. She had placed a foot onto the first step when they both heard it:

A guttural moan from the deck below.

"Did you hear that?" Sarah asked.

Nathan's eyes were wide open, "I wish I hadn't."

As silently as they could against the pitching of the ship, they crept down the stairs. Nathan pointed to a red box on the wall. Sarah placed her index finger against her lips and Nathan nodded. He eased open the case and retrieved a fire axe from inside.

Sarah pushed open the hatch. Her hands still on the latch in case she had to close it quickly, she lent over to peer through the crack in the door.

What she could see of the corridor was empty. As nothing leapt out at her, Sarah decided to open the door fully and step into the corridor. She looked over her shoulder to Nathan. His knuckles were white, clenched around the shaft of the fire axe. Sarah took a hand off the door latch and gestured her intention to go through. Nathan nodded in agreement.

Pushing the door half open, Sarah stepped over into the corridor.

There was a wet smack from behind her like a wet sponge being dropped. Sarah whipped round to see the back of Doctor Robertson. She was sitting on the floor in a pool of blood beside a sailor. The blood waxed and waned as the boat tossed from side to side, like the ocean in miniature.

Doctor Robertson seemed to be examining something as Sarah stepped up to her.

Sarah reached out a hand to touch the doctor's shoulder. Her mouth dry with fear, her voice was barely more than a whisper. "Doctor Robertson?"

Doctor Robertson turned her head towards the voice. Her grey face was smeared with fresh red blood. A long strip of pink flesh from the dead marine on the deck dangled from her mouth. The dull dead eyes of the marine stared at the ceiling, but Doctor Robertson's looked directly at Sarah.

With a throat full of fresh blood, the zombie snarled and twisted round, its blood soaked hands lashing out.

Sarah lunged backwards, missing her step. She threw her arms out for balance but the pitch of the ship tipped her and she crashed to the floor. Ignoring her throbbing coccyx, Sarah propped herself up and started to scramble backwards.

But the zombie that was once Doctor Robertson had turned to pursue its new prey. With one swipe the creature snatched hold of Sarah's left foot and hauled herself up into biting range. Sarah kicked out her right foot, smashing her heel into the zombie's nose. The cartilage crunched loudly from the impact and when she pulled her foot back Sarah could see the nose was spread flat across its face. But this alone would not deter the zombie from its victim.

Nathan rushed forward, axe raised above his head.

"Look out!" Sarah cried as a second zombie lunged at Nathan from the gloom of the cabin.

Caught by surprise by the second creature, Nathan was pinned against the wall with no space to swing his axe.

The second zombie had most of its face gnawed away. Flaps of skin hung down its cheek, revealing glistening gums and bone white teeth. Nathan tried to push the monster away, leaning his hip into it. He forced his axe down in front of its gnashing mouth as the zombie slapped and pawed, trying to reach its prey. A damp hand slapped between the handle of the axe and Nathan's arm. Its fingers strained to claw at his face. One of the creature's digits was missing and the fresh injury was still seeping. Nausea welled up inside Nathan's gut as his cheek was prodded by the stump of the finger. The sensation of wet muscle and hard exposed bone sent torrents of convulsions writhing down his spine.

Sarah backed up, skittering down the corridor on her backside, kicking at the approaching ghoul as she went. In spasmodic kicks, Sarah endeavoured to keep the bare skin of her legs away from Doctor Robertson's infecting nails. All too soon she felt the cold impasse of a bulkhead at her back and Doctor Robertson pulling herself ever closer.

A flash of red and Doctor Robertson's head thundered to the floor. The handle of the fire axe quivered gently for a moment. Sarah looked at the doctor lying face down on the deck, axe embedded in the back of her skull. She looked up at Nathan half way down the corridor.

"You fucking idiot!" Sarah screamed, tears flooding down her cheeks. "You fucking idiot!" she screamed again, wedging herself into the corner.

"What?" Nathan said. He looked down at the remains of the now decapitated marine, then swivelled, looking about, worried by Sarah's reaction that he'd missed something.

"You threw that!" Sarah screeched even more loudly than before pointing at the axe.

"Um... yeah," Nathan replied, confused.

"You could have fucking killed me!"

"What?"

"What if you'd missed?! What then?!"

Nathan shrugged, mystified by Sarah's attitude. "I was saving your life. Are you okay?"

Sarah stopped dead. She looked down at her legs and brushed her hands over her shins. She let out a sigh when she realised the skin was unbroken. Relieved she was okay, she looked up at Nathan. Only now did it register there was a bloody streak down one side of his face.

"Oh, Nathan," Sarah sighed, releasing a saddened gasp.

"What?" he asked, brushing his cheek. He inspected the blood on his fingertips. "Oh, that." He smiled. "No, it was that one." He pointed to the beheaded corpse on the floor. "It was missing the end of a finger. It's not my blood."

Sarah spat on the sleeve of her shirt and wiped Nathan's face clean like a mother before a school photo.

"I'm fine," Nathan protested.

"Thank God," she said, satisfied that he had avoided being scratched.

A command shot out, "On the deck now!"

Nathan and Sarah turned to see a marine with pistol drawn standing a few metres down the corridor.

It was Sarah's turn to be stunned. "What?"

Nathan looked down at the three bodies in the corridor. "But—"

"On the deck now!" the marine shouted again. "Hands behind your head or I will fire!"

The door to the stairwell opened and a second marine appeared. Within seconds of surveying the scene he had his gun drawn and aimed at the survivors.

"Okay," Nathan said softly as he raised his hands. He and Sarah lowered themselves onto the deck, careful to avoid the unsavoury patches of blood.

"What's going on, corporal?" a familiar voice asked.

Sarah craned her head round to where Captain Warden had appeared.

"I heard screams, sir, and the sounds of a scuffle." Not once did the soldier take his eyes or firearm off Sarah and Nathan. "When I got here Doctor Robertson and the other two crewmen were dead."

Sarah lifted her head off the deck. "We didn't kill them. They were already dead."

Captain Warden squatted down in front of her. "What are you saying then?"

"They were both dead when we got here," Nathan said. "They had already turned."

The Captain seemed bewildered.

"They were walking dead," Sarah elaborated and corroborated.

Without acknowledging either of them, Captain Warden bent down over the corpse of Doctor Robertson. He tucked his finger around to the side of the cadaver's neck.

"Cold," he pronounced.

He stepped down the corridor to the detached head. Unceremoniously he picked it up by the hair. He brought the dripping trophy up to eye level. With a casual air he swivelled the head, examining the incisions on its cheek. As it hung there, its jaw worked up and down and its eyes kept a lock on the Captain.

The pitiful animation of the decapitated zombie did nothing to phase Captain Warden's stolid composure. Satisfied that the bite marks were human, he placed the head back on the deck.

"Marine," he beckoned and went back to Doctor Robertson.

He placed his heel on her shoulders and the rest of his foot upon her neck. The old sailor's weathered hands grasped the hilt of the axe and with one powerful tug freed it.

Captain Warden threw the axe to one side. "Marine, help me get this woman undressed."

The marine was so bewildered by the order he only just managed to stutter out, "Wh—What?"

Warden was already down on the ground yanking off the Doctor's pyjama bottoms.

"What's going on?" Nathan said as he started to sit upright.

"Get down!" the second marine barked as he waved his gun.

Nathan lay back down but shot a concerned glance at Sarah.

The deceased doctor's body now naked, Captain Warden sat there staring at her like a punter at some macabre peep show. He pulled a pen from his shirt pocket and used it to move her blood-soaked hair. His fixation ceased. "Turn her over."

The two men rolled her on to her back. Doctor Robertson gazed up at the ceiling, her mouth agawk.

Again Captain Warden studied her body. Like a sick necrophiliac he scanned every inch of the dead woman's flesh.

"Sir?" the marine whispered, hoping the sound would break the uneasiness he felt.

"What's that there, son?" Warden asked, using his pen as a pointer.

The marine blurted out, "I don't know, sir."

"Take a closer look, for Christ's sake!" Warden bellowed.

The marine lent in. Doctor Robertson had an attractive figure in life and the marine was finding it hard to disassociate that with the nude corpse before him. The captain had insisted he look at her breasts. He took in a deep breath of air as if he were about to dive underwater, and started to really look at her body. On her right breast on the curve halfway between her nipple and her ribcage there was a dark patch of skin.

"Is it a bruise?" the marine asked.

Captain Warden prodded it with his pen. "Looks like a love bite and there's a smaller one up by the shoulder."

"A hickey? Is that how she got infected?" the nervous marine asked.

"Getting a love bite wouldn't get you infected," Sarah said.

"How do you know, lady?" Warden snapped.

"Because Doctor Robertson told me. The infection is passed in bodily fluids like blood and saliva."

Warden walked over to Sarah and Nathan. "Someone needed to use their mouth to do that, and correct me if I'm wrong, but that's where you usually find saliva."

Sarah started to get up. The marine pointing his gun at her, taking his cue from the Captain, let her rise.

"The virus doesn't get in through the skin—it's an effective barrier. She told me."

Captain Warden didn't look convinced.

"It's like most other viruses," Sarah explained. "You can't get it from touching it. Remember all the myths about catching AIDS?"

Warden nodded slowly.

"You wouldn't catch it from sitting on a toilet seat because your skin keeps it out. It needs to get into your bloodstream. The same is true here—you won't catch it from shaking hands. And you won't catch it from a love bite."

"But the infection is carried in saliva!" Warden countered.

"But they have to bite you to get the saliva into your bloodstream. All a love bite does is bring blood to the surface. It doesn't break the skin, so it's not transmissible."

Warden was frustrated. "So if there's no bite mark how did she get infected?"

Sarah wanted to speak, to say anything that might defeat this man's ignorance, but she couldn't. Captain Warden was right. There was no bite mark, no fresh scratch or cut on her body. No obvious cause of her infection. Nothing.

"It must mean the contagion has gone airborne!" Warden surmised.

"Not necessarily..."

Captain Warden spoke over her, "I'm no scientist, but I don't see any other explanation."

Sarah opened her mouth to speak, but he cut her short again. "I may not know as much as you about how viruses spread," he conceded, "but I know you can catch a cold from breathing in after someone sneezes." He looked down at Doctor Robertson's naked corpse. "Now it don't take no degree to figure that she must have breathed it in."

Sarah was stunned into silence. She wanted to offer up another explanation but she couldn't think of one. The thought that Captain Warden was right was terrifying.

"We could all be infected by now," said an obviously spooked marine.

"Corporal." Captain Warden snapped at the marine, giving him a verbal slap across the face. The marine straightened up and let his worried expression be replaced with a look of obedient passivity. "Check Frankenstein's lab. Make sure the specimen is secure. And you get this mess cleared up."

"Yes, sir!" the marine barked.

Captain Warden turned to the second marine. "And you take these two to the brig. Then wake up Dr. Frankenstein. I want to speak to him in my office."

"The brig?!" Nathan blurted. "But we've got nothing to do with this!"

Captain Warden stepped over to where Nathan lay. "Yesterday I had six more crewmen than I do now. And you're the only reason I can figure."

"But we're not infected!" Sarah protested.

Warden pointed a rigid finger at her. "Until I know that for certain you're spending your time in the brig."

Nathan strained his neck to look up at the Captain, unsure whether he should just get up or wait to be ordered. His neck hurt from the strain, so he let his head rest on the cold metal deck. As he did something caught his eye. He looked at the dead sailor Doctor Robertson had been feasting on when he had come in. Something felt wrong. Something had changed, but what was out of place was oblivious to his conscious mind. He stared at the body, trying to work out what had drawn his attention. Then he saw it. The man's hand twitched.

Captain Warden took a step back so he could punctuate his next statement with a wave of his arm. "Get them out of here, Corporal."

The dead sailor on the deck reanimated. His eyes shot open and with bared teeth it lunged at Captain Warden's calf.

Nathan screamed a warning but all it succeeded in doing was to make the Captain look down just in time to see the zombie clamp its jaws onto his leg.

Warden howled as he collapsed to the floor. The zombie pulled back, bringing with it a chunk of fabric and muscle.

The scream which boiled out from Captain Warden broke abruptly, silenced by the deafening gunshots. One of the marines had opened fire on the zombie, hammering a dozen bullets into it.

After the din of the shooting, the corridor was quiet for a moment. Sarah's eyes were transfixed by the bloody mess the marine had made of the zombie. Several bullet holes were smattered across its upper chest and neck, but its head had been reduced to a pulp.

The silence was broken by a grunt forced out from behind clench teeth.

"Captain!" The marine bent down by the side of his stricken commander.

"Get them into the brig!" Warden hissed, looking at Sarah and Nathan. He then grasped the shirt of the marine bent over him. "Go get Doctor Frankenstein! Make sure he brings his med kit and his antidote!"

Sarah had to warn the captain. What Doctor Robertson and Professor Cutler had been working on was a vaccine, not a cure. She opened her mouth to speak, but Warden shouted over her.

"What are they still doing here?!" he bellowed. "Get them locked up!"

"Yes, sir!"

The marine whipped round. He grabbed Nathan by the arm and threw him to his feet. Still stumbling to find his balance, he found Sarah scooped up beside him as they were marched off to the brig.

Cell

"COME ON, those were gunshots! Something's wrong!" Bates protested. He stood at the door to his cell, gripping a bar in each hand.

"I've phoned the bridge, Bates. What more do you want me to do?" the guard asked.

Bates rattled his cage. "Let me out and we can go take a look."

The guard shook his head vigorously. "Oh no, Bates. And end up in there with you when the old man finds out?"

Bates was about to protest again when the intercom buzzed. There was a short exchange before the door to the brig was opened and Nathan and Sarah came tumbling into the room.

"Busy tonight," Bates commented.

"Would you can it, Bates?" The guard turned to his newly arrived colleague. "So what's the story?"

"Found our new arrivals here standing over Doctor Robertson's dead body," the marine said.

"Shit!" the guard exclaimed.

The marine went on, "Gets worse. Kelly and Suneil are dead, too."

The guard, still open mouthed, let slip a quieter, "*Shit*."

"Look, we walked in on that. We didn't kill them," Sarah protested.

"Maybe so, lady, but how do you think it looked to me?" The marine pushed Sarah and Nathan deeper into the brig. "Three fucking bodies and you two. They'd been bitten." The marine nodded over to Sarah and Nathan. "They reckon Dr. Robertson was a W.D."

"Shit!" the guard let slip again.

Nathan pushed back against the marine. "Why the fuck would we bite them?!"

The marine continued, "Captain wants 'em locked up because he thinks they're the source of the infection."

The guard looked them up and down. "They don't look dead to me."

"The old man got bit to so I can't hang around," the marine said.

"What?!" Bates voice was pitched high with shock.

"Warden's been infected?!" The guard was just as shocked as Bates.

"Yeah the old man's been bit. Anyway, get these two locked up. I'm off to get Frankenstein." The marine gestured with his gun for Bates to move back and covered the doorway as his prisoners were secured.

As the barred door clunked shut on her, Sarah felt her anxiety rise.

"I'd better get moving. The old man wants me to fetch our ship's mortician." The marine opened the door of the brig to leave. "He's got some kind of an anti-zee shot the Captain wants."

Sarah shouted through the bars at the marine who was about to leave, "Professor Cutler doesn't have a cure—it's only a vaccine!"

The marine paid no attention to her as he left the brig.

"You've got to keep an eye on the Captain! He's going to turn!"

The door to the brig shut and Sarah's shoulders sank.

"My high school biology's a bit weak—well, more accurately, it was a bit of a week. I only turned up for four classes," Bates admitted. "But vaccines don't cure, do they?"

"No, they just boost the natural defences by stimulating the immune system," Sarah said.

"So won't that help?" Nathan asked.

"The vaccine is usually a weakened strain... Something the body can fight off." Sarah looked off at the closed door of the brig, feeling trapped. "The immune system remembers the virus and recognises it as an invader, so it's more effective against a stronger infection."

Bates looked thoughtful for a moment. "But the Captain's been bit, so it's too late for Frankenstein's shot to do anything."

Sarah nodded.

"But there is no mild form of the big zee. You get it, it turns you," Nathan said. "You get a little, it just kills you later."

"Look, I don't know how it works!" Sarah snapped

"You know more than the rest of us," Bates said. "And I think you understand more about this than you're willing to give yourself credit for."

"Some vaccines use viruses that are similar rather than using the real thing. Something that mimics the real contagion. Maybe it's not the live virus... I don't know." Sarah shook her head. "I'm not a biologist—I did some chemistry, that's all." She made to punch the bars in frustration but sensibility refrained. She stepped back and ran both hands through her hair. "I don't know... maybe it will work. I just can't tell from what little I know."

"The Captain is as good as dead, isn't he?" Nathan said in a flat voice.

Bates pressed up against the bars again and called out to the guard, "You hear all that?!"

The guard sat at his desk, arms crossed, looking in at the cell.

"You've got to let us out of here," Bates said. "The Captain's probably wandering around biting people."

"I've had enough of you, Bates," the guard said firmly. "You're relieved of duty, so it's none of your concern."

"If Warden starts biting, how quickly do you think the shit will hit the fan?" Bates asked.

"If there's anything going down, the bridge will call us. Now sit down and shut the fuck up."

Bates backed away from the door of the cell, resigned to the situation.

"Come here often?" Nathan quipped, trying to dispel the tension.

Bates let out a huff. "There's been a few occasions; never this sober before," he admitted. "Since the cable TV went off we've had to make our own entertainment."

Sarah flumped onto the cot in the cell. Its weak mattress dissolved under her weight, crumpling the coarse green blanket into canyons around her. She lent back and let out a sigh.

Something didn't add up. She couldn't work out how Doctor Robertson had become infected. Sarah rubbed her temple and tried to ignore the headache that had set in.

When she tuned back in she realised Nathan and Bates were making idle chat.

"Doctor Robertson didn't get bitten," Sarah interrupted.

"She didn't have a mark on her," Nathan said, confirming Sarah's statement.

"So the infection has gone airborne," Bates said.

Nathan shook his head. "If it had wouldn't that mean we were all infected?"

"Cutler!" Sarah straightened up as she said it.

Bates and Nathan looked at her.

"He's the carrier!" Sarah said, voicing the epiphany.

"We've had crew infected before because of Frankenstein's specimens," Bates said, "but you said there were no bite marks on Doctor Robertson."

"His vaccine," Sarah said. "What if they've tried the vaccine and it doesn't work?"

"That's a hell of a jump, Sarah," Nathan said.

"You said it yourself, Nathan: A little dose will kill you, it just takes longer."

Nathan obviously wasn't convinced. "Sarah, we don't know that it doesn't work. And we don't know how it works and neither of them said they had taken it."

"Frankenstein's reckless enough to try it, but not Doctor Robertson," Bates added.

"The love bite," Sarah said.

Nathan walked over to the cot and sat down next to her. "You said you couldn't catch it through a love bite."

"I know," Sarah said, "but don't you get it."

Looking round, neither Bates or Nathan did.

A voice came from across the brig: "They had sex," the guard said.

"Doctor Robertson had sex with a corpse?!" Nathan squealed in revulsion.

"No, she and Cutler are—*were*—lovers," Bates said. "You're suggesting Frankenstein gave it to her during sex?"

"What—like the clap?" Nathan finally twigged.

"Safe sex is virtually outlawed as part of The Plan. The ABC to save humanity," Bates rhymed off.

Sarah and Nathan gave him blank looks.

"Coalition of the Living speech," Bates added. "Ammo, Babies and Concrete."

The other two occupants of the cell looked dumfounded.

"It's how we're going to win the war," Bates tried to explain.

"No, we get it... it's just a bit... well, you know." Nathan shrugged.

"World's gone to hell in a hand basket and we're still getting fed slogans by fat assed politicians," Sarah said.

"So you reckon Frankenstein gave it to Doctor Robertson," Bates said, bringing the conversation back round.

Sarah nodded.

Bates continued with his line of thought, "But if that's the case, why hasn't Frankenstein turned?"

"I don't know," Sarah admitted. "Maybe he has. I mean you don't just turn the moment you get bit. It works its way through your system first. Who knows how long that would take. And if he's injected himself with some kind of serum he must have manipulated it in some way."

"What would that mean?" Bates asked.

"I don't know." Sarah pushed her tongue against her lip piercing, trying to think. "It might mean nothing. It might mean it works differently." She shook her head. "It could be he's a symptom-less carrier. He could be wandering about feeling fine, spreading the contagion. He could have turned hours ago and has been shambling around trying to find someone to bite. I just don't know."

"Either way, he's not going to save the Captain," Nathan offered.

* * * * *

The rest of the deck dogs had been dismissed and none of them had volunteered to help Patterson with a line check. Resigned to the fact he couldn't get any wetter, he had circled the deck, double-checking nothing else had been damaged or knocked loose by the storm. Satisfied everything was fine, he walked back round to the helicopter pad where he had started. He looked at the ugly repair job. A flash of lightning from behind illuminated the shambolic carpentry. The weather and the absence of the joiner meant that the work had taken three times longer to complete and was a hell of a lot more unsightly that it should be. Patterson, however, was sure it would hold the few days it would take for Kelly to recover.

He trudged through the spray back to the main hatch, a journey made all the more arduous by the weather and the roll of the boat. Every few seconds the ship would pitch, with the waves making walking an impossibility. With his fingers numb and pruned from the wet, holding the guide ropes was agony. But every few steps Patterson was forced to stop and hold on for fear of being tossed overboard. His stiff orange survival suit made him take ugly steps to stop the rubber clinging. He hated the garment; it's ungainly weight, the restrictive joints, even the chemical smell of it conjured up feelings of dread and revulsion. He knew that if he were to lose his grip and be swept into the sea he would be dead in minutes without it.

Finally, wet from the spray and the sweat of the effort Patterson, reached the deck entrance.

The jolt of the lever opening the door screeched all the way up to his elbows. The door groaned as it swung open. Quickly, before the swell shifted the centre of gravity, Patterson ducked inside. As he shut the door behind him his thoughts went immediately to a hot shower and bed. He pulled back the tight sleeve of his suit to check the time. By his estimate it would be well after two in the morning. The sudden warmth of the ship coated his glasses with steam, making it impossible to see. He unzipped the neck of his bright orange survival suit and pulled out the damp hem of his polar-neck jumper.

Popping the glasses into a fold, like he was tuning a violin, he started to clean them in an awkward manner under his chin. He looked up, alerted by the sound of footsteps. Squinting through his myopia he saw a figure limping towards him. Even with his terrible eyesight he could make out the telltale white Captain's cap.

"The landing pad has been temporarily repaired, sir," Patterson reported, still rubbing his glasses. But even without them he could see that the Captain walked with a pronounced limp. "Unfortunately, Kelly injured himself. Nothing serious, so I'd like him to check the work over once he's fit for duty." He finished wiping his glasses. "I was going to retire for the night, unless there was anything else you felt needed my attention, sir?"

As Patterson finished, Captain Warden stepped directly in front of him.

A hand on each leg, Patterson put his glasses back on and focused through the streaks on the lenses. Warden stood before him, his face grey and his jaw hanging open. Patterson's stomach plummeted in the split second of realisation before the zombie attacked.

As the dead Captain lunged forward to bite, Patterson threw his arms up in front of his face. Cold dead hands slapped against the rubberised fabric of the survival suit. Patterson felt the zombie's teeth clamp down on his arm. The force was tremendous, crushing the muscle against his own bone. He screamed out in shock at the pain and realised that his skin hadn't been broken. The cloth of the survival suit didn't yield and the infecting bite of the zombie couldn't break through.

Patterson rallied from the shock and punched his ex-captain in the face. The dead captain's grasping hands occasionally deflected Patterson's blows, but the punching did nothing to deter the zombie's attack.

Captain Warden's sluggish brain realised that its biting wasn't finding flesh. His jaw unlocked just as Patterson's fist connected. The force and the unexpected success of the blow threw Patterson off balance. He found himself stumbling to maintain his steadiness while fending off the Captain's flailing slaps. His feet tangled up with the zombies and he tripped, crashing hard against the deck. Patterson's head cracked against the steel and immediately his senses were overwhelmed by the jolt of pain. He forced his eyes to focus, pushing back the encroaching blackness. Through the muffled ringing he heard a moan and then felt frozen fingers grip his hair. He knew he had to dispatch his dead Captain but he didn't have any weapons on him. His hand brushed over Captain Warden's holster. If he could get enough purchase he could snap the holster open and use Warden's gun.

Against the weight of his assailant and the resistance of his rubberised suit, Patterson heaved himself up. He heaved against the extra weight of the zombie sprawled over top of him. With one arm he pushed himself up, the other fumbling with the catch on the holster. Patterson felt something wet against the side of his face. Opening the holster he grasped the hilt of the gun and yanked it free. The ghoul bit down and this time it found flesh. In one action its teeth clamped together and it pulled back, tearing a chunk of skin from Patterson's jaw line.

Through the pain of the bite, Patterson's only thought was that even if he won his struggle with his dead Captain, he had already lost.

***** *

Sarah was awake and standing by her bunk even before she knew what had woken her.

"Did you hear that?" Bates called out at the guard.

The guard was wiping his eyes and looking confused. "What the hell was that?"

"Just a minute—I'll go out and check," Bates offered. "No, wait— I'm locked in a fucking cell!"

"Just wait there," the guard instructed.

Bates cocked his head. *Ya think?*

There was a heavy clunk then the lights flickered. The fluorescents tinkled and plinked, growing dim and then sparking bright again. Suddenly the electrical hum stopped and the lights went dead.

Sarah gasped, shocked by how complete the darkness was. With a clunk the red emergency lights popped into life. The red glow made the surroundings and everyone around look darker and more sinister than the stark white fluorescents.

Everyone froze as a second spray of shots rang out. The noise was stifled behind walls, but it was still clear enough to be unmistakable.

"I'll phone the bridge," the guard said nervously. His hand shook as he lifted the receiver.

As he was about to dial the number the klaxon burst to life. The guard almost dropped the phone.

"Come on, let us out!" Bates implored.

The guard adamantly stuck to his orders. "I'm calling the bridge."

Shouts, screams and weapons fire now seemed to come from all over.

"Come on," Bates urged.

The guard shook his head. "It's just ringing out."

"You've got to let us out! The shit's going down out there and we're caged up!" Bates rattled the bars for emphasis.

Scraping and scratching sounds accompanied by guttural moans emanated from behind the brig door.

Everyone took a step back deeper into the brig.

The guard pressed up against the bars and looked over his shoulder into the cell. "I... I..."

In the midst of the guard's stammer a stream of machinegun fire opened up from somewhere in the corridor and a line of bullet holes erupted across the wall.

Sarah felt a hard blow across her shoulder and she fell to the floor. The impact with the cell floor knocked the wind from her. Coughing, she tried to breathe but there was a weight on her chest.

Bates slid off Sarah's back and onto the floor beside her.

Laying almost nose to nose with her he whispered, "You okay?"

Catching her breath, Sarah just nodded.

"Sorry if I pushed you down a bit hard," Bates said. "Instinct."

Sarah whispered out her thanks and lay there happy it hadn't been a bullet that had slammed into her. Bates still had his arm around her in a protective hug and he was looking off to the door of the brig expectantly. Sarah found herself examining his face. The stark red lighting sent a dark shadow down from his narrow nose across his elegant, almost feminine chin. Pulses of warm breath blew across Sarah's lips as Bates steadied his breathing. The darkness around his eyes pulled her gaze in. He had long, elegant eyelashes for a man. With the saturating hue of the emergency lights, Sarah couldn't make out or even remember the colour of his iris, but they had a seductive quality to them in this light.

Bates looked away from the door and caught Sarah's gaze. From just inches apart they stared at each other. Sarah was startled by the intensity of the connection between them. His pupils dilated as she watched and she became aware they had both stopped breathing.

Suddenly Sarah became painfully aware of how long she had been staring at Bates. The red light saving her blush from being spotted, Sarah batted her eyelashes and looked away, a nervous smile curling on her lips.

"Everyone okay?" Bates whispered, breaking the nervous quiet.

There was a round of hushed replies.

A second roar of machine gun fire forced the brig's occupants to stay flat against the deck. With the sound of popping of steel, a spree of shots punctured their way through the corridor wall. Through the arc of jagged perforations, glimpses of light and shadow could be seen flickering on the other side. And with the presence of the holes, the noises from outside were no longer muffled. A chorus of undead wails echoed around the ship. Sporadic gunfire in the near and far distance could be heard. Occasionally a scream or a curse could be distinguished above the noises.

"What the hell do we do?" Nathan asked.

No one answered.

Bates pushed a finger through the bars and prodded the guard. "And for fuck's sake don't say *I'll call the bridge.*"

"Well?" Nathan asked.

"The first thing to do is let us out." Bates had kept his voice low but the clipped words conveyed his anger.

"I'm going to check the door," the guard said.

Reticently he got to his feet. He stood there for a moment listening out for danger—or trying to find an excuse to lay back down. Slowly he crept his way to the door, freezing at the slightest sounds.

He reached the door, unholstered his gun and cocked the weapon with a sharp click.

Sarah could see beads of sweat across the man's forehead caught by the unnatural red light.

He stood at the side of the door and reached out for the handle. Turning the lock, he eased the door open a fraction to peer through. The door flew open and in burst a zombie. The guard leapt back, firing wildly as he did.

Sarah instinctively ducked, covering her ears against the thunderous noise of the gun. The din of the gun blast seemed to be amplified against the cold metal bulkheads, with the sound smacking around the small brig almost as violently as the shots themselves.

Two more cadavers heaved their way into the brig and towards the guard. All of the zombies wore military uniforms and all of them looked freshly resurrected. Panicking, the guard fired repeated shots at the creatures. Some of the shots struck the dead crewmen but none of them delivered a coup de grâce.

"Take aimed shots!" Bates shouted above the clamour. "Just one at a time!"

Backed up against the wall, the guard took careful aim at the lead zombie. He pulled the trigger and the bullet found its target. A neat hole erupted just above the bridge of its nose. The exit wound was not as neat. The back of the zombie's skull shattered.

The guard swung his aim round, but the other two zombies were too close. He tussled with them, trying to get his gun in a position to fire while avoiding a bite. The gun went off and the second zombie dropped, but before the guard could switch his attention the third creature clamped its jaws around his neck.

The guard's face contorted as his scream threw his mouth open. The zombie pulled back, ripping open its victim's neck. Seizing back the initiative, the guard shoved the gun into the zombie's face and pulled the trigger.

The corpse crashed to the floor.

Blood gushed from the guard's wound, pulsing out with the rhythm of his heartbeat. Stumbling over to the entrance, blood pouring from his neck, he pushed his shoulder into the door, heaving it closed. Exhausted by his exertion, he slid to the ground, his back to the door, one hand on his gun and the other clamped over his neck, the blood flooding out from between his fingers.

Sprawled against the door, the guard looked into the cell. "I've been bit."

His voice was weak and even in the red light his face looked pale. He lifted up the gun, opened his mouth and pushed the barrel inside.

"No, wait!" Bates screamed as the trigger was pulled.

There was a sharp click as the hammer struck the firing pin, but nothing else. The guard removed the gun from his mouth and looked at it in confusion. The magazine was empty.

Bates let out a sigh as he blew out the breath he'd been holding. His muscles slackened in relief. "You've got to let us out off here first!"

Sluggishly, the guard fell forward onto his knees, one hand covering his wound, his gun hand knuckles down supporting him he shuffled forward like a lame dog. His eyes flickered as if fighting against sleep. His head fell limp and his joints buckled, sending him crashing to the deck. His hand fell free of his neck and the very last few drops of blood trickled out to drip onto the brig floor.

"Ah, fuck man!" Bates kicked the bars in frustration. He spun round, both hands running through his hair. His well defined muscles were ridged with tension and he looked as if he would start tearing his hair out at any moment. He stamped his foot on the deck. "Fuck!"

"What do we do now?!" Nathan exclaimed.

"Not much to do," Bates said, pacing the length of the cell. "Hope we get rescued before we starve to death in here."

"We'd die of thirst first." Sarah said, looking through the bars in dismay.

Bates rubbed his head the way he had when he'd taken his helmet off in the chopper. The action seamed to calm him down. "Die of thirst? That's comforting... I think."

Sarah got down on her knees.

"I don't think praying's going to help," Bates said.

Laying down on the cell floor, Sarah squeezed up to the bars. She laid side on so as to get as much reach as possible with her arm. "I think I can grab him."

"The keys!" Bates rushed over. "You're going to pull him in and get the keys off his belt."

Nathan stood with a pinkie in his ear, waggling it to try and subdue the ringing from the recent gun shots. "You're doing what?"

"She's getting the keys," Bates said slowly and with exaggerated mouth movements.

"That's the idea." Sarah huffed as she adjusted her position and stretched out her slender arm.

It slipped with ease between cold metal bars and out towards the dead guard, her fingertips just touching the man's shirt. She tried jamming her shoulder into the gap between the bars to get that little bit further.

Wedging herself further, Sarah grunted as she pawed for the shirt, but he was just too far away. Shifting her position slightly, she turned her head away from the corpse and stretched her left arm out across the floor for purchase. Her head tilted away, putting her neck in a more relaxed position, affording the muscles around her shoulder joint more flexibility and mobility. Using her left hand for purchase, Sarah pushed her shoulder flat and eased it out through the bars. She walked her fingers onto the dead guard's shirt and up to a seam. Again she couldn't get far enough up to grasp the shirt. Pushing her fingertips against the fabric as hard as she could, she tried to snag the cloth and pull it back. She reasoned that if she could pull enough back she could then maybe get a proper grip. Her nails rasped against the cloth trying to gain purchase as she pulled her hand back. Her knuckles blanched with the pressure and the muscles turned first pink, then red, until finally turning purple from the pressure. Her whole arm trembled from the exertion.

Nathan and Bates whispered their encouragement. Slip followed tug over and over again. Sarah closed her eyes, frustrated by her lack of success and the hindrance of facing the wrong way to be able to see what she was doing.

She screwed her eyes up tight and let out a hiss of breath to convey her annoyance. With her eyes closed she could concentrate on the feel of cloth beneath her fingertips. The lactic acids burning in her arm told her she would have to give up very soon.

Then the fabric began to crumple and slip. It was working. Millimetre by millimetre, Sarah was pulling more and more of the shirt towards her, all the time gaining momentum, almost enough for her to get a proper grasp.

Facing away from the corpse, Sarah couldn't see the dead guards eyes flicker open. The words of encouragement ended abruptly and in the same instant a hand grabbed her. It grasped around her forearm just below the elbow.

Sarah turned and tried to pull away. The freshly resurrected zombie lurched forward, grabbing her arm with both hands. An excited gasp of air hissed out from its lips as it brought its gaping maw snapping down at Sarah's flesh. Sarah felt a second pair of hands grab her but this time it was her other arm. Before the newly reanimated zombie could snap its teeth shut, she had been yanked free of its grasp and pulled deeper into the cell.

She looked up to see Bates towering above her, extending a hand down. She accepted his hand and he lifted her to her feet.

Sarah felt the strength in his muscles as he wrapped a supportive arm around her waist to steady her. She looked up into his eyes, grateful for her rescue. Her heart was hammering from the shock and she could still feel the impression of the zombie's hands around her arm. All of the terror collapsed, dispelled by the presence of the man standing in front of her. She felt soothed by his closeness. He placed his right hand on her shoulder and slowly let it slip down her arm. His fingers gently raked their way down, past her elbow, down her forearm and onto her wrist, until his hand clasped hers.

Sarah couldn't hold back the shudder that tingled through her or the soft gasp of air as he turned her hand over. Bates brought his left hand down the soft white skin of the underside of her forearm until his hands met. clasping Sarah's between them.

"You look clean," Bates said in a firm voice. "No scratches."

The dead guard slammed up against the outside of the cell, snarling and flailing. Thrusting his arms between the bars, the ghoul snatched at the air in a forlorn attempt to seize its prey. Wild with fury, his lips curled back, the zombie lashed out, its gnashing teeth dripping with saliva. He snarled like a rabid dog.

"Don't look too happy at having his meal interrupted," Bates quipped.

Sarah took a couple of deep breaths. She knew her cellmates would assume she was trying to regain her composure after the fright, but in truth Sarah had felt a different primordial reaction.

She granted herself a fleeting smile, a physical acknowledgment of the brief moment of arousal she'd felt for Bates, before returning to their situation.

"I thought when you resurrected you were brain dead, but that fucker looks real pissed," Nathan said.

"Animals get angry," Sarah offered. "Doesn't mean they're intelligent. It's just an instinct."

Bates stepped a little closer, but still out of reach of the zombie. He stepped from side to side, watching as the zombie followed him with thrashing arms.

"He's working on autopilot," Bates said without taking his eyes of the zombie. "Like the knee-jerk reaction. It doesn't take any thought. If he could think, he'd just take his keys and open up the door."

"We've got to get those keys." Nathan pawed at his chin as if trying to find a solution.

"Anything for a quiet life, eh!" Bates signalled to Nathan. "You grab his right arm. I'll grab his left."

"My left or your left?" Nathan asked.

"What the fuck?! We're facing the same way!"

"I mean our left or his left?"

"His left." Bates stood agog. "Look, just grab the one on your side. When we do, Sarah can get the key. Okay?"

"Sure," Nathan said, nodding his head in agreement.

Bates looked over at Sarah for consent.

She nodded.

Taking up a stance with his weight on his front leg, Bates started swaying as if he were about to try to leap a chasm. "One... two..."

"Whoa! Whoa!" Nathan shouted, his hands raised in front of him, palms facing out. "On three or after three?"

Sarah stepped between the pair. "Boys..." She paused and looked them in the eye, in turn. "Just grab him *now!*"

The two men lunged at the zombie. Its arms lashed out, trying to haul them into its maw. The bars rattled and clanked as the two men battled to subdue the creature.

Bates managed to get a two-handed grasp, one below the wrist and the other gripped onto its forearm.

"Fuck me, this bugger's strong!" Bates gritted, fighting to restrain it.

"Shit!" Nathan cursed as he completely lost control of the zombie's other arm.

The dead crewman used his freedom to get closer to Bates. It pushed its snarling face hard against the bars. The metal rods jammed into its cheeks. Only the bone beneath prevented it from forcing its way through.

Bates stared into the snarling creature's eyes. Its irises were still plain to see, unlike the clouded white that old zombies seemed to turn.

The creature used Bates' grip against him. It flexed its dead muscle and started to pull him closer to the bars.

Bates could smell the fresh blood that glistened black in the red light on the cadaver's neck.

"Have you been working out?" Bates joked as he struggled against the zombie.

Bates was a military trained man. He was strong and he was practiced but the creature he fought struggled harder than any living man could. It didn't feel pain, it ignored fatigue, it fought until its muscles ripped.

Bates had an epiphany.

"Fuck it!" he snarled as he pulled the zombie's arm fully into the cell and snapped it back against the bars. Its humerus split in two with a sickening crack. The zombie still flailed unabated, but without the bone for leverage the arm was useless.

Bates held onto the struggling zombie. The arm still tensed and contracted, but deprived of its anchoring the muscles had no purchase. The zombie shoved itself at the bars again and Bates felt the two ends of raw bone rasp together. The crunching ragged edges of bone sent shudders down the zombie's arm each time they grated together. Bates too shuddered at the sound of bone against bone.

He shouted, "Grab the other arm!"

Nathan danced in and grabbed the ghoul's arm.

"Now, Sarah!" Nathan barked.

Sarah lunged between them, falling onto her knees. She thrust her right arm through the bars and grabbed for the keys clipped to the cadaver's waist. Although pinned by both arms, the creature still writhed with considerable force. It threw its weight left then right, fighting not to break loose but to break through. The keys on its hip jangled and bounced as the zombie flailed.

Sarah grasped hold of the keys and yanked hard to dislodge them. The serrated edges of the metal dug into her palms as she pulled, but instead of feeling a jolt of resistance the keys came away easily. Then the cord reached its full extension and snapped taut. Sarah lost her grip and the keys whirled back, drawn by the keychain reel clipped to the guard's belt.

Sarah reached through the bars again, this time grabbing the whole reel. She pulled down at it, but the backing clip held firm, simply tugging at the guard's trousers. Again she tried, this time pushing the reel up and over. The unit slipped up and was almost clear when the zombie twisted, snagging the keys against a belt loop. The whole thing was wrenched from Sarah's grasp and fell clattering to the floor. The zombie's foot clipped the bunch of keys and with a loud jangle they went skittering across the deck. Terrified that they could be knocked out of reach, Sarah plunged her hand down and clutched her fingers over them. Just as she did, the zombie lurched against its restrainers and brought its foot down on Sarah's hand.

For an instant Sarah couldn't work out what had went crunch. Then the pain hit her.

A scream punched its way out of her mouth as her eyes welled up with tears. The zombie shuffled and Sarah snatched her hand back through the bars. She sobbed, cradling her hand to her chest, too scared to look down at where the pain was coming from, too worried by what the damage would be.

"I've got it!" Nathan called as he let go of the zombie's arm. He ducked down and made a grab for the keys.

"Hurry up!" Bates screamed as the zombie tried to pull away.

Bates felt something tear—something soft. He looked down to see the zombie's bicep ripped open by the jagged end of the bone underneath. In the tug of war between them, it was the zombie's flesh that was giving way. The skin was being sawn open from the inside by the frantic heaving.

"I can't hold him!" Bates warned.

Nathan threw himself to the back of the cell, keys held aloft in triumph. "Got 'em!"

"Thank fuck," Bates said as he let go of the half severed arm and stepped out of reach.

The frustrated creature let out a plaintive moan. Its face pressed against the bars, drool dripping off its chin. Its arms outstretched through the bars, the mangled and broken arm swinging limp from the bicep, twitching spasmodically as it dangled.

Bates knelt down. He felt nauseous. Remembering the feeling of the bones grinding together sent kicks of revulsion to his stomach. He swallowed back the taste of bile and turned to Sarah.

"Let me see," he said, softly looking down to where Sarah hid her hand.

Still too scared to look, Sarah took her good hand away, and turning her head she held out her injured hand.

"Okay," Bates said as he looked at her crumpled fingers. "It looks like the index and middle fingers are broken."

He stood up and walked over to the bunk he'd been using before Sarah and Nathan's incarceration. At the foot of the bunk there was a metal cup with the hilt of a spoon protruding from the lip. Bates picked up the spoon and wiped it on the bed covers.

He called over the noise of the whining zombie, "Nathan, pull the covers off that bed and rip me some strips off to use as bandages."

Nathan nodded and started about his task.

Bates sat down next to Sarah again. He had the spoon in both hands and was bending it at the neck. "I'm going to splint those two fingers. It's not going to stop them from hurting but it'll make it a bit more comfortable." He looked over his shoulder at the snarling zombie. "Well, as comfortable as you get given the situation."

Sarah nodded as Nathan passed over a wad of stripped linen.

"This is going to hurt," Bates said as he snapped the head off the spoon.

Nathan held out his hand "Here. Squeeze it as hard as you like."

Sarah clasped her good hand into Nathan's and started taking some deep breaths.

"I'll be as quick as I can," Bates said.

He took firm hold of Sarah's broken fingers and pulled.

Sarah screamed. She screamed so hard even the zombie was stunned. Blackness rushed in around her vision. Her head giddy and light, it rolled onto her chest and she passed out.

✱ ✱ ✱ ✱ ✱

When she woke up, the first thing she heard was the zombie's wheezy moan.

"Don't get up."

It was Nathan's voice she heard. Sarah started to regain her bearings. She was still in the cell, but now she was laying on one of the cots, coarse woollen blanket on top of her.

"You passed out," Nathan said.

Sarah raised her head to look at her bandaged hand. Her fingertips and the ragged end of a broken spoon poked out from the dressing.

"Not the best looking bandage I know, but it will do," Bates said. "How are you feeling?"

"Okay I guess. How long was I out?"

"About half an hour."

"So what's the plan?"

"Get the fuck out off here!" Nathan offered.

Sarah slowly sat up in bed, careful not to place any weight on her injured hand. "I had expected a little more planning than that, Nathan."

"Get the fuck out of here and off this ship!" Nathan replied unhelpfully.

"We don't know if the whole ship's been overrun," Bates said. "But I think we should assume the worst for now. If I'm wrong then life's easy, but its been quiet except for moaning, so my guess is we've been overrun."

Sarah nodded. "Agreed. We need to get out of here and get to Jennifer."

"Well," Nathan said, pointing at the zombified guard, "our first problem is him."

"Same as with the key," Bates said. "Two of us hold him by the arms through the bars. The other person opens the cell door and dispatches him."

"With what?" Sarah asked.

"The gun?" Nathan said, pointing at where the discarded weapon lay.

"Gun's empty," Bates reminded them. "You saw that when he tried to off himself."

"Is there any more ammo?" Sarah asked.

"It's a possibility, but not a certainty," Bates replied. "He was just guarding us, so no need for more than one clip... *normally.*"

Sarah swung her legs round to sit on the edge of the bed. "If there is any ammo, where is it likely to be?"

"In a pocket or in the desk drawer," Bates said. "If it's in the drawer, it might be locked." He started to pace the cell. He ran a hand through his hair before adding, "If there is a reload, it'll be quicker for me to do it."

Sarah nodded. "Okay."

"Jeez, volunteered again," Bates said, trying to lighten the mood. "I should just keep my big mouth shut."

Sarah took his attempt at humour as a disguise against nervousness. She couldn't blame him; a bite or even a scratch could be enough to kill him and turn him into one of them. It was a prospect none of them relished.

Bates spun the keys around on their chain, familiarising himself with what was there: A key for the cell, a key for the main door and a key for the desk. The desk key was a small thin silver thing with a reference number stamped on the head. The other two keys were more sturdy, heavier and longer, with a block of teeth at the end. There was no way of telling which were for what lock. He would just have to try both and that could mean a delay in getting the ammo. He knew the longer he took the more chance there was that the zombie would get loose and attack him. He'd never fought a zombie barehanded before and it wasn't something he was keen to try.

Nathan placed his hand flat on Sarah's leg. "Are you up to this?" Sarah nodded.

"If you can't keep a grip on him you holler and let me know," Bates said, just as concerned about Nathan's abilities as Sarah's.

"Sure thing, Bates," Sarah said as she stood up from the bed.

Bates held the two likely keys in front of him. "Okay... go!"

Sarah and Nathan raced forward, Nathan grabbed hold of the creature's left arm, leaving Sarah to take its partially severed right.

Bates knelt down in front of the lock and reached round, key in hand, to feel for the entrance of the lock. Neing a prison cell, the door only opened from the outside. The tip of the key danced around where Bates thought the opening should be. He swirled the key round, desperately trying to locate the opening. All the while Bates could hear the slap, and grunts and undead groans as his comrades struggled to control the monster mere inches away. Finally the key snagged. He gently eased it over and found the entrance. He pushed the key home, but the angle was too steep. It jammed against the cylinder inside. He pulled it out slightly and tried again at a shallower angle. This time the key found the seating. He twisted it and met with resistance. Again he tried a little harder but still nothing.

"Shit!" Bates hissed as he pulled the key from the lock. He quickly selected the next one and found the keyhole. Something felt different. There was no play with the second key. It wouldn't even turn. "Shit, shit, shit!" He realised the first key had been the correct one. He slipped it back into the lock and felt it connect. He turned it and again it stuck. He applied more strength to the turn and there was a deep clunk from within the lock as the key moved. Twisting it further and harder, Bates worried that with every extra ounce of force the shaft would snap, sealing them in.

The bolt slipped out of the lock and the door swung open.

Pulling the key from the lock, Bates sprinted over to where the gun lay discarded, and in all the excitement and adrenaline his boots lost traction on the blood-soaked deck. He threw his arms out to try to keep his balance as he went skidding across the floor, but it was too late. With his centre of gravity too far back for him to right, Bates threw his hands down to catch himself. His palms slapped the deck, spraying a fountain of half congealed blood into the air. His backside jolted to an abrupt stop in the pool of spilt blood. He sat in shock, feeling the droplets of blood splatter against his face. Instinctively he drew the back of his sleeve across his lips in an attempt to remove any of the infected blood. Placing his palm to steady himself, in one smooth action he swooped up the gun, turned, and dashed to the desk where he hoped to find ammunition.

Every time the arm Sarah clutched moved, she could feel the muscles tear a little further. With every jolt the limb came a little freer. But Sarah dare not try for a grip further up. If she tried to hold the zombie at the shoulder her hands would be through the bars and perilously close to being bitten. The zombie jerked to the side, catching Sarah off guard. She stumbled, trying to keep hold of the ragged limb without ripping it further. The zombie pulled back, trying to get closer to Bates and Sarah tripped forward. Instinctively she threw her right hand out to stop herself, forgetting about the bandaged fingers. Her hand slapped against a metal bar. Pain stung at her hand then bolted up her arm, obliterating all of her other senses. She screamed, falling back into the cell. Her left hand still held the zombie by the wrist. As she fell backwards she felt the slightest tug from her left side before the last tendons snapped, severing the zombie's arm.

The sudden yank of the arm ripping free sent the zombie lurching backwards. Abruptly the direction of force changed, catching Nathan off guard. The arm Nathan held onto broke free of his grip, sliding back beyond the bars. As the zombie's hand drew back its nails scraped along Nathan's forearm, gouging out ragged furrows. Wincing, Nathan yanked his arm back. As he looked at the underside of his forearm, blood started to well up through the broken skin. He stared, frozen by the sight. The zombie's hand had been soaked in blood—the blood the guard had tried to stem from the open wound on his neck—the blood which had poured out of his artery after he had been bitten open by a ghoul. The blood that almost certainly carried the contagion.

Nathan looked up to see the zombie turn and shuffle off after Bates. He cried, "Look out!"

Sarah threw the twitching limb into the far corner of the cell and sprung to her feet to see the zombie stagger towards Bates. A loud crashing sound filled the cell.

Sarah didn't take any time trying to figure out what had caused the noise. Instead she sprinted out of the cell and up behind the zombie.

As she reached the shambling corpse, it stopped.

Sarah froze. She hadn't planned how to help Bates; only that she should. Slowly the zombie turned and she had no idea how to fend it off.

As the creature spun round it corkscrewed its way to the floor.

"Thank fuck!" Sarah heard herself say as the zombie fell to the deck, a broken chair leg embedded in its eye socket.

She looked past the corpse to Bates. The desk drawer behind him was wide open, but empty, and across the floor lay the splintered remains of the guard's chair.

Bates smiled. "Adapt, improvise and overcome."

Oblivious to what was going on outside the cell, Nathan was transfixed by the blood on his arm. Some of it was his, some if it was the zombie's. He heard himself bemoaning the fact that his leather wrist strap was on his right arm rather than his left. If only it had been the other side, the thick leather band would have protected him. It would have saved his life. *There's still a chance*, Nathan told himself. It was a scratch, not a bite. With a bite you were a goner for sure because the infected saliva always got into the wound. With the saliva round the wound some was bound to get in. But with the scratch, Nathan told himself, it could be different. The only fluid was from the guard's blood, but that had pumped out before he had turned. The chances were there was very little contact with the contagion. Nathan assured himself that because it was a scratch and not a bite it hadn't severed any veins. The blood on his arm had welled up through the skin and surely that would flush any contagion out.

Bates bent down and started checking the guard's pockets. "Bingo!" He held aloft a full clip of ammunition.

Nathan stepped out of the cell. "Okay, so what's the plan?"

"Get some weapons, get Jennifer, and get into a life raft," Sarah offered.

"No good," Bates said as he loaded the ammunition into the gun.

"Sure it's good," Nathan protested. "This storm can't last much longer and at least we'll be safe from those things."

"The weather and the W.D.s are the least of our worries." Bates swung his arm up to check his watch. "We'd all be dead in five hours."

Sarah's voice was flat. "What do you mean, Bates?"

"This is a research vessel. Dr. Frankenstein and Dr. Robertson were working on the virus to find some way to beat it. There were concerns about the safety of the research."

Nathan jumped in, throwing his words out with nervous quickness, "So they stuck you on a boat so if this happened, it could be contained. We get it."

"No, you don't get it," Bates said. "They weren't overly concerned about an outbreak on ship. Hell, the top brass figured a fuckup was inevitable."

In her most measured tone, Sarah asked, "So what's the catch?"

"An adrift ship infested with W.D.s wasn't a concern. The *nature* of the infection was."

"I'm not following you," Nathan said. "What do you mean, *nature of the infection?*"

"Top brass were worried that Frankenstein's tinkering would make the virus more deadly."

Nathan threw up his hands as if he were about to start pulling out his own hair, before slapping them down by his side. "How exactly could it get more deadly than fatal?!"

Bates corrected himself. "Well, not more deadly—more dangerous."

"That's the fucking same thing," Nathan squabbled. "You don't get worse than undead."

"You mean more *contagious*, don't you?" Sarah clarified.

"Again with the *how*." Even in the red light it was obvious that Nathan was becoming flushed. "One bite and you're a goner."

"What if they didn't need to bite you?" Sarah looked over at Bates. "They're worried it'll mutate. They're worried it'll go *airborne*."

"That's why they have a safety protocol in place," Bates replied. "We need to radio our status every eight hours. If we miss one, then it's kaboom!"

"It obviously hasn't gone airborne or we'd be contaminated by now," Sarah said.

Nathan was hopping around like a child bursting for the toilet. "Okay, so there's a self destruct. We disarm it. You know, cut the red wire or the blue wire or whatever."

Bates shook his head. "Wouldn't work 'cause we're not in charge of the explosion."

"Okay, so what's there to stop us taking a life raft and abandoning ship?"

"You couldn't paddle fast enough," Bates said. "If we don't make that radio call in time, there's a Russian sub with orders to nuke us."

Nathan pawed at his chin where his stubbly beard used to be. "Shit..."

"We're no closer to a plan," Sarah interrupted.

"Armoury is on this level but at the other end of the ship," Bates said. "The radio room is halfway between the two, but a level up."

"Jennifer is two decks above us," Sarah added.

"Is she a smart girl?"

"Yeah, but I don't want to leave her alone." Sarah's thoughts went to the small girl locked in her cabin alone. "She must be terrified."

Bates read the concern on Sarah's face. "Will she have the sense to keep the door locked and to stay quiet?"

"Yeah, I think so," Sarah said. "Why? What have you got in mind?"

Bates turned to face the door out of the brig as if he were trying to peer through it with x-ray vision. "Get to the armoury first. We can't rescue anyone until we can protect them and ourselves. Agreed?"

"I guess," Nathan said with a shrug.

"Once we have Jennifer, we radio the sub. We'll be able to call from the bridge and bypass the radio room altogether." Bates programmed in a countdown on his watch. "We should have just over four hours to check in."

Sarah walked up to the bullet holes in the wall and peered through to the darkness in the corridor beyond. "What can we expect out there?"

"Your guess is as good as mine," Bates said.

"Worst case scenario?" Nathan asked, rubbing his injured arm.

Bates puffed out a shot of breath. "Let's say the whole crew have got themselves killed then decide to get up and go for a walk. We'll have around forty W.D.'s, give or take. With a little luck, some will be trapped in cabins too dumb to get out. There may be some so badly mauled they can't resurrect."

"That's not bad." Nathan pointed to the weapon Bates held. "I mean, we've got a gun. You've got, what, ten shots?"

"Fifteen," Bates corrected.

"Christ, that's enough to put half of them down."

Bates held the gun in front of him, twisting it, slowly examining it. "Problem is, though, if we meet any former members of the crew it's going to be in close quarters. We won't get a clean shot. So don't let the gun give you a false sense of security."

"But there's more than enough guns and ammo in the armoury, right?"

Bates smiled. "Sure, but I'm worried about getting jumped. If we end up going hand-to-hand, chances are you're going to get bit."

Sarah decided to look for the positive. "What's the best case scenario?"

"Hopefully we're not the only ones left alive," Bates answered. "Hopefully a few of the marines have started to clean up. If that's the case, best watch out they don't get too trigger happy and mistake us for W.D.'s."

"The last thing I want is a bullet in the brain," Nathan said.

Infection

"I CAN'T SEE A THING," Nathan whispered, his complaint competing against a dissonance of unsettling sounds.

The emergency lighting in this part of the corridor was sporadic. What lights that did work spluttered and coughed on and off, casting disturbing shadows.

"Close your eyes for a few seconds," Bates said. "It'll help you adjust to the low light."

Sarah placed her good hand gently onto Nathan's shoulder so as not to frighten him. "And try and squint."

Nathan turned in the blackness at the sound of his friend's voice. "You're shitting me, right?"

Sarah spoke softly into Nathan's ear, "No, the cones in your eyes that see colour are at the centre, but they don't work well in darkness. It's the rods at the edge that see in black and white that give you your best night vision."

"Thanks for the science lesson," Bates grumbled. "Now if you've quite finished, can we go with stealth mode here?"

Unfamiliar sounds burst out from the darkness. Metallic creaks from the vessels hull. Resonating clangs and dull clunks carried through the ship's seams. Far off crashing and splintering.

Catching the start of an unusual sound, Sarah's mind half twisted them into screams or moans until she heard enough to identify the sources.

Sometimes the cries were human. The desperation in their tone still carried some hope for Sarah. There were people alive, somewhere onboard.

But even this consolation couldn't allay Sarah's fears for long. Often she couldn't tell the difference between a person or the ship groaning, but the moans. The moaning seemed to travel unattenuated through the ship. That breathy sound forced out across stiff vocal cords. Those whispery vowels that slipped out from between dead lips. The call of the undead that Sarah could always make out.

She listened like she were waiting for the rising thunder clap after a lightning strike. She listened out for each moan, marking it off as being closer or further away than the last one. But in the enveloping darkness everything felt louder and closer. She had no way of judging how accurate her guesses were.

Bates suddenly froze. His gun raised, he cocked his head, looking up the corridor.

Sarah squinted through the shadows, and there up ahead was a dark mass swaying from side to side.

Bates let his finger slip from the trigger guard onto the trigger. A trickle of sweat formed on his upper lip but he suppressed the urge to wipe it away. Pushing the crook of his index finger against the trigger, he eased it back gently. The trigger pivoted backwards until a slight tug of resistance told Bates he'd found the biting point. He could squeeze a shot off from here aimed at head height. He couldn't make out a head, just the rhythmic swaying of a shape in the darkness. If he shot and missed, the creature would turn and come for him, in which case he would shoot it in the head when it got closer. But that would mean wasting a shot. Bates knew he had to conserve his precious ammunition if there were to be any chance of reaching the armoury.

Keeping the gun levelled, he took his supporting hand away from under the butt of the pistol and wiped the annoying sweat from his lip. He smeared his damp fingers across the breast of his shirt, drying them, before returning his hand to the gun.

He edged forward, determined not to fire until he could see his target.

As he drew closer he could hear a strange high pitch groan. A squealing like rough hinges in sync with the rhythm of the movement.

Pushing closer, the dark shape seemed to be surprisingly straight-edged.

Bates let out a sigh of relief and turned to his companions.

"It's just a door," he said in a light tone.

The voice in the darkness registered in a zombie's ears. It shambled out from behind the swinging door and into the corridor.

Still smiling, Bates turned to resume his advance. As he brought his gun up to renew his stance, Professor Cutler lurched out from behind the swinging door and bit into Bates' forearm.

Bates screamed and pulled back, tearing his flesh from the zombie's mouth. The zombie fell into the corridor, snatching at Bates as it did.

"Fuck!" Bates shrieked and he fired wild shots at the cadaver.

In the dark of the corridor the muzzle flashes sent out pulses of light like a strobe in a night club, the snapshot glimpses burning bright green amorphous after images into their eyes.

The deafening bark of the gunshots added to the disorientation. The noise bounded off the walls of the corridor and smacked into Sarah's ears. Each violent stab of sound made Sarah wince, squeezing her eyes shut as if they could form a barrier against the sound. She tensed against the cacophony pounding her eardrums, but shrieks of migraine-like pain still shot through her head.

The gun fire stopped, leaving an aftermath of rising tinnitus. Opening her eyes and peering out through her blurred vision, Sarah could make out more figures shambling towards her and her companions.

"Quick in here!" she shouted over the ringing in her ears.

Grabbing Bates by the shoulders, she pulled with all her strength, hauling him into the room the zombie had emerged from. Bates didn't resist, but paralysed with shock he didn't aid Sarah either.

As she frog-marched Bates into the room, Sarah felt Nathan jostle into her as he misjudged his footing in the dark.

"Get the door!" she shouted.

Nathan pushed into the room, and pivoting, he took the door handle, heaving the door closed with one big slam. One hand still on the handle holding the door shut, he ran his free hand along the jamb. He fumbled around the frame and the handle, searching for a key or a latch or any other means to lock the door.

After a frantic doublecheck he called out to Sarah, "There's no key!"

"Find something to the wedge the handle with!"

"Shit, I've been bit." Bates' voice was weak and distant. "I been fuckin' bit."

"I can't see a thing in here!" Nathan screeched as he bashed around in the darkness.

Sarah looked around, not knowing what she was searching for. Then her eyes came to a tiny green light. Above it was a dusky yellow light. She felt her way through the blackness up to the source of the green glow. Taking a step forward, she bumped into something at her waist. The object gave way from the collision with the clear squeak of wheels on tile. *A trolley or something*, Sarah thought as she put her hands out to feel her way around. Her hands came across cold metal struts. Beyond that, hard plastic, like the type school chairs always seemed to be made of. Her fingers met with the edge of a rough linen sheet with a thin plastic tube running across it. There was a weak judder as if something on the gurney had shifted its weight.

Sarah held her breath.

Moving her hand further along to where she hoped to find an end to the obstruction, she brushed her fingers against a strap of thick leather. She placed her hand on something cold like a lump of meat but as she did it twitched.

Throwing her hands in the air, Sarah screamed.

"What is it?" Nathan asked.

The trolley rattled and shook.

"I think it's the specimen Doctor Robertson mentioned," Sarah said, her voice full of revulsion.

"Where?!"

"I think it's tied down..." Sarah worked up the courage to check. "Yes, it's strapped down on a trolley or something. I'm going to see if I can get some light."

Careful to keep out of the juddering zombie's reach, Sarah edged round the gurney to where she could see the green and yellow glow.

The yellow light was a LED on the face of a computer. She groped around near the green light and found a round button. As she pressed it in, there was a hard thunk and a jagged rip of light dashed across the screen. The glassy cathode ray tube gasped out a metallic *plink* and the screen erupted into life. The screen lit up the room with its television-like luminescence.

"There must be a UPS in here," Nathan said as he hunted for something to use as a barricade.

There was a loud thump against the door, followed by another.

Both Sarah and Nathan froze, waiting—hoping—for a human voice to call out.

Another thump and then a moan.

"Why do they moan like that?!" Nathan cursed, not expecting an answer.

"Just hurry up blocking that door, Nathan!" Sarah yelled, the growing pounding at the door giving urgency to her demand.

She whipped round and started scanning the room for something—anything—useful.

Then, by the light of the computer, she saw what she needed. She reached up to a shelf and pulled down a large silver flask. She placed the container on the desk next to a Bunsen burner.

"Where are the matches?" she muttered to herself as she opened the desk drawer to rummage inside.

There came a loud crashing noise from the door. The room was filled by the sound of breaking glass and crumpling metal.

Sarah screamed with fright and jumped back.

Standing to the side of the door, Sarah could make out Nathan's form. Across the doorway there now lay a large refrigerator, its doors fallen open, its shelves and contents spewed across the deck.

"Nathan!" Sarah screamed.

"What?! You wanted the fucking door blocked!"

Sarah couldn't reply. She had wanted to chastise him for giving her a shock but he'd been right. She'd barked at him to get it blocked she could hardly complain when he had done what he was told.

Returning to the flask, Sarah unscrewed the lid slightly, just enough to make it easy to open but not enough for the contents to spill out.

"I've been bit! I've fuckin' got bit," Bates repeated, looking at the blood trickling from the wound. He cocked his weapon, checking there was a round in the chamber, and pushed the barrel of the gun into the soft flesh underneath his jaw.

"Bates!" Sarah snapped. "Give me the gun."

He looked at her with moist eyes. In a far off voice he said, "I've been bit."

"Give me your gun," Sarah said in a harsher tone. When Bates didn't comply, she barked, "That's an order, soldier!"

Reluctantly Bates lowered his weapon. "*I've been bit...*"

"I'm sorry, Bates," Sarah said.

She grabbed his hand and whipped off the lid to the flask.

"What for?" Bates asked.

"This," Sarah said as she plunged his arm into the container.

Plumes of mist rolled over the top of the flask and Bates screamed. He shuddered and tried to pull his arm free, but Sarah held it down with all her force.

The noise Bates made hardly sounded human. It was more high pitched and primordial like a jungle creature caught in a trap.

"What the fuck?!" Nathan cried.

"Help me hold him!" Sarah shouted back, struggling to keep the arm submerged.

Nathan rushed up and clamped his arms around Bates.

The liquid nitrogen in the flask bubbled like boiling water. Plumes of icy mist bellowed over the rim of the flask and around Bates' arm.

Between the piercing screams and trying to subdue his thrashing, Sarah watched as the skin turned white. A thick frost was climbing up the limb. It froze every hair it touched, leaving a crystalline sheen of ice over the skin and crept onwards accompanied by swirls of fog.

"Okay!" Sarah shouted. "That's enough!"

She let go of the arm and pulled the flask out of the way.

Now the pounding at the door had become more frenzied, spurred on by the wailing on the other side.

His eyes wide open from the shock, Bates was transfixed by his ice-covered limb. His fist, his wrist, and a good part of his forearm including the bite were frozen solid.

Sarah picked the gun up by the barrel, and using it like a hammer, she smashed it down onto the frozen arm.

The arm shattered, sending chunks of pink ice skittering across the table. Some of the lumps collided, splintering still further with the impact.

Nathan let go and stepped back. He let out a dry cough and felt his whole gut cramp up. The force bent him double and he retched up what little he had left in his stomach.

Bates' eyelids flickered as his eyes rolled back. His muscles went limp and he crashed to the floor.

"We need to cauterise the wound," Sarah said, searching for a box of matches with which to light the Bunsen burner. Frantically she started pulling out drawers until finally she found a lighter wand.

"Try to find a first aid kit," Sarah said to Nathan as she lit the burner.

An eerie yellow light flickered across the lab. Light ebbed and flowed with the flickering of the flame, sending shadows dancing across the opposite wall.

Sarah stretched the burner's rubber hose as far as it would go. "Help me get Bates over here."

Unceremoniously Nathan grabbed the unconscious soldier under his armpits and hoisted him up.

Sarah turned the baffle at the base of the Bunsen burner, changing the flame from a licking yellow to a roaring blue head. Bates moaned as Sarah waved the flame over the stump. The flesh and blood crackled as it scorched and Sarah feared Bates would wake up and start screaming again. A foul odour—a mixture of burnt hair and roast pork—wafted up from the wound.

"First aid kit?" Sarah asked.

"Goddammit, one thing at a time!" Nathan snapped. He laid Bates back on the deck and returned to his search.

"Try near the door," Sarah offered.

Nathan's footsteps crunched over to the door, pulverising still further the discarded contents of the fridge.

The light in the room changed as behind him Sarah flipped the Bunsen burner back to its yellow flame. With the extra light, Nathan's eyes caught the reflection of the saffron flame on the shoulder of a fire extinguisher secured to the wall. Above it there hung a green plastic box with a white cross in its centre. The first aid box slipped out of its bracket easily and Nathan turned back to Sarah.

As he did the light from the flame caught his arm. The scratch he'd sustained in the cell looked inflamed. Even in the warm hue of the burner, his skin bordering the welts looked pale, not red as he would have expected. A dry cough found the back of his throat and the seasickness still clawed at his stomach.

"Here," he said as he passed Sarah the first aid kit.

He took off his wristband and swapped it over. The tattered leather strap covered most of the inflammation and would serve to camouflage the wound from Sarah.

Sarah turned to the Bunsen burner, and using its bright yellow light, fished out a wound dressing from the green box.

"That door isn't going to keep them out," Nathan said as the banging behind him solidified into a constant droning.

Even through the residual whining in her ears from the earlier gun play, the hammering at the door was still louder than Sarah's tinnitus.

Trying to ignore the noise, Sarah applied the dressings, but she couldn't stop herself from glancing up every few moments. It was impossible to tell if the door was actually shaking or whether the flickering shadows just gave that impression. Either way, there were zombies on the other side of that door and it would only be a matter of time before they forced their way in.

"We still have to get to the armoury and then get Jennifer," Sarah said, looking back at Nathan.

"Yeah, and radio that sub and ask them nicely not to nuke us!" Nathan added. "Oh, and not get eaten in the process."

Sarah picked up the gun she had taken from Bates and examined it. It was heavy. More so than she had expected. Looking at it closely, she realized that it was also smaller than she would have thought a gun should be.

She turned her attention to the mechanisms of the gun proper, desperately needing to know how many shots were left.

There were three latches on the gun, and if there were annotations on the casing Sarah couldn't tell in the dim light. The top catch was directly in front of the hammer and she guessed it must be the safety catch. She drew her fingers down the gun onto the middle latch. It was long and slender and seated directly above the trigger. She tried to remember if she'd seen any of the soldiers load their pistols. She knew that in the past day she must have seen dozens of guns being loaded, but she couldn't conjure up any of them. She ran her fingers along the clasp for a moment, and not knowing why decided it wasn't the catch for the magazine. Where the trigger guard met with the handle of the gun there was a small button. She nudged it forward and the clip glided out.

Caught off guard by the speed of the clip, Sarah fumbled to stop it hitting the floor. As she did she skiffed a broken finger across the butt of the gun.

"Shit!" she cursed through pursed lips.

The magazine tumbled to the deck and clattered to a stop.

"Do you know what you're doing there?" Nathan asked.

"Sure," Sarah lied, trying to sound confident. "Just banged my finger, that's all." She reached down and grabbed the clip even before she'd finished speaking to Nathan.

The magazine was slender and long. From the movies she'd been dragged to by tiresome boyfriends, she had the impression that all ammo clips were square chunky things. A copper bodied bullet with a dull gunmetal grey head sat at the top of the magazine. The ammunition was tiny, like it should belong in a toy, not a real firearm. Sarah dispelled that thought; having already witnessed the power of these unimposing shells, she knew how deadly they were. She had hoped that when she removed the clip it would be obvious to her how many shots were left, but it wasn't. There were a series of small holes up the face of the magazine but she couldn't angle enough light to see if there were any bullets inside. She surmised that there would be some kind of spring arrangement that pushed the bullets up into the breach of the gun and that theoretically she would be able to unload and reload the clip. But she had paid enough attention during those bad dates to know that guns jammed and she didn't know enough about guns to trust herself to reload the clip correctly.

"Are you *sure* you know how to use that thing?" Nathan asked again.

"Yeah, I had every season of *Twenty-Four* on DVD." Sarah slapped the clip back up into position with a satisfying click and tried to look nonchalant holding the gun.

Nathan sat himself down next to the Bunsen burner. "So we're just going to walk out there?"

"We have to," Sarah said.

They both found their gaze had settled on the Bunsen burner's flame. The primordial comfort of the fire wasn't enough to dispel their fear. The door still shook as the groaning zombies tried to force their way in.

Sarah took a deep breath, signifying the end of the respite.

She stood up and waved the gun at the door. "You open the door and stand back. I'll shoot them as they come in."

"How may shots you got left?" Nathan asked.

Sarah looked at the gun. "Enough... I hope."

Nathan presented the palms of his hands to the flame from the Bunsen burner to warm them up.

"You cold?" Sarah asked.

"Freezing. What about you?"

"I'm fine." Sarah paused for a second. "But then I haven't just heaved my guts up. Are you up to this?"

Nathan shrugged. "I'm going to have to be."

"Here, take my shirt," Sarah offered.

"Are you sure?" Nathan half-heartedly protested. "I mean, won't you get cold?"

Sarah unbuttoned the garment, revealing a tight white vest underneath. "I'll be fine. It's too big for me anyway," she said, handing it over.

"Thanks," Nathan said as he put it on, carefully rolling the sleeves down to further hide his injury.

"Okay, let's do this. You get the door and I'll shoot them," Sarah said as she took up position a few feet from the door.

"Will you be okay to shoot that?" Nathan asked, looking at Sarah's bandaged fingers.

"I'll just fire left handed. How much more difficult can it be?"

"Fuck." Nathan shook his head as he crunched his way over to the broken fridge. He bent down squat and with his hands hooked around the top of the fridge he hauled it out of the doorway.

The noise of the fridge scraping along the deck excited the zombies even further and they increased the ferocity of their pounding.

Nathan stepped to the side of the door and nodded to Sarah.

"Go!" Sarah ordered and Nathan tipped the door handle.

The door flew open, spilling a torrent of cadavers into the room. The first few, unbalanced by the push behind them and sudden opening of the door, toppled to the deck. Before they could make to get up the creatures behind had surged forward, trampling their compatriots.

Sarah aimed the gun at the lead zombie and pulled the trigger. The gun bucked wildly in her hands, throwing her aim up and off.

The explosion from the shot made her blink, shutting her eyes instinctively and the thunderous bark of the gun meant that she recoiled as much as the weapon. When she opened her eyes the uninjured zombie was still advancing on her. She fired again, blinking her eyes shut at the sound and the flash of the shot. When she looked at the zombie she'd been aiming at, it was struggling to its feet, a smouldering hole in its shoulder.

She aimed and fired again. This time the bullet found its mark and the zombie crumpled to the ground. The next zombie in line stumbled forward, showing no regard for the corpse it trampled over. Sarah aimed the gun again, this time with a stiffer grip, and fired.

The shot missed, but this time she hadn't flinched. Levelling the gun at the zombie's head she fired again.

A huge chunk of scalp flew out from the back of the zombie's skull and it collapsed to the floor.

Three more zombies were still bearing down on her. One shambled ahead, its arm outstretched pawing at the air. The other two were staggering to their feet, having been knocked over as the door opened.

Sarah took a couple of steps back to keep her distance from the approaching corpse. She took aim and this time her shot hit home.

The two remaining zombies behind simply pushed passed their fallen brethren and continued to advance.

Sarah tried to step back but her retreat was over. She had reached the hull. Cornered against the wall, she fired at the closest one. The shot burst its skull open, sending it tumbling to the deck.

The last creature, undeterred, reached out its arms to grab her.

The ghoul was so close that the barrel of the gun touched its forehead. Sarah pulled the trigger and heard an empty click.

Her heart sank and she became suddenly aware of the pounding in her ears and her shortness of breath.

The zombie grabbed Sarah by the hair and started to pull her in.

There was a loud crack.

"Ow!" Nathan screamed.

The zombie collapsed to the floor and behind it stood Nathan, nursing his right hand.

"What happened?" Sarah asked, trying to catch her breath.

"I smacked it one with the fire extinguisher and the fucking thing's taken a chunk of skin off my knuckles."

Sarah stepped forward. "Let's see."

Nathan held out his hand. There was a tiny gash across the joint of his first two fingers. "It was the squeezy bit." He could see Sarah hadn't understood what he was talking about. "The trigger thing... I was holding it." He shook his head. "Ah, never mind."

"Get a dressing from the first aid kit. You'll be fine," Sarah said as she opened the cupboard beside her. "Oh, and thanks."

"Anytime," Nathan said, rooting around the first aid box. He glanced over at Bates. "What are we going to do about him?"

Sarah opened up a second cupboard. "Take him with us."

Nathan looked anxiously at the open door. "Not just lock him in here?"

Sarah was pulling out bottles and squinting to read the labels in the dim light. "I don't want to double back if we can avoid it. And we'll need him to radio the Russians and stop them from nuking us."

"Okay, but we can't carry him... What are you doing anyway?"

"This." Sarah opened up a small bottle and knelt down next to Bates.

"Jeez, what the hell is that?" Nathan asked, screwing up his face. "It smells like rat piss."

Sarah was wafting the bottle under Bates' nose. "Ammonia. It's what smelling salts used to be made of."

Bates took in a gasp of air followed by a long splutter of coughs. His eyelids fluttered open.

Sarah shook him by the shoulders. "Bates? Bates?"

All Bates could manage was a groggy, "Uh..."

"You've been bit," Sarah reminded him. "But we've stopped the infection from spreading. We need your help. You're going to have to walk."

Bates held out his injured arm in front of him. There was a fresh white bandage a few inches below his elbow where his arm now terminated.

"My hand! My fucking hand! Fuck it hurts!"

"I had to stop the infection from spreading," Sarah said as justification.

Nathan looked down at his own arm. The whole thing ached and felt numb. He tried to suppress his dry cough and shivered from the effort. His throat was scratchy and the headache from being seasick was getting stronger. He had hoped the oppressive cold was from the storm outside, but seeing Sarah comfortable in a vest made him realise just how sick he had become.

"Now on your feet soldier!" Sarah barked.

"Yes, ma'am," Bates replied back out of instinct.

Sarah extended her arm and helped Bates to his feet. "I couldn't find any morphine. Do you know where it will be?"

"There'll be some in the infirmary, but that's backtracking," Bates said. "I'll be fine."

"You need to lead us to the armoury," Nathan said. "Are you up for it?"

"Sure," Bates replied with a pained gasp.

"This is yours," Sarah said, passing Bates the gun. She added, "It's empty."

Bates reached out with his severed arm. He looked down at the empty space where his hand should have been, and snorted.

"Don't matter," he sniggered. "I can't fire it anyways."

"Use your left hand, you idiot!" Nathan snapped. "Now can we get out of here?! That door's wide open and those shots will draw every zombie on board!"

"Okay, let's go," Bates said, and stepped out of the lab.

Sarah and Nathan followed.

∗ ∗ ∗ ∗ ∗

As the three figures moved down the corridor, a zombie shuffled after them. Something caught its eye—a flickering movement from the room beside it.

Professor Cutler shuffled into the room. There were a number of bodies lying on the ground which made getting into the room difficult for the stiff-legged zombie. It ambled over to the source of the movement. The creature which once spoke four languages fluently let out an unintelligible grunt. The noise was made all the more horrific as it gurgled out past the mashed-up flesh and bone that used to be his lower jaw. Part of the professor's ear had also been obliterated from the shots Bates had fired at him. Drawn deeper into the room, he bent down to see the dancing yellow shape more closely.

The light from the Bunsen illuminated what was left of Professor Cutler's ashen face. The only colour was his brown hair and the crimson ooze around the edges of his ragged flesh. He seemed ignorant to the fact a large portion of his face had been blasted away by a gunshot. All that captured his attention was the dancing light in front of him. He reached out a hand to grasp the movement but he couldn't clutch hold of it. Instead it ran up the sleeve of his crumpled and gore splattered white shirt. This astounded the professor, who stood and watched as the yellow flame engulfed him.

Swatches of the burning shirt sloughed off and floated to the floor. Flame dripped onto the gurney where the tethered zombie lay concealed under a sheet. The covers ignited. Flames gusted up, touching the ceiling and dripped down, wafting to the floor. In turn, these offspring ignited the clothing of the corpses on the deck and within moments the whole lab was burning.

Strapped to its gurney, the specimen zombie could do nothing but watch the flames engulf him for as long as his eyes still worked.

Professor Cutler shambled out of the lab, his body a flaming torch. The movement and light from the flame had caught his interest for a moment, but his primordial drive compelled him to search out victims to infect, regardless of his physical state.

✳ ✳ ✳ ✳ ✳

"It's not far now," Bates said. "Just a few more feet."

"Fuck!" Nathan swore as he stumbled. He tried to hold his balance by pushing his foot out, but it slipped on a wet patch. Nathan threw his arms out and landed on something cold and soft. A tirade of mono-phrase profanities spilt from his mouth as he jerked back up to his feet.

Sarah bent down to see what had caused such panic in her friend.

"What is it?" Bates asked.

"Dead bodies." Sarah looked up at Bates. "Or should I say dead W.D.'s." She turned her focus to Nathan. "You okay?"

Nathan blew out a puff of breath. "I'm covered in shit."

"Are you okay though?" Bates repeated Sarah's question.

"Yeah, sure, I suppose." Nathan replied, punctuating his answer with a dry cough.

"You sure?" Sarah asked softly. "You don't sound too good."

Nathan snorted and wiped his nose. "Yeah, I told you I'm fine. It's just this seasickness."

Sarah stood up and went to place her hand in Nathan's, but in the darkness she misjudged his location and instead touched his

arm.

Nathan winced and jolted away. "I'm fine!"

"Well, it's kind of good news," Bates said.

"What do you mean?" Sarah asked, shrugging off Nathan's reaction.

"These W.D.'s have been dispatched..." Bates paused to let the significance sink in. "If we didn't waste them, that bodes well."

"You mean there are others still alive?"

"Look, it doesn't mean they're still alive, but at the very least there are—what—three, four less to deal with?"

"Are you always so pragmatic?" Sarah asked.

"It's what's kept me in one..." Bates stopped. "It's what keeps me alive."

Sensing the change in mood, Sarah pushed past. "Where's this armoury?"

"This door down here," Bates said, pointing the way. "You'll need both hands to open it."

"Won't it be locked?"

Bates drew level with her at the door. "Nah, there's a locker room inside and an anti-room like the brig."

Sarah swung the door open. She had reacted even before she had consciously registered why. Her instinct had thrust her into a tight ball the moment the gun fired. A familiar ringing peeled through her head but she could make out shouts over the noise.

"Ustanovaka! Hold your fire, French, they're uninfected!" Angel bellowed. "Don't stand about get in, get in!"

The thick, east European accent stressed the vowels, stretching them, while her brusque consonants brought a harsh quality to the end of her words. All the same it was a voice Sarah was pleased to hear.

Inside the brightly lit room stood Angel and the two marines who had harangued them at the landing pad. Angel's previously white plaster cast was now adorned with drawings and scribbles, most of which were friendly jibes at her misfortune.

Sarah looked around the armoury. It was a room only a few metres square. Against one wall was a cage like the one in the brig, but instead of holding captives there were racks of guns and ammunition.

"Thought my arm was bad," Angel commented as Bates stumbled into the room.

"Yeah, I lost it," Bates said mournfully.

Angel ignored his tone and slapped her comrade hard across the back. "You were always shit at gambling."

"How come you've got lights?" Nathan asked as the door was shut behind him.

"What happened you?" Angel asked as Nathan stepped into the light.

"Huh?" Nathan said, then he followed her gaze down the front of his shirt. The whole thing was soaked in the blood from the cadavers outside.

"He fell over into your handiwork," Bates said.

"He still looks like shit," Angel said.

"He's been seasick all night," Sarah said in Nathan's defence.

"And it's been a rough night," Bates added, holding up his bandaged stump.

Angel looked at the mutilated arm. "Does that not hurt?"

"No, it feels great," he answered dryly. "I recommend it for everyone."

Angel nodded over to a pile of equipment. "There is some Tramadol with my kit."

"Thanks," Bates said, walking over to the pile.

Nathan looked over to where Bates was heading. On the floor there was what looked like a car battery. Attached by crocodile clips and hung from the wall was a stark white bulb caged in an orange plastic housing.

Nathan nodded. "High tech."

Bates addressed the room as he rummaged for the drugs, "Are we all that's left?"

"Looks like it," French said.

"Been quiet for some time. We heard shots about five minutes ago," Angel added.

Sarah raised a hand as if she were at school. "That would have been me."

"You know how to use gun?" Angel said more than asked.

"The answer's no," Bates said, brandishing the pistol. "Otherwise there'd still be bullets in this thing."

Nathan continued his casual survey of the armoury. He turned round to look at the way they had come in. As he did he saw a figure slouched against the wall. The open door had obscured the body as he had come in and Nathan peered past the other occupants to get a better view. It was the body of a dead sailor slumped on the floor of the armoury.

"What happened to him?" Nathan asked nervously. The spray of red blood on the wall behind him had already told him his answer, but Nathan needed to hear it.

French pulled back the sailor's collar to show a deep bite mark. Sarah asked, "Did he kill himself?"

The marine huffed, "Good catholic lad, or something. Couldn't bring himself to do it."

Bates and Sarah looked at French. Angel had her eyes down.

Nathan covered his mouth and stifled his cough. His head pounded and his body ached. He felt asthmatic, unable to get enough breath and the wound on his arm burned. It burned through the muscles and down into the bone.

"Don't you give me any crap," French said. "Hey, if there had been a few more people like me when this all kicked off, things would be totally different."

"God only knows," Sarah blurted out.

French stepped closer to Sarah. "You got a problem, lady?"

Sarah gave him a trenchant stare. "Was it you who took the pot shot at us on the way in?" There was a lingering silence and a good few hard looks before Sarah continued, "If it was, I wouldn't trust you to aim straight enough to shoot me."

French surged forward, "Why you—"

"Shut up, Lawrence!" Angel said, pushing in front of him.

Bates stepped up to Angel, adding to the human barrier between the marine and Sarah. "So have you dogs got a plan?" he asked.

"Sure," Angel said." We wait here few hours, let things settle down before we make our way to radio room to send mayday."

"We had much the same plan, but we need to get up to our cabin and rescue Jennifer," Sarah added.

"If you going out there you better take precautions," Angel said, throwing open the door to the armoury.

"How many vests do we have here, Angel?" Bates asked as he walked into the locker.

"Three. One I'm wearing and the spares." Angel looked Bates up and down. "Can I assume yours in your bunk?"

"Sorry, I didn't get an invite to this party," Bates said, hauling out the vests.

"Yes, you were in brig again."

Bates threw the first vest to Sarah. "Funny," he said as he gave Angel a reluctant smile. "Seem to remember that the last time I was in there you had warmed the bunk for me."

The second vest snagged by one of its straps. Bates yanked it free but his one-armed clumsiness sent it dropping to the deck. He bent down and picked it up, frustrated by his disability.

He thrust the second vest at Nathan. "Here."

Sarah protested, "Bates, I don't know what to do with this. Aren't you guys better off wearing these?"

"The lady's right, Bates," French added. "What are you doing that for?"

Bates ignored him. "Sarah, these aren't just ammo vests." He poked at the material behind the ammo pockets. "It's made from a stab-proof weave. We wear them in country 'cause if they stop knives they stop bites."

"Do you smell something?" the other marine asked.

"Smoke?" Angel replied.

"Cover me," French said as he stepped up to the door.

French eased open the door to a trill of soft clicks as safety catches were disengaged.

A thick cloud of black smoke clung to the ceiling of the corridor and further down the ship the plumes were backlit with a rolling orange tint.

"Aw, shit," French said as he slammed the door shut. "We'd better get out of here."

"Isn't there a fire suppression system?" Sarah asked.

"Yeah," Bates said as he pocketed useful items. "But it's linked to the power and the manual system assumes there'll be more than six of us to deal with it."

"What are we going to do?" French asked, anxiety rising in his voice.

"We need to abandon ship," Angel said, her voice calm and steady.

"Not before we—" Bates fumbled a lump of yellow tinged plastic. Half out a pocket and left-handed he couldn't stop it from falling to the floor. "Shit!"

Sarah could see he was annoyed at himself for the awkwardness he had working one handed. She bent down and passed him the wayward object.

Bates shown Sarah a sheepish grin. Sarah watched as his lips arched, plumping his cheeks as he smiled. She looked up into his eyes and realised that she was smiling back at him. His eyes were hazel, she noted.

Bates took in a sip of breath and broke eye contact, his cheeks a slightly redder hue than a few moments before. He cleared his throat and continued, "As I was saying, we can't abandon the ship before we've sent that sitrep."

Sarah turned and saw Nathan staring at her. His mouth was slightly open and his eyebrows were furrowed. His pale, clammy complexion stressed the hurt in his expression. Sarah cast her eyes down, suddenly ashamed. She had no reason to feel guilty; she had never led Nathan on, but she knew he had always carried affection for her. She had always brushed off his advances with excuses about their situation rather than the truth. Nathan was a nice guy, but not the type Sarah found attractive. Now she saw the harm of that lie in Nathan's eyes.

"Do we risk the bridge or just go straight to the radio room?" asked a nervous looking marine.

"Radio room our best bet," Angel said.

"Okay, Nathan and I will go get Jennifer," Sarah said. "You guys make the radio call before abandoning ship and we'll meet you up on deck."

"I'm coming with you," Bates said.

"But you're wounded."

"You'll be quicker with someone who knows the ship," Bates argued. "Besides, Angel can't shoot straight right handed. I'm safer off with you two."

A huge grin on her face, Angel flicked a slap across the back of Bates' head. "Tool-up, people. Let's get out of here."

The soldiers quickly loaded guns and ammo, passing equipment to Nathan and Sarah.

"Shall I show them how to clear a jam?" the nervous marine asked Bates.

"No point," Angel chipped in before Bates could answer. "If they have jam they won't be quick enough to clear it. Give them two guns instead."

"And no John Woo stuff," Bates added.

"Take one of these so we know how we're all doing," Angel said, placing a walkie-talkie and headset into her hand. "I've set the channels so all you need to do is press this button on the headphone cable to talk."

Sarah pushed the button and there was a hiss of static on the radio Angel still held.

Nathan and Sarah loaded their vests with ammunition and both slipped their spare gun into an integrated holster inside.

Bates handed flashlights around and asked, "Are we all ready?"

There was a muttering and a nodding of heads.

"Good. See you all on deck," Bates said.

He nodded for French to open the door.

The door swung open and in the corridor a flaming zombie staggered towards them.

Angel stepped forward.

"Mine," she said as she rested her pistol's muzzle on her plaster cast and squeezed the trigger.

The ghoul collapsed to the floor, flames sweeping behind it as it fell.

"Happy hunting! See you on deck!" Bates called out as the two groups went their separate ways.

Abandoned

THE BEAMS OF LIGHT SWEPT through the increasingly deepening smoke.

Nathan rasped out a cough.

"Should have brought gas masks," Bates complained.

Bates had mistaken Nathan's cough as irritation from the smoke. Nathan chose not to correct him.

"Is this it?" Sarah asked, unsure of her bearings in the dark.

"This is it," Bates confirmed.

Sarah reached out and tried the handle. It was still locked.

"Jennifer, it's Sarah," she said as she knocked on the cabin door. "You in there, honey?"

"Sarah!" came the muffled but excited reply.

Sarah smiled to the rest of her companions. "Yeah, it's me, honey. Open up."

From behind the door came some grunting and scraping.

"Are you okay?" Sarah asked nervously.

Jennifer's anxious voice came back, "I can't move the bed! It's stuck!"

Bates looked at Sarah with a puzzled expression. "The bed?"

Sarah called through the closed door, "Jennifer, what's going on?"

Jennifer sounded close to tears. "I pushed the bed against the door, but I can't move it. It's caught on something."

Suddenly shots rang out. The noise caused Jennifer to scream from inside the cabin.

Bates and Sarah spun round, guns at the ready. Before them, Nathan stood, his gun smoking, and on the ground a few feet down the corridor lay a motionless zombie.

"Whoa!" Bates shouted, cuffing Nathan's arm a little too strongly.

"What?" Nathan protested.

"You scared the shit out of us!" Sarah chastised.

"But I got him," Nathan said, gesturing at the corpse on the deck.

"Next time let us know so we don't wet ourselves or step into your line of fire," Bates said.

"Would you quit raggin' on me?!" Nathan retorted. "There was one of them. I wasted it. Simple."

Sarah interjected, "Boys! How do we get into the room?"

"It's not a bulkhead door," Bates said. "We can just smash it open."

"But there's a bed against it," Nathan reminded him.

"The bed's what, two feet high? We can break open the door above that."

Sarah looked around. "Okay, let's find a fire axe or something to use as a battering ram."

"Got a quicker plan," Bates said, holding up the lump of plastic he had fumbled with back in the armoury.

Sarah pressed herself up against the door. "Jennifer, go into the bathroom and shut the door. Crouch down in the shower into a tight little ball."

"And cover your ears," Bates added.

"Okay," came the reply through the door.

"There's going to be a loud bang in about fifteen seconds, so get going." Bates adjusted the primer. "Okay, let's go!"

The group scurried off back down the corridor.

"Cover your ears," Bates instructed and waited for his companions to comply. "Fire in the hole."

When the plastic explosives went off, the noise was disappointing. In comparison to the deafening gunshots, the explosives were pedestrian.

Sarah uncovered her ears and ran back to the shattered door.

"Jennifer, are you all right?" she called through the splintered hole.

The figure of the eight year-old girl emerged through the dust.

"I'm fine," Jennifer said, climbing onto the pile of debris that had once been her bed.

Sarah stretched out her arms and the two connected in a massive cuddle, but their embrace was wrecked by the distant bark of gunfire.

Nathan jumped. "What the fuck was that?!"

"Is that the only word you know?" Bates asked.

"It's the *best* one," Nathan replied.

"Shall I radio Angel?" Sarah asked, marking how nonchalant Bates was.

"No, she doesn't like it when you call her at work."

"What if she needs help?"

"She'll call if she needs us," Bates explained. "And if she's busy she won't thank you for the distraction."

Nathan heaved up a hoarse cough. This time he spat out a wad of dislodged mucus onto the deck. He spluttered, "Let's get to the life boats then!"

A rip of static burst across Sarah's earpiece. She asked into the mic, "Angel, is that you?" When there was no answer she looked at Bates for confirmation that she'd done everything right.

"Try again," Bates suggested.

Sarah toggled the transmit button. "Angel, come in. Can you hear me?"

"The shooting's stopped," Nathan observed.

There was silence. No shooting, no hiss across the radio. Even the ship seemed to be holding its breath.

Bates kicked the bulkhead next to him, hard, sending a dull clunk through the wall. "Aw, shit. Angel's down."

"Then we need to go after her," Sarah said.

"What?!" Nathan squawked.

Sarah started to repeat herself, "We need to go aft—"

"No," Bates said firmly.

"What do you mean *no*?"

"If Angel couldn't hack it down there, neither can we," Bates said, trying to keep his composure. "And besides, the lower decks are on fire. We might not even be able to get to her."

"But we don't know if they've radioed that Russian sub," Sarah pointed out.

Nathan coughed to clear his throat and tried to make it sound as if he'd only done it to attract attention. "We can do that from the bridge, can't we?"

Bates nodded. "As long as the fire hasn't damaged any of the equipment."

"What do you mean?"

"Look, there's no power," Bates explained, "but the radio has backup batteries, only..."

"Only what?"

Bates shifted uncomfortably. "They're in the radio room."

"But you said we could call from the bridge!" Sarah said.

"Only if the wiring is still intact."

Sarah felt a gentle tugging at the hem of her vest. "Sarah," came Jennifer's soft voice.

Bates continued to explain the situation. "If the fire has severed the connection, or damaged the transmitter..."

The tugging at Sarah's vest grew stronger. Jennifer's voice sounded more frantic. "Sarah."

"Just a moment, Jennifer," Sarah said without paying her any attention.

"Isn't there a spare?" Nathan asked.

Jennifer tugged again. "Sarah!"

The adults were too engrossed talking through the problem to pay attention to the little girl.

Bates put pay to Nathan's idea: "It's in storage and that's in the hold. We'd—"

Tired of being ignored Jennifer let out a scream, "Zombie!"

The three adults spun round to see Jennifer pointing at a figure lumbering down the corridor.

With a shower of muzzle flashes, hard booms filled the corridor. The zombie jolted with the impact of the shots before collapsing to the deck.

"Thanks, Jennifer!" Sarah shouted over the buzzing in her ears.

Jennifer stood with her head shrugged down to her shoulders and her hands clasped over her ears. The sound of the guns had been painfully loud for the small girl.

Sarah holstered her pistol and stretched her arms out. Jennifer immediately recognised the offer of comfort and let Sarah lift her into her arms.

The pair embraced in a strong supportive hug. Sarah sensed her young ward relax, at which she bent down, letting the girl stand on her own.

"Okay?" Sarah asked with a smile.

Jennifer nodded and smiled back.

"Lets get to the bridge," Bates said, leading the way.

Nathan let the rest of the group pass him, mustering a smile for Jennifer as she passed. He shone his torch on the globule of mucous he had spat onto the deck earlier. It was brown with streaks of blood through it.

Unbuttoning the sleeve of his shirt, Nathan popped the hilt of his flashlight into his mouth. He angled the beam onto his forearm and apprehensively unrolled the cuff up past his elbow. The blue veins stood out against his pale skin, but the network of blood vessels darkened the closer they got to the scratch mark. Hidden under his wristband, Nathan couldn't see the wound and he wasn't brave enough to look. All around the wrist band the skin was cracked like a dry riverbed, the flesh black and the split canyons a raw red.

"Nathan," a sweet voice called out.

He looked up to see Jennifer standing a short distance away, looking back at him.

"Is your arm okay?" she asked in all innocence.

Nathan hastily covered it back up. "Yeah fine, just banged it... bruise... you know, the one from giving blood."

"It looks sore," Jennifer said.

"No, it's fine," Nathan replied. He stepped over and rubbed his hand across Jennifer's head, mussing up her hair. "Come on, squirt. We'd better catch up to the others. Don't want to get them worried."

✳ ✳ ✳ ✳ ✳

Bates shone his flashlight across the corpse. The dead body wore an all-in-one bright orange survival suit. Beads of water had dripped off it to form a brackish pool on the deck. He'd never liked Patterson, tight assed moron that he was, but he suddenly realised he'd always trusted him. Patterson had always been true to his word and predictable in his action and that was more than Bates could say about most of his friends.

Seeing the second in command lying dead on the floor shook Bates more than all the zombies he'd encountered.

He turned to Sarah and said simply, "Patterson."

Sarah looked down at where Bates was shining his torch.

Bates tracked the torchlight over the deck to a second corpse. "And over there Captain Warden."

"Both dead," Sarah said absentmindedly. "I wonder what happened."

"Patterson came round the corner or out of a room right into Captain Warden. The captain must have turned by that point 'cause he bit Patterson." Bates shone his torch over the bite marks on Patterson's face. "They scuffled. Patterson got to the Captain's side arm. Judging by the number of shots..." Again Bates moved the beam onto Captain Warden's body, pointing out the areas of note. "Stomach, chest, neck and head. I'd say the two of them were in a close scuffle. That's why Patterson couldn't get a clean shot to the head." Bates swung the torch back to Patterson. "Commander Patterson, feeling weak from the blood loss, sat down there and decided he wasn't coming back as one of those things, and shot himself."

"Did you get a merit badge in making that shit up or what?" Nathan jibed.

"Shut the fuck up!" Bates snapped.

Nathan recoiled, surprised by the weight of emotion.

"You okay, Bates?" Sarah asked.

Bates shook his head, staring at Patterson's corpse. "We'd look at the W.D.'s from the chopper. We'd joke about them. How come so many of them were naked?" Bates pushed out a laugh. "Do W.D.'s get undressed when they reanimate? Shit like that." Bates let his shoulders sink, dispelling the pretence of his forced joke. "I always wondered, did they see a loved one turn and just not know or believe what was happening? Did they go down fighting, or scared, or what? Every one of these poor bastards got bit. Made me wonder how. See them standing there in the clothes they died in. We'd make up little stories about them, you know, based on what clothes they were wearing. Shirt and tie: office worker from some soulless corporation cubical. There's a commotion outside, the receptionist screams. Next thing he's rammed up against a filing cabinet fighting those things off him. It was always easy to dehumanise them. Hell, most of them didn't look human anymore. They just wander about in a trance when they're not trying to eat you." He tapped a finger to his temple. "They don't think like us—they're dead, they're not us—they're the enemy. But it ain't even like a real fucking war 'cause you're not shooting a real fucking person, are you?" Bates wasn't looking for vindication; he was just stating the facts as he saw them. "It's not killing to put a bullet through their brain, 'cause they're dead. Right? Ain't no worse than shooting a deer. Hell, shooting an animal is worse, right? 'Cause it's a living, breathing creature like you or me. Right?"

This time Bates was looking for approval.

Sarah nodded, too frightened by Bates' growing mania to speak.

Bates sniffed back a tear. "But these ain't rotting corpses like on the mainland. These are fresh. These are the people I lived and worked with for years. I know *their* stories." He stared at Patterson's corpse, and added, this time a little louder and with a tinge of desperation in his voice," I know these people. I know they were human."

He turned around to look Nathan in the eye. The muscles around his mouth were tough and he snorted sharp breaths through his nose. His anger exploded. "I don't have to make shit up because I knew them!"

He lunged forward, pushing Nathan against the wall.

Pinned under the chin by Bates' forearm, Nathan squirmed for room to breathe. He grappled hold of his assailant's arm and tried to prise it free, but the soldier was far too powerful and rage-fuelled to budge.

"Bates!" Sarah shouted.

Bates stood, his eyes wide, taking panting breaths.

"Bates," Sarah said more softly as she stepped up beside him. She put a gentle hand on his shoulder.

Bates looked up at her with tears in his eyes.

Sarah wanted to say something warm and comforting, but all she could say was, "Bates, let Nathan go."

Bates relaxed his hold and took a pace back.

Nathan slid down the wall gasping for breath.

Wiping his eyes with the back of his hand, Bates mourned, "Shit, this is fucked up."

Sarah looked down at Nathan as he sat crouched over and coughing.

"You okay?" she asked.

"No!" he rasped back. "That psycho tried to kill me!"

Sarah bent down. "Let me take a look."

"No!" he snapped as he recoiled away from her.

Sarah lent in and touched her hand to his cheek, "Jeez, you're burning up, Nathan."

"I'm *fine*. And I'll *stay* fine if jerks stop trying to kill me."

"Will you be okay?"

Nathan nodded back at her. He felt terrible, but it wasn't because of the throttling, and the last thing he wanted was Sarah taking too close a look at him.

When she stood back up, Bates was gazing at the bandage over his stump.

"Let's keep going," Sarah told him, gently rubbing the bicep on his good arm. "You said the bridge isn't far."

Bates didn't move.

"Bates," Sarah said a little louder.

The soldier flicked his eyes up to make contact with her, almost as if he'd been startled to find her there.

Sarah lowered her voice. "The bridge?"

"It's just up here," Bates said, snapping out of his trance.

As they walked away, Nathan raised his gun and aimed it at the back of Bates' head. The muzzle of the gun shook as the frenzy rattling around inside Nathan's mind manifested in his muscles. His lips pursed, Nathan snorted out a half whispered, "*Bastard.*"

He pulled his finger against the trigger.

"Nathan," Jennifer said in a sharp, stern tone.

Nathan flicked his finger off the trigger and lowered the gun. He looked down at the young girl, a frown still clenched on his face.

"You don't understand," Nathan protested.

Just then a voice called back down the corridor.

"Nathan, Jennifer this way!" Sarah called.

Jennifer stretched her hand up for Nathan to take. Ignoring her gesture, Nathan stormed off down the corridor.

* * * * *

The bridge door was unimposing. A small metal plaque was all that announced it.

Bates shot Nathan a cold stare as he coughed again. He hissed, "*Can it.*"

Nathan flipped his middle finger up at him but kept quiet.

Bates ignored Nathan and signalled for Sarah to open the door. Positioning himself to be the first inside, he nodded his readiness.

In time to a mouthed countdown, Sarah threw the door open. The corridor flooded with light and Sarah watched as Bates disappeared inside.

"Clear!" Bates called out.

Sarah stepped onto the bridge. The lights were still working, something Sarah found just as creepy as the dark corridors. Raindrops peppered the panoramic window. The blackness of the storm outside and the bright light from the room turned the window into a mirror. This little island of functionality protected from the squall outside was pristine except for two things. Firstly there were no people here and secondly the blood. Long streaky smears of blood swept around the bridge. It wasn't a slaughterhouse, just a dozen or so dragged handprints or spurts of blood, but in the stark light the crimson was harsh.

Nathan spun around to take in the whole room. "What the hell happened here?"

"Good news: battery power is up," Bates said, looking up at the lights.

"What about the radio?" Sarah asked. "Where do we start?"

Bates walked over to a station at the back of the bridge. "Be quicker if I do it. You two stand guard. One of you on the door we came in and one of you watching the access to the deck."

Nathan gave a weak nod of agreement to Sarah.

"You managing okay, Nathan? You look like shit," Bates said.

"Is that your way of an apology?!" Nathan snarled. "What the fuck do you care anyway?"

Bates was worried by the green tinge to Nathan's skin. "I mean if—"

"Just fucking leave it!" Nathan growled back.

Bates put his hand in the air in mocking surrender.

Nathan turned his back on Bates to look out of the window onto the deck.

"Guess I'll take the door we came in then," Sarah said, taking up position.

Bates placed his gun down next to the console he was operating and started checking the radio.

Nathan was staring at a blood streak across the windowpane. "I don't get it. If there's blood, where did the bridge crew go?"

"Abandoned ship maybe?" Sarah offered.

"Ah, shit!" Bates cursed.

Panic rose in Sarah's voice. "Is it broken?!"

Bates stood over the controls, his shoulders slumped. "I don't think so. It's just..."

"Just what?" Nathan demanded.

"It's just so difficult with only my left hand," Bates said, looking at the dressing on his stump.

Sarah could sense the despair and frustration simmering inside him. She knew he had to keep it together, otherwise they were all lost. Now that there was a lull there was time to reflect on what had happened to him. He was going into shock, but Sarah knew they were far from safe. She had to keep him focused.

"Jennifer, go help Bates," Sarah said. "He'll tell you which buttons to press."

Jennifer walked over to Bates, slipping her small hand into his. She stood on tip-toe to see the radio. Bates looked down at the elfin face and smiled.

"Come here," he said, lifting her up.

After a few giggles and a bit of instruction, Bates announced, "This should be it."

"We can get a signal out?" Sarah asked.

"We can try," Bates said with a shrug. "There's no guarantee."

Nathan leapt back from the window, his gun raised. "What was that?"

Sarah levelled her gun and scanned the room. "What was what?"

Nathan stepped forward and tried to peer past his reflection. "Outside the window."

The radio crackled behind them.

"This is the research vessel Ishtar calling the Pskov. Come in please." Bates let go of the talk button on the microphone.

Eerie white noise of static filled the bridge.

Sarah tried to listen for a reply while looking through the reflection-glazed window.

The static waxed and waned, the odd blip catching the ear, the survivors all trying to twist the sounds into something audible.

Outside a surge of rain lashed the bridge window, sending thick streams of water trickling down the pane.

"Was that movement?" Nathan asked.

"Could have been the spray from a wave," Sarah said.

Satisfied he wasn't going to talk over a response, Bates tried again. "This is the research vessel Ishtar calling the Pskov. Respond please."

"Sarah, turn the lights off." Nathan waved at her to go to the wall switch.

Sarah hesitated.

A ghostly voice wafted from the radio, "This is the Pskov. Go ahead."

Bates looked over at Sarah, a triumphant grin across his face.
Smack!

The bridge glass vibrated from the force of the impact. A bloodstained and pale crewman threw himself at the window right in front of Nathan.

Nathan jumped and from shear panic shot at the zombie.

"No!" Bates screamed as the panoramic window burst open.

The millions of shards of glass crashed to the floor and the raw elements forced their way through. The rain-laden wind wrapped itself around the new access and came howling into the bridge.

The sudden gust of icy wind blinded everyone—everyone who was alive.

The zombie, pushed by the wind and no longer excluded by the window, fell into the bridge. Behind it, more of the deceased crew clambered over the shards of glass, lured to the bridge by the noise and the light.

Nathan pointed his gun at the zombie as it tumbled through the open window. He yelled, "Fuck you!" and pulled the trigger at point-blank range. A spray of blood exploded into the air and up his face. He recoiled and spit in revulsion. "Shit."

Sarah caught Nathan drawing back from the corner of her eye. She turned for a fraction of a second, concerned that he was all right. When she turned back a zombie was upon her.

The dead crewman's hands lashing out at her, Sarah pushed the gun up at the creature and fired. The shot sliced through the zombie crewman's shoulder, pushing it off balance. Still striking out at the human in front of it, the zombie fell forward, crashing into the warm flesh.

Hit by the full weight of the drenched dead man and trying to defend herself at the same time, Sarah couldn't step out of the way quick enough. The two of them toppled to the deck. Sarah hit the ground hard. The gun slipped from her grasp and skidded across the floor.

A pair of dead hands grabbed Sarah by the shoulders as the zombie hauled itself up for a bite.

Through a throbbing head and double vision, Sarah saw the cadaver bear down on her. She threw one arm out wildly grasping for her dropped gun. The other arm she wedged under the zombie's chin hard against its throat.

She screamed as her broken fingers jarred against the zombie's neck. The whip of pain caused her to lose her grasp. The zombie slipped down her arm and landed on top of her.

Water trickled of its sodden hair, down over its snarling face, dripping onto Sarah's chest. Its eyes fixed on Sarah, its jaw chewing the open air. It raised itself up for a bite.

Sarah wedged her forearm under the gnashing jaw, pushing the creature away from her. If this had been a living person the pressure on their windpipe would have suffocated them, but the zombie continued to bear down, snarling and snapping its teeth.

Gulping in exhausted breaths, Sarah knew she couldn't fend off the ghoul much longer.

"Aim your shots!" Bates bellowed at Nathan furiously.

Nathan was firing shot after shot at the encroaching zombies. Most of his shots were wild. His gun stalled. The covering over the barrel slid back and stayed there, exposing the empty chamber.

Nathan fumbled with the ammo pouch, desperately trying to release a fresh clip.

A zombie lurched forward, bringing itself face to face with Nathan. Nathan gasped and threw his empty gun down. He pulled the zipper on the vest pocket that held his second gun, but the zombie had already sprung its attack. The dead man's teeth bit down hard on the collar of Nathan's tactical vest. He felt tremendous pressure as the zombie's teeth bore down.

Ignoring the second gun, Nathan elbowed the creature off him, and with the extra space between them he put his whole body behind a shove. The palsied muscles of the zombie couldn't react against

Nathan's aggression and it stumbled backwards, falling over the window frame back out of the bridge.

Nathan looked down at where the zombie had bitten. On the thick weave of the vest was an imprint of the zombie's dentition and a glistening pool of saliva. The vest's fabric was indeed bite proof.

Bates grabbed for his gun sitting on the console. But his left hand wasn't as dextrous as his lost right. In his clumsy attempt to snatch the gun, he nudged it from its seating and the weapon skidded off the desk onto the deck. Bending down to retrieve it, Bates was confronted by a deceased sailor. His blue fatigues were rain soaked and clung to his dead body. His face was vacant and a shrivelled ghostly white. The misty eyes looked down, but passed Bates.

The zombie flung itself not at Bates—but at Jennifer.

From his squat position on the deck, Bates leapt sideways with an explosive burst of strength. He threw his left arm around the girl as he lunged.

Jennifer screamed as she was tossed across the room, landing at the doorway they had come in.

Bates flipped round to see the zombie lying where Jennifer had stood. Behind the animated corpse lay the gun Bates had fumbled.

The zombie crawled forward with wet slaps of its sodden hands and knees. Its advance was checked by the hard smack of rubber-soled boots. Supporting himself on his good arm, Bates kicked out with his sturdy military boots. Blow after blow fell about the zombie's head and face, the hard slap of rubber joined by the squelching crunch of snapped cartilage as the zombie's nose was repeatedly stamped flat.

With no regard for the ferocity of the pounding, the zombie crawled on through the blows, intent on its meal. Following it now were a group of equally ravenous corpses.

Jennifer stood flat against the door out of the bridge. There were zombies everywhere and only Nathan was still standing. Suddenly she felt a change in pressure behind her. The door at her back fell away. Jennifer turned to see it swing open, revealing an ominous figure looming over her.

Angel stepped onto the bridge. Her plaster cast on her left arm was blood splattered, her uniform grimy and dishevelled. Strands of her long auburn hair had been wrestled free from her tight ponytail. The sniper's porcelain skin was smudged with dirt, but her light brown eyes looked like burnished bronze.

Angel looked down at Jennifer and gave her a reassuring wink as she stepped onto the bridge.

Bates kicked out at the zombie at his feet but the cadaver keeled over. He froze in surprise, then saw the bullet hole. He saw a figure out of the corner of his eye and braced himself for another attack. Angel walked passed him and he realised where the shot had come from.

Sarah's arm trembled with the strain, her strength ready to fail at any moment. A black army boot kicked the zombie square in the ribs, sending it tumbling from her. The action was just enough for Sarah to stretch out and grab her lost firearm. She swung round in time to see the zombie steel itself for another attack. Before it could surge forward again, Sarah sent a round into its skull.

Wading into the bridge, Angel fired precise shot after precise shot. With brutal efficiency she floored zombie after zombie. The last creature in the room lurched forward to sink its teeth into the human. Angel threw out her left arm as the creature's jaw clamped down.

The cadaver's teeth met with the rigid casing of Angel's plaster cast. Confused by the lack of flesh, the zombie looked up at Angel.

Angel shoved the barrel of her pistol hard between the zombie's eyes.

"Bite me," she said as she squeezed the trigger.

"Angel!" Bates shouted as he pulled himself up from the deck. He rushed up to her and planted a wet kiss on her forehead before wrapping his arm around her and hugging her tight.

Sarah too hauled herself to her feet. She looked around the body-strewn bridge. The florescent lights flickered with the salt-water spray blown in through the broken window.

"Everyone okay?" she asked.

A chorus of affirmative answers filled the bridge.

Bates finished pounding Angel on the back. "What happened?"

"Didn't get to radio room," Angel explained. "We got jumped. There were too many, too close."

Sarah looked down at the radio. "Bates."

"Oh, yeah. Sure." He picked up the receiver and resumed his radio call. "Research vessel Ishtar to the Pskov. Come in, please."

This time the radio came to life instantly. "This is the Pskov. What can we do for you?"

Bates spoke into the microphone. "Stand down targeting. The ship has been overrun. Requesting assistance. Remaining crew abandoning ship."

There was a long pause.

"And the virus?" the voice from the Pskov asked.

"The virus remains the same," Bates answered. "It has not—I repeat, *not*—gone airborne. The outbreak is by direct contact only."

There was another worrying silence. The survivors looked anxiously at each other.

The radio sparked to life again. "Will contact Ascension command regarding your situation."

"What does that mean?" Sarah asked.

Bates slammed the microphone into the console. "It means they're too chickenshit to come and help us."

"It means they might still nuke us," Angel added.

"You mean they're just going to fuck us over!" Nathan's voice was hoarse and crackly.

Sarah couldn't tell if it was sweat or rain that drenched him, but Nathan had a definite tinge of green to his flesh.

"No, no. That's not what she means. We still stand a chance. It's military protocol, that's all." Sarah looked over at Bates for confirmation. "You always have to check with your superiors, right?"

Bates stood with his head hung low and a dejected look on his face. He caught Jennifer looking up at him. She was thin and wiry, her hair ruffled from the evening's trials. But behind the muck and scruffiness, her doey brown eyes were bright and clear. Bates raised his head to look at Nathan and then Sarah in turn. They were all hoping for an answer.

Finally he looked back down at Jennifer. "Yeah, that's right. They have to check with high command."

Angel saw the optimism Bates was trying to foster. "There might be a vessel close to us that could be diverted to pick us up, or a rescue chopper from aircraft carrier."

Bates nodded his head to reassure everyone, including himself. "They're not going to nuke us. They need to get intelligence reports and debriefings from us."

"And they'll want Frankenstein Work," Angel added.

Sarah brought a smile to her lips. "Okay, what now?"

"Pressure is rising," Bates said. "This storm hasn't much strength left in it. We head for the life rafts and wait for them to come rescue us."

"Which way to the life rafts?" Nathan coughed out.

"This way," Angel said as she made towards the opposite door.

＊ ＊ ＊ ＊ ＊

Outside it was dark and windy. The rain had eased off, but the waves threw lashes of spray across the decks. A thick plume of smoke made its lazy way out of several broken windows. Behind the smoke could be seen the flickering light of orange flame.

A zombie deck hand shambled its way over to the group, only to have its head obliterated by a shot from Angel.

Ignoring the freshly decapitated corpse, Angel walked over to the railings.

"You two are going to have to do the bulk of the work," she said to Sarah and Nathan.

Sarah nodded, looking at the woman's plaster cast. "What do we do?"

Nathan coughed violently. Bent double, he crashed to his knees, spitting out mucous and blood.

Not noticing the crimson fluid by the dim emergency lighting, Angel patted Nathan on the back.

"Smoke getting to you?" she asked.

Nathan wiped a sleeve across his mouth. "Uh... oh, yeah."

"Everybody quiet!" Bates barked.

Sarah and Angel stood up, guns in hand.

The excited moan of a zombie called out from within the smoke. The wind changed, whipping spirals of smoke towards them and with it more sounds of the undead.

"Stay close, Jennifer," Sarah said, pulling the young girl close.

"Where are you, you dead fuck?" Bates muttered, levelling his gun at the murk.

Jennifer screamed as out of the smog a dark figure emerged. The zombie was scorched from head to toe, its flesh a crispy black shell. Its left jaw was partially missing, but it still had enough teeth to deliver an infecting bite. Its jerky motion split the seared skin from its muscles as it lurched at Sarah.

The blackened corpse lunged. The ship rolled, amplifying the force of the creature's attack. Thrown against the guardrail and tilted back by the ships pitch, Sarah felt her body pivot rearward. Her hands were out in front of her, keeping the zombie at bay. She threw down a han,d trying to grasp the railing.

"Sarah!" Jennifer cried.

Sarah tried to seize hold of the railing, but her splinted fingers wouldn't grip. Already falling backwards from the initial collision, the zombie fell into her, sending them both over the railing.

Sarah fell open-mouthed, watching as the outreached hand of Jennifer hurtled away from her.

The swelling ocean punched her in the back as she landed. The force and the cold shock thumped the breath out of her and Sarah sank into the freezing blackness.

Feeling her strength drained by the cold waters, she let out a scream. A gulp of icy liquid rushed into her mouth, fuelling her panic.

She kicked out and felt her head breach the surface. Retching out the seawater, she thrashed her arms against the encompassing waves, trying to suck in a full lungful of air.

A scorched but cold hand slapped her in the face and grabbed hold. She screamed in horror to see the burnt zombie reaching out of the water to bite her. Its blistered and peeling hands grabbed onto her and pulled her back under the water.

Sarah punched and kicked, trying to free herself from the cadaver's grasp. As they sank deeper she managed to dislodge its grip only to have the creature latch on to the bottom of her combat vest. She looked up to see the burning ship fade to the water overhead. Paddling with her arms, she fought to maintain her buoyancy while kicking at the undead anchor that pulled her down. The creature's hands were knocked free again and Sarah kicked out hard, propelling herself to the surface. She started to rise back up but then she felt a clawing at her ankle. Pulling itself up to get a bite, the zombie had its scorched mouth open, eager for its repast.

Sarah's cold and tired muscles couldn't struggle any longer. She tilted her head up to see a bright light floating down towards her.

Her lungs were scorched.

Her energy was spent.

An angel coming to take my soul, Sarah thought.

The flare sank past Sarah's face, quickly followed by a hand that grabbed the fabric of her vest.

The strong hand yanked Sarah's motionless body free of the zombie's grasp. The creature descended down into the depths, arms outstretched in a vain attempt to seize back its prey.

With gritted teeth, Bates heaved Sarah's limp body above the water. Angel hung over the side of the life raft and added her own strength. They laid her down in the middle of the raft.

"How the fuck do you do CPR with one arm in a fucking rubber dingy?!" Bates shouted.

The rubber raft gave way with each blow, dampening the force of the compression. Bates knelt forward and placed his lips around Sarah's.

The flesh was cold and tasted salty. He pinched her nose and sent a breath down into her lungs. He lent back, ready to try again, but before he could Sarah's eyes jolted open.

Bates whipped round, and grabbing his gun, thrust it into Sarah's face.

Sarah's mouth opened and she vomited seawater.

"Thank fuck!" Bates proclaimed.

Sarah coughed and spluttered, trying to get her breath as Bates cradled her in his arm.

She looked up at the sky. The rain had stopped and the clouds were lit pink from the sunrise. In the raft with her, Bates, Angel, Jennifer and Nathan looked weary and wet.

"I'm okay," Sarah finally managed to whisper out.

Bates rocked her as he sat clasping her tight to his chest.

"I thought I'd lost you," he whispered back to her.

"Look!" Jennifer shouted. She pointed towards the rising sun.

The survivors looked out across the ocean, past the burning hulk of the Ishtar. Gradually the sound of rotor blades brought their eyes to what Jennifer had spotted.

The ship's helicopter was on its inbound flight.

"Idris! He's back!" Angel said in amazement.

"We're saved! Here's the rescue!" Sarah said.

Jennifer stood up in the rocking raft and started waving at the chopper.

Sarah looked over at Nathan, who was lying at the far corner of the raft. He looked exhausted.

"You hear that, Nathan?! We're saved!" Sarah said, a little louder for his benefit.

Nathan let out a soft moan.

Jennifer looked down at Sarah. "Nathan is sick, Sarah."

"I know, honey. It's the sea." Sarah pulled herself up to join Jennifer in waving. She croaked, "Over here!" before starting another coughing fit and spitting out leftover seawater.

"No, *real* sick," Jennifer said, plaintively looking back at Nathan's necrotic hand. But her fear was lost to Sarah's coughing and the noise of the chopper.

Bates sat rubbing Sarah's back to help ease the coughing.

"We're saved!" she said looking at him with a smile.

The expression Bates wore wasn't quite as cheerful.

"'Fraid not," he said apologetically. "That's our chopper and we burnt down their landing pad. He's going to have to ditch."

Sarah's smile melted. "What?"

"There's nowhere in three hundred miles for him to land, and even if he could there's nowhere to refuel." Bates reached over and picked up an oar. "Grab a paddle. We're going to have to rescue them."

Behind them, Nathan let out a last laboured breath, his fight against the spreading infection lost.

After a few moments, slowly edging closer to the waves, the helicopter touched down on the water. Its top-heavy engine pulled the craft sideways and it started to sink.

Bates, Angel, Sarah and Jennifer paddled furiously to reach the sinking helicopter. As they watched, the tail rotor sunk out of sight beneath the ocean. In the distance thoug,h between the rise and fall of the waves, there could be seen objects floating in the water. Buoyed on by the hope of survivors, all but one of the life raft's crew paddled.

Behind them, Nathan's body lay still and lifeless.

Then his eyes sprung open.

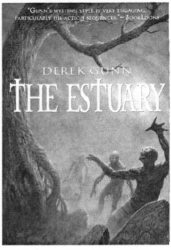

BY WILLIAM D. CARL

Beneath the dim light of a full moon, the population of Cincinnati mutates into huge, snarling monsters that devour everyone they see, acting upon their most base and bestial desires. Planes fall from the sky. Highways are clogged with abandoned cars, and buildings explode and topple. The city burns.

Only four people are immune to the metamorphosis—a smooth-talking thief who maintains the code of the Old West, an African-American bank teller who has struggled her entire life to emerge unscathed from the ghetto, a wealthy middle-aged housewife who finds everything she once believed to be a lie, and a teen-aged runaway turning tricks for food.

Somehow, these survivors must discover what caused this apocalypse and stop it from spreading. In their way is not only a city of beasts at night, but, in the daylight hours, the same monsters returned to human form, many driven insane by atrocities committed against friends and families.

Now another night is fast approaching. And once again the moon will be full.

ISBN: 978-1934861042

EDEN

A ZOMBIE NOVEL BY TONY MONCHINSKI

Seemingly overnight the world transforms into a barren wasteland ravaged by plague and overrun by hordes of flesh-eating zombies. A small band of desperate men and women stand their ground in a fortified compound in what had been Queens, New York. They've named their sanctuary Eden.

Harris—the unusual honest man in this dead world—races against time to solve a murder while maintaining his own humanity. Because the danger posed by the dead and diseased mass clawing at Eden's walls pales in comparison to the deceit and treachery Harris faces within.

ISBN: 978-1934861172

MORE DETAILS, EXCERPTS, AND PURCHASE INFORMATION AT

www.permutedpress.com

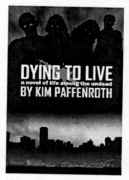
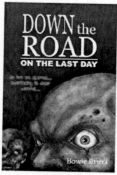

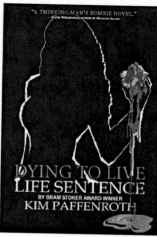

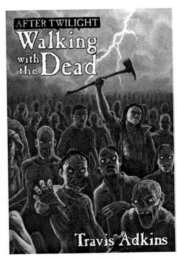

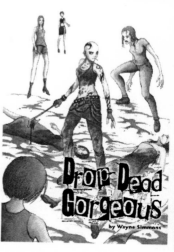

CPSIA information can be obtained at www.ICGtesting.com
Printed in the USA
LVOW060346141211

259316LV00001B/95/P